Praise for
Retellings of the Inland Seas

Anyone who can envision Atlantis as a doomed space-faring civilization about to be engulfed by rogue AI, or who has wondered what a bombastic, battled-hardened Odysseus would do when faced with unknown aliens while trying to escape an asteroid field, should take a look.

— Sarah Rice, *Booklist*

In this gorgeous, intelligently edited anthology, Athena Andreadis offers fiction that draws on the past to illuminate future imaginative possibilities. Readers of science fiction and fantasy will find both beauty and solace in these eloquent, well-told tales.

— Pamela Sargent, editor of *Women of Wonder*,
author of *The Shore of Women*

The stories are universally strong and well written. There are no repeats, and the use of the source material by each of the authors is subtly different. // The stories in this anthology take classic, often familiar narratives and present them in modern forms that recapture and re-empower stories long obscured, polishing them into gems on the shore for readers to pick up and discover.

— Paul Weimer, Hugo finalist SFF reviewer, *Nerds of a Feather*

This anthology provides a great feast for readers, whether they are steeped in the classics or just love good fantasy and science fiction. Several of these tales should win places on the upcoming award ballots, but this grouping deserves the ultimate compliment for an anthology and its editor: there's not a bad story in it.

— Nancy Jane Moore, author of *The Weave*
and the forthcoming *For the Good of the Realm*

Classic myth meets feminist spec fic in this crunchy, challenging anthology. My favourite stories were the most science fictional: Furies on Mars! Argonauts in space! But I found them all all thought-provoking, providing fresh interpretations of some of our oldest stories.

— Tansy Rayner Roberts, multiple winner of Ditmar and WSFA awards

The Feral Astrogators series

The Other Half of the Sky

To Shape The Dark

Retellings of the Inland Seas

Retellings of
the Inland Seas

edited by Athena Andreadis

Candlemark & Gleam

First edition published 2020

Copyright © 2020 by Athena Andreadis

Individual contributions copyright © 2019 by the respective authors

For information, address
Candlemark & Gleam LLC,
38 Rice Street #2, Cambridge, MA 02140
eloi@candlemarkandgleam.com

Library of Congress Cataloging-in-Publication Data
In Progress

ISBN: 978-1-936460-95-3
eISBN: 978-1-936460-94-6

Cover art and design by Eleni Tsami

Book design and composition by Athena Andreadis

www.candlemarkandgleam.com

To my father,
who shared his birthplace of Chios with Homer,
and whose entire line of ancestors plied the Inland Seas.

To my mother,
whose mother's family came from Trapezous,
the imperial capital-in-exile on the Black Sea,
and whose ancestral home may still stand
across the bay from Constantinople.

Though we smashed their statues,
though we drove them off their temples,
doesn't mean at all that the gods are dead.

— Konstantínos Kaváfis, "Ionian"

Contents

Ancestral Campfires, Distant Beacons

Athena Andreadis

"…we have a place where we belong, no matter where we are, that is as invisible as the air and more real than the ground we walk on." — Linda LeGarde Grover, *The Dance Boots*

My entire life I've fallen between too many stools to avoid or count, but one rift marked me decisively: my departure from my native culture at age eighteen, and my subsequent sojourn in a radically different adopted culture. Even before that tectonic shift, I had started sailing out of sight of familiar coastlines. I had discovered science fiction and fantasy (henceforth SFF) when infinitely malleable, even before I had taught myself to read. After all, what were the world myths and epics I pounced upon, even in simplified form—the Odyssey, the Kalevala, the Heike Monogatari, Inanna's Descent, the Eddas, the Mahabharata, the Dighenis Akritas lais—or, earlier yet, the lullabies of far away deeds, that I found out later were often based on history?

So here I am today, a zero-generation immigrant at the cusp of old age, an unfeminine feminist poised between science and art, a dedicated bookworm who writes in two languages and reads in four, a nurturer of others' speculative fiction stories and a determined non-jumper of bandwagons, in an era when terms like appropriation, ownvoices, censorship, stereotypical, authenticity, policing, identity, "stay in your own lane" constantly lock lightsabers. What of SFF as the genre of imaginative exploration, as the de facto realm of the liminal? What of the double vision, of seeing merit in seemingly irreconcilable positions, that becomes an obligatory attribute of a lifelong wanderer in the Between? What of my own roots—and blossoms—in this struggle? Who speaks for "my people"—and who are "my people" to an exile? I've had these discussions in the previous Feral Astrogator journeys, in *The Other Half of the Sky* and *To Shape the Dark*. *Retellings of the Inland Seas* is a resumption of these conversations, compass needles in labyrinths and starry lanes.

I undertook my voluntary exile in a youthful spirit of eagerness to explore (though there were additional reasons: a military junta in power, with my family known for participation in several resistances; my divergence from local gender rules/roles; my desire to become a research scientist). Like many diasporans, I became a feral orphan belonging to neither culture: I sang of love and strife like the nightingale pressing its breast against a thorn, in a tongue I learned after infancy—and languages learned past that threshold are processed differently by the brain/mind, "through a glass darkly"; I've had my first and last name mispronounced my entire adult life; and the tales of my ancestors became constant whispers shadowing my path, tinged with the incurable nostalgia of idealized neverwheres/whens that nevertheless kept me intact as I inevitably got buffeted and bruised while making my way.

It's my great luck, and equally great burden, that I come from a civilization that is millennia old and has had half a dozen flowerings—and that the ripples of this civilization have been formative for a large portion of humanity. This means that stories from my part of the world are deemed common property, with all the outcomes implicit in this categorization. All too often, when I read SFF I see layers of my own native stories peeking under the surface like imperfectly scraped palimpsests, like submerged ships: from the "surprise" in *The Empire Strikes Back* (which I guessed as soon as I heard there was one) to the space-opera retelling of the struggles of the Hellenic city-states against the Persian empire in Jack McDevitt's *A Talent for War.*

In today's rush to promote diversity, it has become topical—and to a significant measure justified—to ask: who will/should tell culture-specific stories, especially if most of such telling is still done by the equivalent of tourists, omits or glosses the exploited, enslaved, slaughtered, and uprooted, and confers accolades and rewards for "originality" that is in fact a metric of collective readership ignorance? What does "write what you know" mean for a far-roaming genre, for the lucid dreaming of a complicated species that migrated throughout its entire planet, ceaselessly cross-fertilizing? Is indeed "nothing specifically Greek about the Odyssey" as Neil Gaiman opined, to defend being selected to write the tale of the Monkey King?—though the wish of the Chinese producers for a name well-known in the Anglophone West to anchor the effort is entirely understandable.

In this regard, SFF has a more acute problem than mainstream fiction due to two persistent characteristics which flatten the stories borrowed from the "public archive" that aspire to appear new or at least renewed: parochialism and neoteny. This is without even discussing the commissar/inquisitor-style scorched-earth purity patrolling that has been going on at various borders best left nebulous and porous.

Despite its claims to universalism, SF remains firmly embedded in US paradigms and the unique advantages (and limitations) of the English language, as witnessed from its interpretations of slavery to most of its attempts to create "unusual" socio-political systems and languages. To give just one example, it remains largely undiscussed among devotees of both Star Wars and social justice that the Jedi practice Ottoman-style devşirme ("blood tax"), a.k.a. forcible childgathering that produces emotionally stunted janissaries. Authors from beyond the US are expected to write exclusively about their backgrounds, becoming willy-nilly exoticized representatives of their entire "kind" (plus subject to authenticity checks by their own group/s) while they must also homogenize their offerings to render them palatable to a readership that's usually entirely unaware of the unfamiliar context, too often resulting in embarrassing hymns to derivative works.

SF also doesn't have collective long-term memory except for auto-worship of the Leaden Era trinity of Asimov, Heinlein and Clarke. Many up-and-coming writers express righteous hope that the "dinosaurs" will soon limp onto their designated ice floes, thereby solving all the genre's problems (if only). So the genre keeps reinventing and grinding wheels, including concepts borrowed from other times and places—and in particular from stories that have become foundational and get retold in infinities of flattened versions leached of all resonance and potency. Most SFF readers vaguely recall that Athena sprang from the forehead of Zeus; too few know that she had a Titan mother, Metis (Wisdom), Lilith to Zeus' Adam and metalsmith of her daughter's helmet—which gives a different hue to this genesis myth and makes Athena a mixed-blood offspring.

The relatively recent insistence in SFF to write only "what you know" has at least one valid reason: the shallow, mediocre portrayals of other cultures (broadly defined) that too often descend to cardboard caricatures—and not of Wayang or Karaghiozis shadowplay quality either. At the same time, this injunction is potentially lethal for non-Anglo writers. We are no longer full citizens of our natal culture—we're not up to its current idioms and customs—nor are we ever accepted as full citizens of our adopted one: many of us read our works in legacy accents; these works have the giveaway shimmer of submerged harmonies, of unexpected word couplings; we have to create while wrangling with the dissonances and glass-shard barriers in our minds and hearts; and we tend to produce uncategorizable (and hence unmarketable) hybrids unless we happen to hit Pavlovian buttons of fashions du jour and Chosen One anointments by the Big Five (Four? Three?).

So do/should stories divide us or unite us? The answer, of course, is "both"—because they help us figure out who we are;

and who we are is informed by every aspect of our context, though we do have a core self that remains fixed, courtesy of the brain neurons that never multiply or divide after birth but constantly create new synapses and hence new connections and paths. For exiles, the core self is always diffracted through yearning, in part because we're more culturally hardwired than we'd like to think. SF is theoretically an ideal storytelling medium for those who walk the wind between the stars, who act as scouts and bridges. And just as SF will not prosper if it turns completely inward and abandons knowledge of real science (something I discussed in *To Shape the Dark*), neither will it flourish if it abandons the tales humanity has told around campfires from the moment they realized that memory is crucial to survive and thrive. We have immutable need for such tales as a species that evolved in small multi-linked groups, hence our endless fascination with family sagas from the Atreides of Mycenae to the Atreides of Arrakis.

People who know me are aware that I'm unabashedly unibrow in my art tastes. I enjoy—and deem completely valid and worthwhile works whose foundations are rooted in older stories regardless of cultural provenance and creator affiliations, provided that their makers have enough skill, sensibility and knowledge (whether innate or acquired) to transmute the material into something "rich and strange", to add new threads and perhaps new functions to the old tapestry. It will come as no surprise that I've used motifs from the inexhaustible Mediterranean legacy in my own stories: the singer in the underworld ("The Stone Lyre"), the crucified nonconformist ("Dry Rivers"). But I also wanted to hear other voices, reweaving tales from the Inland Seas which were the cradle to much that still defines us decisively no matter how globalized we've become.

So I lit my mountaintop signaling fires, as I did before for *The Other Half of the Sky* and *To Shape the Dark*, and relatives of the heart responded. Again without any urging from me, as with the scientific disciplines of the protagonists in *To Shape the Dark*, each contributor chose a different story to transmute.

I put a list of correspondences after the stories. As is the case with all quality art, the stories can be enjoyed fully without any knowledge of their original source—but such knowledge deepens appreciation. Ranging from the Crimean peninsula to the Maghrib, from a Minoan exodus through wormholes to Furies on Mars, from space Argonauts to cloned twins to Scythian and Imazighen warrior queens, crackling with fallen angels and defiant women, the unquenchable ancestral beacons burn with renewed vigor and limn new paths alongside the old ones.

Those who embark on such journeys are "my people" if I have any—those who honor collective memories by (re) shaping them with passion and flair while aware of their siren-like allures and dangers. Some of the contributors have first languages different from English; some half-remember languages spoken by their grandparents while growing up; others spoke English from the get-go. But all still hear and follow the beating of great wings from distant times and places, the dreams that nourish us while they trouble us, and keep us exploring.

> "Here we moored the ship to mend the broken oars,
> to drink water and to sleep.
> The sea that embittered us is deep and unexplored
> and unfolds a boundless calm.
> Here among the pebbles we found a coin
> and threw dice for it.
> The youngest won it and disappeared.
>
> We put to sea again with our broken oars."
>
> — Ghiórghos Seféris, *Mythistorema,* 12: Bottle in the Sea
> translated by Edmund Keeley

Into the Wine-Dark Sea

A.M. Tuomala

That long breath when we came
unmoored, aurorae in our wake. Thermosphere
broke against the bow and
parted, shedding fire—kindling—we slipped
into the great cold sea of stars.

Ungirdling, we
floated free. Medea, long
hair streaming, eyes dragontooth bright. *Jason,*
I've never seen so many stars. Tears
pearling the air; Orpheus hailing
the earth, the heavens, the sea:
This is the Argo, turning
back for one last look.

Earth haloing Coronus, hurricanes spiraling
up from Haiti to lick Lisbon's ear—
Mopsus cartwheeling ears over atmosphere,
Laughing jay-wild, lit from inside.
Hey, he said. *Look*, he said. *I'll be*
damned, he said, fingers spread like pinion
feathers.

I'm flying.

Canthus catching his hand, tender, tethered.

I've got you.

Titanium girders gleaming; Atalanta's
apple cheeks golden and
Eurytus and Eurytion and Eurydamus all speared
across with light. In our dozens, be
holding the sun through the nightless void.

Proud brave strangers, we.
Some great voyage lay before us
And before us
And before

Sirens

Melissa Scott

Perseis stood at the outer edge of what had been Aptera's Observation Lounge, stripped now of everything that could have helped to repair the ships that had taken Aptera's staff and residents on their one-way journey to what they hoped was safety. One by one she had launched them, flinging them out into the night to enter the adjacent possible on the courses she and what was left of Gray Promised Tree had calculated for them. Whether they had made their planetfalls safely or not, she didn't know, and likely never would, and she glanced over her shoulder at the nearly empty space. With only the most basic built-ins left behind, it looked as though a great slice had been removed from the station's wheel, open to space on the viewing side.

That was deliberate, of course; Observation was designed to quick-seal in case of disaster, but it made the nanites shiver in her blood, aware of the empty spaces, of the crippled stub-AI at the station's heart. That had been her doing, her hand that had severed the link between Gray Promised Tree's full self and the share that managed the station's systems— her responsibility, as Firstborn and Holder of the station— because the moment she had seen that attack was led by the greatest of the quantum AI was the moment she had known that the station was doomed. She could stave off disaster long enough to save its people—perhaps, if all had gone well— but she could not save Aptera, which she had loved for the best part of her working life, and if she could not save it, she would not save herself. Or so she had thought, in the first hot pain of betrayal.

She turned back to the transparent steel that formed the viewing port, staring at the stars that blazed beyond it. Aptera was currently positioned 45 degrees off galactic vertical, the optimum launch position for the last escapees, and she hadn't wasted fuel returning it to its more conventional position. The plane of the galaxy crossed the window at a matching angle, a great slash of light that frayed into darkness only at the edges, where the galaxy's heart trailed away into lesser streams of stars.

That glory, that spectacle, was a lie. The light of those stars was old, a past image no longer valid; present truth followed behind, a black nothing where those stars had been. The Event was coming, propagating through the adjacent possible, traveling through normal space at near lightspeed. Already, many of those stars were gone, and soon—within three months, within a year—the Event would reach out to envelop Aptera. Its sun, too, would vanish in a swirl of unreal energies, snuffed like a candle by whatever it was the rebel AI had unleashed. Or, just possibly, not: she had only stub-AI to work with, a fragment of Gray Promised Tree, and without Promise's full power—without the full power of quantum AI—her calculations were imperfect. Aptera might be just beyond the Event's reach; the impossible unmaking might lap at their doorstep and leave them be. Or the wave might break over them at full force, destroying them all. She could not be sure without more powerful AI, and that was the one thing she could not risk.

I could ask. I'm capable of discretion.

That was Gray Promised Tree, a whisper at the back of her mind, soft and—if it was possible—faintly amused. "We can't risk it," she said aloud, and felt the equivalent of a sigh wash over her.

I am incomplete. Imperfect. I would be more use if I were whole.

How many other AI shares had made the same complaint

in the moments before the AI War erupted? Perseis wondered. Quantum AI existed as least as much in the adjacent possible as in normal space/time; they could divide and subdivide their attention, their very selves, in ways that even the Firstborn could not fully imagine. The whole could betray the parts, override loyalties and desires... "It's too much of a risk," she said again, and stared up at the blinding stars.

Captain Harsharin has accepted your invitation. She will meet you tonight.

That was also Gray Promised Tree, relaying a message from Aptera itself, and Perseis nodded, letting the nanites relay her agreement. "Open my workspace."

Ulrike Harsharin stood in the docking bay's control room, overlooking *Nostos* as it hung in the cradle. The worst damage was repaired, the cracked plates and strained sections of the frame cut away and replaced from the seemingly endless stock Aptera Station concealed in its depths. The stressed environmentals had been overhauled, blown components replaced, and the entire system reconfigured to accommodate triple the original rated passenger load: Aptera had spare stock and seemingly endless power for that as well.

She remembered what it had been like getting there, falling, endlessly falling along the edge of the adjacent possible, systems screaming, until at last they'd managed a controlled failure of the FTL envelope, and *Nostos* had tumbled out of the adjacent possible into normal space/time just close enough to Aptera to limp into the docking bay. The station had been empty, except for its Firstborn chatelaine, and she had welcomed them with open arms. It had been standard rations for the first month, but then the Eki Perseis had coaxed the Gardens back into production, and *Nostos*'s survivors moved out of the bay and into the station's generous living space.

"We can't stay," she said, mostly to herself, and her chief

engineer looked up from his data board.

"Sorry?"

"Nothing. Talking to myself."

Isa-Myrgori gave her the look that deserved. He was Facienda, one of the waterfolk designed to help exploit the middle reaches of Ithaka's oceans, and they had worked together for years. "I half wish we could," he said. "Stay, I mean."

She sighed, dropping the pretense. "But we can't. We've been over that a hundred times."

Isa-Myrgori nodded, rubbing the gill lines closed tight along his long neck. "We've determined that the anomalous energy wave that passed us two weeks ago is definitely the same kind of energy that we saw when we left Canosa. The Eki has confirmed that. She's calling it a harbinger wave, and says we can expect more of them, and stronger ones as the Event's leading edge comes closer. And it's propagating in the adjacent possible, not just realspace."

"I know." And that meant they needed to leave soon, if they were to have any chance of reaching Ithaka: they had barely managed to escape Canosa when the Event ate the system's sun, and Harsharin had no intention of risking anything like that ever again. "We need a course."

"You said the Eki would write us one."

"She said she would." If only that were enough, Harsharin thought. Bad enough that they couldn't risk contracting even a stub-AI to pilot them through the adjacent possible—the way they'd always done it, back when things were normal, when the AI and the Firstborn were locked in a reluctant truce—but they'd jumped from Canosa in company with a dozen other ships, and seen them all ripped apart in the adjacent possible. She was still not sure how *Nostos* had escaped, except sheer blind luck.

"We don't have any choice," Isa-Myrgori said. "We can't stay, the Eki's made that clear. But if she gives us a course, if we cling to it, don't let anything force us to deviate... That's more or less how we got here, anyway."

Thirty people in the crew and crew-family, Harsharin thought. Three hundred forty-seven more random residents of Canosa who'd fought their way onto this escape ship and not another, including twenty-three children under sixteen with no accompanying adult. Three hundred seventy-seven souls she'd promised to bring home, or at least to safety. She was a freighter captain, under contract to the Barba Sisters, a perfectly ordinary trading combine, not some hero out of a travel-tale; and for the thousandth time since the War began, she felt the weight of her own inadequacies.

She was Secondborn, part of the great middle of humanity, neither exalted like the Firstborn who had unlocked the secrets of space/time nor purpose-built like the Facienda, a plain captain with a decent record and no profound ambitions beyond being a good provider to her kin. To be thrust into this was, she felt, asking more than was reasonable—and yet there was no choice. But she wanted more than a course—needed more than just a course—and she'd told the Eki Perseis exactly that, when they'd last argued over the best way to escape. "How long will it take us to get packed up?"

"Ideally? People have spread out, settled down." Isa-Myrgori shrugged. "A ten-day?"

"Let's plan for that," Harsharin said. "If the ship's ready."

"She's better than ready," Isa-Myrgori answered, with a fond look at the transport gleaming in the worklights, and Harsharin couldn't help smiling. If anything could bring them through, it was her crew.

It had taken Perseis the better part of a month to come up with a solution, and even then it was a makeshift, a fragile construct that could too easily melt away into disaster, not improved by the extra hours she had spent checking the calculations one last time. Because she was unsure, she asked Harsharin to come to her, not in Observation this time, or any other neutral space, but in the segments of the Inner Ring where the Firstborn had made their home. It was optimized for them, delicate colors and carefully harmonized shapes, channels that ran with light and water and a twist of *indevillia tarensi* that clung to growth medium just below the center point of the arching ceiling, and trailed cascades of golden flowers that reached almost to the ground.

Light filtered through the *indevillia*, diffuse and pleasant as a cloudy day, leaving the gray-plush inclines the center of attention—the shared low table set with tea and a covered dish and a plate of the small cakes she had coaxed from Aptera's production systems. The edges of the space were in shadow, and Harsharin's access tube rose into them, a catch-field forming to accept and hold the cylinder as she disembarked, and then flicked out as she left the tube and came forward into the light.

"Eki."

"Captain." Perseis gestured to the other incline, and Harsharin perched uneasily on its edge. "I have a course for you."

Harsharin nodded. "Isa-Myrgori and Juliel say you agree that we need to launch soon if we're going to get ahead of the harbinger waves."

Isa-Myrgori was the ship's engineer, and Facienda; Juliel was the mate, as Secondborn as Harsharin herself. "Yes," Perseis said. "They'll only get more powerful as the Event's leading edge approaches." She paused, trying to read the captain's expression. "If I thought we'd survive, I'd urge you to stay. But there's only a thirty percent chance that Aptera itself will survive, and that's only if it doesn't have to protect inhabitants as well as itself."

"You talk about it as though it's alive." Harsharin sounded faintly startled.

"It is," Perseis said, startled in turn. Surely even the Secondborn understood the nature of the great waystations. They were not artificial intelligence, that was reserved for the AI share that mediated between them and the Firstborn and the far-flung network of stations, but they were artificial life, with feelings and a complexity that defied the circumstances of their creation. She had loved them since she had first entered one—Devashi, lightyears and most of a lifetime ago—and when she had been sent to Aptera, it had been the fulfillment of a dream. Her own station, where she could grow into its unique attributes just as it would be shaped by her... She swallowed sorrow, knowing that world had ended, and made herself concentrate on the business at hand. "In some sense, anyway. It's not quantum AI, of course, or even ordinary AI—it's not what you'd call sentient—but it's a coherent thing."

"But it can't protect us," Harsharin said.

"As I've said, it's more likely that the Event will indeed reach us, that this entire system will be destroyed. If it isn't, I'd like to give it every chance."

"Which—you know, fair enough," Harsharin said. "But there's still the problem of getting through the adjacent possible. I told you what we saw."

Perseis nodded. "I have a solution." She reached for the dark-blue dish and lifted the cover, revealing a tiny iridescent ball the size of her smallest knucklebone. As the light hit it, it began to glow faintly, shimmering from blue to green to gold to red and back to blue again.

"What is that?" Harsharin sounded uneasy.

"Nanites," Perseis answered. "A seed dose. The AI are overwhelming FTL ships with unnecessary data, allowing them to infiltrate ships' systems and destroy the envelope. This will allow you and your crew to ignore and override that data in *Nostos*'s systems."

Harsharin lifted an eyebrow, eying the tiny glowing sphere. It was flickering wanly in the room's light, and Perseis crushed the impulse to say more. "What's the catch? If it were this easy—"

Perseis gave a wry smile. "Not a catch, exactly. It's just that it's not been tested, and it can't be tested without showing the AI how you're evading them. They'd rewrite their program to bypass the protection, and I'd have to create another version to block that. So you have one jump, and shorter would be better."

"That's all right," Harsharin said. "It's only eight hours to Ithaka, a straight-line jump—and you said you had the course—"

"Yes."

"So. Side effects?"

"Ah."

Harsharin sighed. "Let's hear it."

"This is the full nanite burden." Perseis touched the sphere gently, rolling it so that it spat tiny sparks, vivid against the cobalt dish. "Derived from mine. There wasn't time to edit it to only provide protection." Nor had she wanted to try: without being able to test the nanites, there were too many chances to get it wrong, to edit out the thing that was needed to protect ship and crew from the AIs' wrath.

"Making anyone who takes it...essentially one of you," Harsharin said. "Firstborn."

"Yes." Perseis let the word hang between them. It wasn't impossible, everyone knew that the Firstborn could share their nanites not just with each other but with the Secondborn and even the Facienda, changing their very nature as the nanites remade their bodies. The process was strictly controlled, forbidden except under circumstances vanishingly rare and tightly regulated, something even the Firstborn rarely considered. She realized she had no idea if it was something the Secondborn desired or dreaded, and scanned Harsharin's expression for a clue.

"That would be an unauthorized and unregulated transfer," Harsharin said. "Which would be forbidden."

"Yes, we can both quote the law," Perseis snapped. She controlled herself, searching for the words that would convince the captain to take her gift. "It will make you one of us, yes, and the transfer is permanent—"

"I don't want to be other than I am," Harsharin said. The gulf opened between them, fragile, short-lived Secondborn defying the Firstborn who had made their existence possible, and Perseis shivered. The Secondborn were just that, always second, always less: she had not meant to open that old wound, and could do nothing to heal it.

"The truth, then," she said. "I can't do anything else. I can't see another way to get *Nostos* safely through the adjacent possible, and I don't have time to modify it so that it doesn't change you, it would take months—years, maybe—that we don't have, and help from true AI to boot."

"Could you fly the ship?"

Perseis spread her hands. "Is your ship capable of being flown single-handedly? Could all of you stand back and let me do the work even when it seems I'm going to get everyone killed? Or would I have to tie everyone to their bunks to make it happen? And—I'm not a pilot. I'm not crew. I'm not trained at all. Even with the ship to help me, I don't know if I could do it."

She saw Harsharin take a breath. "What am I to say? It would take us weeks to rig *Nostos* for a single control point, and it would take an experienced FTL pilot to handle it. We don't have a choice."

"I don't see any other options," Perseis said. Neither one of them spoke of consequences, she noticed, of Firstborn law or Secondborn anger, or what this might do to Ithaka's society, dropping fifteen or twenty newly-made Firstborn into that carefully balanced world. They were far beyond that point, into uncharted territory, with known space, all the known worlds, in tatters around them. Whatever happened after would have to be dealt with after, outside the old laws and customs—and what was a Firstborn for if not to rewrite the rules of existence? Perseis had never particularly wanted that responsibility, she was hardly of the status to have ever expected to make such choices, but she would face them squarely.

"We need to get home," Harsharin said at last. "That— even if it's just to face the end with friends, families, lovers, that's a thing that matters. And..." She hesitated, then shrugged, wide mouth twisting in a half-smile. "I won't deny that it's tempting to become Firstborn. Since we're telling truths."

Say that when you've become one. Perseis swallowed the words—there were truths and truths, and some were never worth sharing—and offered a smile instead, holding out the dish again. "Then here you are."

Harsharin took it warily between thumb and forefinger, a few sparks fizzing against her skin. "And?"

"Let it dissolve on your tongue." Perseis waited.

Harsharin placed the tiny ball on her tongue and closed her mouth over it, all her attention focused inward as the nanites began to do their work, dissolving the bonding medium and filtering through the mucous membranes of her mouth. Perseis rose from her incline, and came to sit beside her.

"Now what?" Harsharin asked.

"I activate them," Perseis answered. "If you'll allow a kiss?"

"And is this how I'll share with my people?"

Perseis dipped her head. "It's the easiest way."

"All right."

Perseis put one finger under the other woman's chin, tipping her head back slightly. Harsharin did not resist as she leaned closer, and brought their lips together. Harsharin's skin was dry, cool to her touch; Perseis touched her tongue to the other woman's lips and felt the spark leap between them. Harsharin's eyes widened, and Perseis would have pulled away, but Harsharin pulled her closer, deepening the kiss. Perseis let her eyes close, feeling the transfer flow between them, feeling, too, the press of lips and tongues, until at last they pulled apart, breathless and wary.

"Why?" Harsharin whispered, and Perseis was startled by her own response, by the answer that came unbidden.

"I don't want to be alone."

"But why all of us? Surely you don't need all of us..."

"That's the Dedalor mistake." Perseis brushed a finger along Harsharin's cheek, feeling the nanites spreading beneath the skin. "They hoarded everything, thought there would be too many of us, but, I think, the more there are of us, the better choices we have…" It sounded foolish, said aloud, and she let her voice trail off before she tried again. "You'll see soon enough."

Harsharin shook her head. "I don't feel any different?"

"You will," Perseis said.

As Perseis had promised, the changes washed over Harsharin in waves, the nanites finding their way into every part of her body—from the marrow of her bones, where they pulsed and throbbed like a second heart as the original burden replicated itself, to the tips of her fingers, which wept pale blood-tinged fluid now and then for no reason she could see. When she was sure she was relatively stable, Harsharin summoned her crew and laid out the bargain. No one was required to take it, she said, but there would need to be a minimum who accepted it in order to make the last jump to home.

In the end, twenty-eight of the thirty agreed, the two abstaining because of children and partners who would be left behind. Three more balked at the last minute, and Harsharin sent them away with the promise that they could try again later. She was not, she was well aware, a particularly good advertisement for the process, her eyes still bloodshot and her body seized by periodic trembling, but there was no time to waste. She was only grateful that she had never run a sibling-ship, where the crew was pledged to treat each other as kin, and sex was taboo as incest. Her ships had always been Old Rule, nothing forbidden unless it interfered with the running of the ship. Now she was grateful for the web of friendships and affairs and loves small and large that had woven them into a crew, a different kind of family.

She had slept with Juliel many times before, though recently Juliel had turned her attention to the engineer. Harsharin had slept with Isa-Myrgori as well, and that was how the three of them ended up tangled in the bed she had scavenged from the goods left in Aptera, awkward at first, and then as the nanites transferred and took hold, more purposeful and certain. Harsharin ended wedged against the cold bulkhead with Juliel in her arms while Isa-Myrgori sat blinking at the end of the bed. She could see both sets of eyelids opening and closing, could see the gill slits for once open enough to show inner flesh and the faint sheen of the nanites. She could feel the echo of his orgasm, and of Juliel's, as well as her own, but when she met his eyes, he looked away.

"That was…very strange."

Harsharin lifted an eyebrow, absurdly offended, then realized that Juliel was weeping on her shoulder, the tears sparkling against her skin. Harsharin stroked the hair back from her face, and saw the tears moving on her face, crawling back toward her ears and nostrils and the corners of her mouth.

"Juliel?"

Isa-Myrgori leaned forward to stroke her ankle, and hissed at the spark where his fingers met her skin. "Are you all right?"

"Fine," Juliel said, though the tears continued to shimmer and crawl. "I don't even know." She sounded more angry than anything, but Harsharin held her until weeping ended and the last of the tears had been reabsorbed into her body.

"Can you carry on?" she asked at last.

Juliel sat up, pushing back her hair. "Well, I have to."

"Not necessarily." Isa-Myrgori was putting his clothes to rights, even now unwilling to show the remade musculature that marked him as Facienda. "The captain and I —"

"We agreed," Juliel said. "The captain's done her share. We agreed, each one take one, and I'm perfectly capable of doing my bit. I'm fine. I don't know why—I don't know what that was about."

"If you're sure," Harsharin said, and closed her hand over Juliel's, feeling the mate's agreement in her bones. They kissed, a chaste brush of closed lips on soft cheeks, and then on Isa-Myrgori's rougher, sandpaper skin, and Harsharin was left to lie awake while her own nanites huddled in her bones and occasionally shivered with the echoes of other people's pleasures.

Perseis swore this was all normal, part of the nanites' acclimatization, and that it would all settle down soon enough. It could have been worse, she said, they could have suffered fevers or rejection necrosis or half a hundred other bizarre complaints, but after the first days of transmission, Harsharin and her crew were just clumsy and tired, distracted by the constant inner drumbeat.

Perseis looked tired, too, more than any Firstborn had any right to be, and when Harsharin taxed her with it, she blamed it first on the culling of her own nanites to provide the seed, and also to the sudden presence—the noise—of other Firstborn. Like having a horde of toddlers on the station, she said, and none of them with any idea how to interact with her or with the station. Harsharin swallowed her immediate sense of insult, and made sure that she and the others practiced safe connections with each other and with Aptera. The station was indeed alive, as she had not expected, a vast, vaguely affectionate presence that reminded her of draft animals she had seen on Ysteris, and she caught herself hoping it would in fact survive.

On Moving Day—she'd taken to calling it that to try to cut it down to size, and the rest of her crew and the refugees had copied her—she was the last to board, just behind Perseis herself. The Firstborn hesitated in the hatchway, and Harsharin started to put a hand on her back to urge her forward, then remembered the nanites and hastily drew back.

"You can stay if you want," she said, and Perseis gave her a quick, almost startled glance.

"I want to give Aptera every chance." She smiled suddenly. "Myself, too, for that matter."

"We'll do the best we can," Harsharin said. Neither one of them mentioned Gray Promised Tree: Harsharin flatly refused to have it on board, in *Nostos*'s systems, and Perseis had run out of arguments to persuade her. Neither one mentioned the truth: that once *Nostos* entered the adjacent possible there was nothing they could do to keep Gray Promised Tree from returning to the adjacent possible and finding them there. Perseis trusted the AI, or at least the share of it that she had worked with for decades, that much was obvious, but after Canosa, Harsharin couldn't bring herself to believe that any AI was anything less than hostile.

They cast off from Aptera without incident, the station depressurizing the bay and opening the clamshell doors as though everything were ordinary. Harsharin let the junior crew handle it, watching from her seat on the control room's upper tier, getting used to the way the nanites interacted with the ship's systems, so that she felt the ship's health like pinpricks on her own skin. There was no room for testing, for fear the lurking AI would use any test to figure out how to overwhelm the nanites, but she was willing to take the chance. *Nostos* had always been a lively ship, eager to respond; with the nanite boost, the effect was exaggerated, as though she sailed a ship without a keel, perpetually ready to slip aside from the intended course..

At least they had time to get used to the new feelings, the new interactions, in the run out to heliopause. By then, Harsharin felt confident that she could handle the ship, and she could see the same certainty in the bridge crew. The juniors stepped down, though they remained on standby— less for anything they could do if things went horribly wrong, Harsharin thought, than that no one wanted to sit this one out in a cabin. Even Perseis had claimed the supercargo's seat rather than retreat to a cabin.

"We're coming up on the jump point," said Marimen, the navigator, and Juliel looked up from the pilot's console. That was her privilege, as mate, and no one was going to argue with her.

"Course is locked."

"Myrgori?" Harsharin asked, and there was a moment's pause as the engineer's fingers skittered over his controls.

"Ready to go," he said at last. "All systems nominal."

"Jump point in five," Marimen said.

"Right." There was nothing to be gained by delaying the inevitable. Harsharin flipped the switch that triggered the all-hands alert, and opened the ship-wide intercom. "All hands, all hands. Jump in five minutes. I repeat, jump in five minutes." She set the words to repeat, and closed the speaker in the control room. Everyone should be secured in their cabins, strapped into the bunks that were designed to provide some protection if *Nostos* split apart on exiting the adjacent possible. There was nothing more she could do for them except bring the ship through. "Systems check, please."

She felt the ship's response before her crew could answer, and heard in their sudden stumbles that they'd felt the same unsettling connection. "People. We're doing this the regular way. Give me a systems check."

She felt the ship's pulse again, but this time the answers came promptly and without mistakes. On the main display, their course drove toward the fleck of light that marked their insertion point, numbers flowing at the corners of the screen to track time-until-jump, alignment, field strength, and capacitor charge. Everything looked good—everything felt good, confirming the crew's quick exchanges, and she checked her screens a final time.

"Capacitor at full," Isa-Myrgori said.

"Jump point achieved," Marimen said.

Harsharin nodded. "Go."

The nanites felt the kick more than she did herself, a massive internal shift as though every cell in her body had leaped a centimeter up and sideways. She gasped, recovered, feeling the same momentary confusion among the rest of the crew, her eyes going to the display. The clock was running, the numbers solid green; the lower right quadrant of the screen swam with numbers as the automatic systems worked through the calculations prescribed by Perseis's course.

"Check in, please."

"Everything's green for go," Juliel answered. "On course and running solid."

"Field and envelope are nominal," Isa-Myrgori said.

She could feel the truth of their words in the warmth in her bones, strange and weirdly familiar all at the same time. "Hold the course."

"Holding course, confirmed," Juliel said.

They were all not saying it, not thinking it. Last time had been terrible from the start, a disaster as soon as they made the jump; she was still holding herself in readiness, waiting for things to slide out of true, but they were locked to the ship's systems, and everything seemed steady.

"Anything impinging on the field?" They had no true sensors in the adjacent possible, but the ship could register changes—the last trip it had been screaming from the start, every readout jumping straight to red and staying pinned there as they careened along the shredding edge of possibility. This was...almost normal, and she cringed inwardly, wishing she could flick fingers in propitiation. There was nothing more superstitious than an FTL captain. Especially Secondborn. Especially Secondborn without AI aboard. Except she was not that anymore.

"All green," Marimen said, and Harsharin made herself nod as though she had expected it.

There was a sound beside her, from the supercargo's chair, soft as a cough and then louder. She turned to see Perseis clutching the arms of her chair, red-faced and staring. She dragged in a breath with a sound like tearing silk, and then her head went back, eyes fluttering. There was a strange sheen on the lower part of her face, over her lips and chin, a smear of iridescence, and a brighter flicker of color crawling back over her hands: something wrong with her nanites, Harsharin guessed, but she'd never heard of anything like it.

"Keep your posts," she snapped. "Hold the course. Whatever you do, hold the course."

She got a mumble of acknowledgment, a stronger pulse from the nanites, knitting them into a loose network, and released herself from the safety webbing. There had to be something she could do, some way to break what was going on—Gray Promised Tree, maybe, betraying them as she'd known it would. She reached for Perseis's wrist, feeling for a pulse, and, too late, felt the shock as the other's nanites met her skin.

She was flung out into nothingness, into light and fire and flickering dark, unable to pull her hand away. She spun in dizzying circles, knowing at the same time that she stood frozen on *Nostos*'s bridge, her hand still touching Perseis's wrist. She closed her eyes, knowing it would do nothing, tried to marshal the nanites in her own bloodstream. She could feel them, yes, flung back from her hand as though it wasn't any longer hers, and she focused on that, determined to reclaim her flesh. The blackness swooped and slowed, steadied, and she felt the nanites at work, barricading, blocking, intercepting and interpreting...

This was the adjacent possible as the Firstborn saw it, not-space reduced to sketch and schematic, lines of light slashing the dark in a pattern she could not read. To her left, there was a line of smoldering orange, like a sunset or an oncoming fire: the Event, she guessed, and hoped it was keeping the AI occupied even while it was consuming as many resources as its brilliance would suggest. There was no sign of anyone else, not Perseis, not Gray Promised Tree—and surely Perseis had to be there, it was her nanites that had seized Harsharin like a drowning man seizes another swimmer. Where was she?

Someone was calling her, the word slowed and dulled by the illusion, and Harsharin thrust her free hand into her hair, pulling hard. The vision faded, but not enough, and she dug nails into her scalp until she could see through the shadow to the shapes of the bridge. Juliel was out of her chair and moving toward her, Marimen now on the conn, and Harsharin fought for control to speak, to form slow words so that she could be understood.

"Don't...touch."

Juliel froze, hand outstretched, and then retreated, eyes wide. "Captain...?"

"Hold the course," Harsharin said again. She could feel the others' nanites reaching for hers, attempting to reestablish contact, to reinforce their loose connection, and she pulled herself inward, refusing the connection. "Don't touch. Any touch."

Juliel lifted her hands in acknowledgment, backing away, and Harsharin held her breath. She was balanced on the knife's edge, could see both the adjacent possible and the sliver of reality contained within the FTL envelope. Perseis was out there somewhere, or some part of her was, bound by her nanites and maybe by the decades she'd worked with AI; the ship, the crew were safe, held in the envelope, unable to receive the attack, and she—she was balanced between. She could let Perseis go, and that would probably guarantee *Nostos* safe passage; she could try to save Perseis, and doom the ship and everyone on it.

She knew what she should do, knew where her primary obligation lay—but Perseis had taken them in when they washed up on her doorstep, had welcomed them and fed them and offered them this way out. If she had transformed them, it was meant to serve them as well. She looked down, seeing her own hand frozen a few centimeters from Perseis's wrist. A glittering thread spun between them, bright and fragile, flashing as it caught the light. Forged by the nanites, she realized, a physical connection between their realities, and she focused all her attention on that strand. Slowly, fumbling for technique, she coaxed her nanites toward that thread, still keeping their barriers intact, impermeable, while strengthening the point of contact. For an instant, she thought she felt Perseis there beside her, a familiar shadow against the dark, felt her touch and cling.

She could go no further, not without tipping the balance one way or the other. All she could do was hold that point of contact, keep that door open, while *Nostos* drove toward the end of its course and safety.

Perseis clung to that point of light, a single solidity in the spinning haze that was her view of the adjacent possible. It was her mistake, she owned it freely—she should have adjusted her own nanite burden so that it also shed the data attack. It was too late now to reconstruct it; if she did so, she'd show the AI-share whose attention was turned their way how to destroy *Nostos*. She didn't think it was Gray Promised Tree, or at least she hoped in some corner of her mind that it wasn't, but there wasn't enough to identify it without letting herself fall deeper into the adjacent possible. *Nostos* would survive, at least, and surely Harsharin would survive with it, but Perseis wanted to live. Even if the Firstborn world was falling to tatters, she found no reason to go down with it. She could be of use, she had already created something new that she would need to tend—and most of all, she wasn't done.

She focused inward, marshaling her nanites, feeling them fraying toward the adjacent possible even as she reached to hold them. There were techniques for that, basic skills she had learned in childhood, and she reached for them, turning and twisting until she found the grain of space and aligned herself against it. The drain slowed to a trickle, a few particles shredded here and there, and she dared to pull herself a little closer to the real.

She could separate herself a little better now, though she could feel the AI-share as a vortex, pulling at her even as it flung mindless data at *Nostos* and her crew, trying to overload their systems. Already it was beginning to make sense of what she'd done, to find cracks and crevices to take its data, and she contorted herself again, trying to block its passage. It swept her aside, ripping away another packet of nanites, and in the vast distance of the real, she heard herself scream.

She twisted again, aligned herself another time, lying across the grain of space, and felt the tug of Harsharin's connection fractionally stronger. Time was passing, time had passed, though the adjacent possible was outside those constraints. She needed to free herself, somehow, and reconnect with her physical self before *Nostos* left the adjacent possible. She could feel the real world close and heavy, tried to kick herself back to it, but the techniques of a lifetime failed her, leaving her hanging gasping in the dark.

The AI-share swatted at her, and she caught a taste of Gray Promised Tree in its complexity, a grief she could not spare the time to feel. She reached for memories buried in the nanites themselves, shaping and shredding a portion of the burden, until she could release it into the adjacent possible like ink in water. There was a momentary swirl, a cessation of pressure, and she hauled herself back into her body, slamming all doors closed again behind her.

She opened her eyes to smoke and shouting, alarms blaring across *Nostos*'s control room, flashing orange and red from every screen. She gasped, choking, then shoved herself upright, feeling the fragile tie that had held her to Harsharin snap. Harsharin spared her a single look, eyes wide and worried, then turned back to the fight. "Course!"

"Still holding." That was the mate, Juliel, and at her side the navigator Marimen pulled hard on his controls.

"Envelope's at seventy," the Facienda engineer called. "We're losing it."

"Time to drop?"

"Twenty minute by the course clock," Juliel answered.

Still outside Ithaka's system, Perseis thought. But not far off. If the damage wasn't too bad… The blaring alarms and the bitter taste of smoke made that unlikely, but surely it wouldn't be beyond repair. They'd rebuilt the systems to accommodate the extra passengers, she'd suggested redundancies that the engineer had seized and expanded on, surely that would be enough…

"Sixty-nine," the engineer reported. "Sixty-five's point of no return."

"Stand by to punch us out," Harsharin said. "But wait. Wait for my signal."

Perseis could feel the ship shuddering, could see the crew's eyes shifting from screen to screen, the AI's data overriding normal function. She could feel Harsharin shaking, too, and reached out to touch the captain's wrist. Harsharin jerked, and Perseis opened herself, offering her nanites, her very self, to be used as needed to bring *Nostos* home. She felt Harsharin steady, her unfamiliar burden stabilized by the connection to its source, and felt the captain tense.

"Now. Punch out now."

The engineer threw switches and both pilot and mate hunched their shoulders as though that could protect them. The ship wailed, a last long groan of stressed metal and fiber, and they were abruptly in normal space again. The air was still filled with smoke, but the worst of the red lights had faded to orange.

"Reports," Harsharin snapped. "Damage control?"

"Working on it, captain."

"Position?"

"Still working," Juliel said.

"Translight envelope collapse successful," the engineer said. "Field stable. Sunlight engines online and on standby."

"I have Ithaka on scanners," Juliel announced, and there was an audible sigh of relief. "We're just inside heliopause. I'll have transit time once Myrgori gets me full engine status."

"Working on it." The engineer bent closer over his screens.

"Damage control?" Harsharin said again. "Where are my reports?"

"Team Alpha here." The voice came from the speakers. "Hull's intact, and we show minor damage to the maneuver engines, should be within limits."

"Beta here. Creeping burnout in secondary electrics, confined to that system and under control."

"Medics here. Some burns in engineering, the nanites are handling that for us. Reports of minor injury among the passengers, bruises and a broken arm so far. We'll follow up."

"Gamma here. Environmentals are sound. Two cut-outs tripped, but the affected compartments are running on backup. We'll have them online again shortly."

Perseis leaned back in her chair as the damage teams reported in, letting their words wash over her. From the sound of it, they would make Ithaka, even if it took a week or more to get there. She closed her eyes, exhaustion washing over her. There were not enough nanites left to compensate, or perhaps they were simply too stressed themselves; she let herself drift, and woke to Harsharin saying her name.

"Captain?"

"Are you all right?"

Perseis blinked. The air already tasted better, and there were fewer orange lights on the consoles; her body felt much the same, cautiously reasserting its normal state, and she nodded. "Thank you. I think—I made a stupid mistake. Thank you for pulling me out."

"Dumb luck," Harsharin said. "I had no idea what I was doing."

"The nanites know," Perseis began, the lesson she had recited since she'd received her adult burden, then stopped. "Or at least they used to. With everything—I don't know how much you can rely on their knowledge."

"I'll remember that," Harsharin said. "We've all got a lot to learn."

"I'd be glad to teach you what I can," Perseis said. "I owe you."

"You saved us first," Harsharin said. "We're even." She paused. "But—we'd all be glad of your help. With everything—we're going to need it."

They would need help with the nanites, learning to use them and their new skills, certainly, and Perseis would need someplace to stay, someone to become: it would balance in the end. Assuming there would be anything left to survive for— but she wouldn't think of that today. "I'm at your service," she said, and Harsharin smiled before she turned away.

Hide and Seek

Shariann Lewitt

e are a race of heroes and we fought the Children of the Gods. You should have seen the place burn, the women scream for mercy. Had a few of them too. Lost them, more's the pity. You know I was the one who came up with the idea that won us the final victory. You might hear about the warriors, the champions, but I figured out how to get us behind their lines. Pattern recognition, that's the thing. You can fool it, you know. Doesn't even take great tech, though we had the best." Then he blinks and comes back to here and now. "You got those calculations yet, nav? To get home? On where home's supposed to be?"

I heard that story plenty times of before. Dear Holy Primes, the Old Man never shuts up. This battle, that crossing, the armada of all time, and especially his very own stealthy plan. Shaalaa, so he picked up a few tricks on image processing. We're all bored to Antares and back by his stories and there ain't no fucking gods. So far as any of us can tell, he only fought First-Lost whose tech isn't even up to ours. I wish he would shut his trap but he holds my contract and I've had worse.

Besides, I don't have much choice just now since I'm wedged half into the access hatch trying to tie together what I can of the remaining nav bits to get us home, and me off this damn tub. Fiddling up around the char makes it a toss-up whether it's worse to try to tie the comp back together or just plot the damn trajectory by hand. It wouldn't be too bad if we weren't in the Belt.

Asteroids. Can't track 'em by eye and can't blast the bloody things to vacuum. Well, not with the blazers at the two thirds energy packs we have left, and we'll need the extra fuel if we run into any trouble with the slingshot maneuver around Mars.

"While we're at it, can you hand me the ion wrench, Commander?" He presses something into my hand. "No, the other ion wrench, the one that says 'Ion 3590' on the handle. Shaayaa, that one."

If only the damn starboard nav hadn't been busted to shit, the port overcompensating, and the main nav comp blown a couple of gaskets in between. Hey, we weren't crushed by that world-chomping hole, density so far through the fucking mags that even now I can't look at the readings without my stomach doing backflips. I got us into the asteroid belt in human homespace and that's more luck than the Old Man has any right to have. How much fuel I managed to save on that maneuver? That's my own pure skill and more than we deserve—but still way too tight on what we need to make me comfortable.

"Hold that steady, would you?" I tell him while I seal the board into place. Six more to go. Be a whole lot easier, too, if these dirtballers didn't insist on all the artificial grav in every Prime damned turn and corner on this hulk. The galley and the head, of course, but in the maintenance shafts, for Holy Numbers' sake? Dirtballers aren't willing to live without their local vertical all the time and it drives us spacers crazy. Walking, climbing, everything takes three times the energy we need, not to mention the drain on ship's reserves.

Yeah, we keep the gravity regs in quarters and work areas so we can survive, we all know how the physiology works. Besides, there's more important considerations. Like the Guild interhall rugby tournament.

Gotta have grav for rugby and we're all determined to win, every one of us, even if most on this excuse of a ship are Greens with a smattering of Whites and Grays. Even Grove, eldest of us all amen, with three rows of mission beads, half of them military, in his long braids, can shove his weight in the scrum. And when Cuddy and Orris get in there, well, there's a reason they're always on opposite squads.

In fact, it's become so popular that some of the Old Man's soldier troops join in our games so now we've got full size teams. Rugby practice in full one Gee doesn't count as part of required grav time. Not when you're White squad. I may be a bit past my prime playing days, but I gotta keep up to partner and coach when I get back home. I swear we're gonna take the Guild Cup this cycle.

"And why exactly am I playing servant to you?" I forgot the Old Man for a moment, lucky me.

"Because I know how to put this thing back together," I tell him, ignoring the part where I'm not sure if anyone could put it back together. I have to cannibalize parts from two wrecks in the fleet that didn't quite make it whole from the hole. Torn up and without a crew (don't like to think about that part), the remnants had been pulled in our wake when we escaped. And lucky for us, or we wouldn't have had the supplies for any repairs at all.

"You know how I ended that war?" he asks. Again.

"You already told me. About twenty times or more. You were tricksy with the damn pattern recog. And you know what's weak in the image processing algorithm. That if it reads only a little of some part off, it'll fill in that small bit and not read around it, so far as I understand."

"That's a crude understanding."

Tell stories to anyone, he could tell stories to me about my own contract. And if I'd known maybe I wouldn't have been so ready to sign up.

Belay that. I'd have signed. Being abandoned on a backwater dirtball like Barker's End, I'd had precious few opportunities to leave the damn gravity well. Naalaa, I was almost ready to hire on as an extra hand to get out of there. End they call it because End it is, and I'm off that place for well and good. I don't think the Old Man is about to dump me on some back-ass world without my pay like my previous Captain did. Not that I thought she was going to do that either. My mistake.

Besides, how many offers of an event horizon was I ever going to see in my life? Surviving the thing will make a great story and kick up my rep by a few lightyears when I get back to civilization, and when I get back to the Guild Hall I'm gonna get the damn finest mission bead the very best lamp artist can make to thread in my braids. Something with a twist and five colors that'll cost me a week's pay.

Now asteroids. Anyone ever tell this guy how damn hard it is to fly the Belt? All that crap hurtling at you, recalibrating speed and angles all the time, and it's all on me, and at all hours. And not even a decent meal on this hulk either. Once I get off this crate, I swear I will never, ever, no matter what, eat dried Veg-O Chick-O Ramen again, even if it means starving to death.

We set two more boards. I test them and they look good. My neck cramps up under that panel. He's a big guy, I'll give him that, big and broad and grizzled, with scars all over his arms when he rolls up his sleeves. His fingers are the size of pool cues. I can barely maneuver even the smallest welder around them, kneeling and bent backwards wearing a headlight so I can see up into the jumble of garbage that pretends to be the innards of a nav comp. I hand him another board and shove it into place with one of his fat, flat fingers to hold it steady while I dance around to hit the weld.

"You wiggle around like that, I'm gonna start to think of you like you're one hot old lady," he says.

"I am a hot lady," I say up into the cavity. How many more of these do I have to do? "And not so old, neither. Under forty beads up here." I tap my head—I must admit I am proud of the thirty-two beads that attest to my experience and expertise along with my full double corona of honor beads. Not one other spacer on this scow has that many, not even Grove, who is most senior here.

"Spacers got stupid standards, then," he grouses. "You in this line of work because no one ever wanted to register commitment with you?"

"That's over the line." Because spacers do their jobs and

do not share personal information. Especially with dirtballers. And I have no desire to tell anyone why I had been stranded on the End looking for any berth I could take.

Maybe someday it'll make a good story, but hiring on to run dark through the Sparks, that shows a lack of judgment. I knew in the back of my mind that had to be some kind of dead op and likely a hit on the likes of Captain Barr (if that legendary pirate really exists). And I should have known that anyone who had the damn nerve to try a dark run in a pirate sector was not to be trusted. And shaalaa, she dumped me on Barker's without my wages after I'd managed to outrun the four skull flags gunning after us.

At least those pirates wouldn't be looking for me on this piece of shit. They'd expect me to have standards. After the run I gave them they'd probably hire me on and right now that sounds pretty good. Their ships, so I've heard, are the very latest spacer spec.

"You're done," I tell him. "I have to make a bunch of connections before I install the rest of it." Okay, that's a bit of a fib. I can do it all at the end but, given the mess in here, it's easier to get some of the tie-ins out of the way before adding even more muck to the mix. Besides, I'm sick of his company. Even if I have to do the final installation on my own.

He leaves me with blessed silence. In the zone I get it done and more, tidy up the transmission lines, run diagnostics, clean up the code that had gone buggy when we hit a magnetic field with all the damage we'd taken. I get that nav comp running as pretty as if it shipped new in the box, so when the dinner bell interrupts my hyper focus, I'm ready to stretch and call it a good day's work.

Even better, the stack in the galley doesn't have the entirely too familiar Veg-O Chick-O green stripe decorated with little pink explosions on the dirty white package. No, today we have the big red bowls with orange rims, Gude Grams Mac N' Teeze Extra Spicee, everyone's prime favorite meal.

"To what do we owe this feast?" Tas asks, cradling the bowl before breaking the heating seal once we all sit down.

I can smell it through the double insulated wrapper and I'm ready to pounce.

We only have the two small scuffed tables that had once been enameled white but have been chipped and scarred over the years of the Old Man's war and the journeys there and back and back again. Not to mention the mismatched leftover seats that we gathered around, crammed close around a single table now that we are so few.

And then Orris shows up and takes my favorite seat, the one with all the struts in the back. He knows I like it and I outrank him. He's only got one corona, not two, and no more than twenty-five beads that I can count if he keeps still. Probably fewer.

"You know Penna likes that chair," Grove says.

Orris looks at his bowl, the seal just about ready to pop. I can see he just wants to eat in peace and not talk to Grove and especially not me. He doesn't like me, which is fine. I don't like him back.

But spacers have respect for each other. We'd better. We learn that early in training, along with Basic Orientation and Craft Identification, when we're still probationer primes.

Grove deserves respect. The oldest spacer on board, Grove holds our history, our link to the Guild. Not that Grove has more than forty-two beads in his hair, but he's still senior spacer here. Or is it forty-six? I always forget.

Then, so slow that I can count off the parsecs to the Toi system, Orris gets up and takes his bowl with the heat seal wrinkling in the finishing steam. He don't say a word, but moves two spaces over. To the other side of where Tas is sitting. He nudges one of the soldiers to get the spot, but the soldier just smiles and winks at him before taking a place further down the table.

I don't like him, but Tas keeps telling me he's just quiet is all. Most of us aren't big on gab. Besides, she goes on about how he graduated top ginny in his year with the best scores in a decade, as if the honor beads woven in his braids aren't plain to see. I think she's got a thing for him. So what is he doing here, I want to know? Old Man got himself one top crew.

"I think we need to toast Penna on the nav," Brayley, our pilot, interrupts. "It looks like a clear shot home, two hundred forty-seven days and change, plenty of fuel to cover, and a nice warm landing. We've got plenty of supplies, Mac N'Teeze, Korma Karma Curry, Vikram's Vindaloo..."

"You mean no more Veg-O?"

Brayley grimaces. "Not quite that good. But only a few days a week, and I can live with that."

Shaa, I can live with that too. But my Mac N'Teeze is steaming and the scent of double hot sauce wafts up my nose. Irresistible. My tongue blisters in ecstasy as the bright red sauce coats and burns all the way down.

"Home!" Tas says, having devoured the entire dinner in record time. "A toast to home!" We all dutifully rise and raise our glasses. Not the big ones full of water, but the tiny ones that hold a thimbleful of tar tasty booze.

"Home," we chorus, and throw the noxious stuff back.

Now, I don't complain about alcohol. I've endured Selene Station brew and Colony wines (from Pyroeis Atlas, Pyroeis Tethys, and Pyroeis Themis, and I can vouch for the fact that no one in their right minds would ever drink any of them). But that stuff, I dunno, rocket fuel probably tastes better. Though it probably don't pack near the punch.

To home. Shaalaa by the Sacred Numbers. The Commander arrives just as we barely take our seats again. No ceremony in the galley, no standing or salutes or military honors.

The Old Man points to me. "Nav," he says, because he never bothers with any of our names. "I heard something. We're going to land."

Shit. I'd just calculated the perfect course. And a course through the Belt is not trivial. Asteroids don't all go in some neatly spaced promenade like a military parade, naalaa, the Belt's more like a rugby scrum at the end of a tied game. Hamilton versus Scorpio in the Malton Bowl, three-three in the last two minutes of the final game. Lost some real money on that one.

"Nav, get over here now and identify the source of the signal," he bellows. Good thing I'd finished my meal. The Old Man stands and I follow as he marches us both to the bridge.

I've been in plenty of spacecraft in my life—decrepit traders, luxury cruisers, floating bordellos, top notch traders, scavengers and trows and trailers, everything short of pirates. And this bridge is the ugliest, most scrap-heap-worthy scow of them all. I thought military issue would be spiff, and maybe it had been once upon a time, but that time was back when the Commander's hair had been dark and his ego hadn't been the size of Neptune's orbit. So I slide into the unpadded nav chair and hit the switches and watch my beautifully restored comp come to life.

"That," he grunts as a signal invaded the entire bridge.

And shaalaayaa, I get it. I itch to go there, too. I don't even need to hear. Just looking at the complexity of the signature takes my breath away, for that thing is truly not made by nature. A thing of beauty it is, as I had never seen before and suspect I would never see again. By all the Sacred Numbers, it brings me to worship.

So perfect it is that I wonder if it has been made by human hands. The intervals, utterly precise in their repetitions and exquisite mathematical intersections, are in base forty-seven. Humans don't gravitate toward base forty-seven by nature. And yet this is so pretty, singing, praising Holy Primes in new voices I almost cry.

"We're going there."

"You got it, boss." Because I don't care what the old goat says, I'm going there and I happen to be in charge of the nav. I hardly notice my fingers sliding over the screen, adjusting trajectory and speed, finding the source of that perfect glory and calculating the approach.

"Too small to actually land," I mutter. "We're going to have to match it and go down to the surface if you want boots on ground. We can do a good scan from here…"

"We are going there," he orders.

"Oh, we are going indeed." Because, for the one and only time, I am in utter agreement. "But we had better get some data while we approach is all I'm saying, laashaa?"

The Old Man only grunts in reply as he stands over my shoulder, watching as I pull the schematics in closer. I can smell the Extra Spicee on his breath as he leans in while I enlarge the asteroid on my secondary screen.

If I don't bother with minor crap like configuration and trajectory, the thing could pass as a rock. The shell has the same mottled brownish greenish surface of most of the asteroids around. And it's big. Not big enough to land on, but plenty big enough for an exploration team to go down and poke around.

Only as I rotate the image through a complete 3-D and see the full contours, I can clearly see that it was nothing like any rock in the Belt. 'Cause this thing is long and regular and tapered on both ends, like it has been made to fly. And, when I get it through the full rotation, it sprouts fins around the middle.

Holy fucking Primes. Fins. The Old Man is breathing hard but I don't care. I fiddle with the resolution, trying to get some detail of the surface under that accumulation of crud.

Are there people in there? As in, alien slime monsters watching us? Or some super advanced civilization with the answers for our tendency to kill each other off every generation or so? Or First-Lost, not that we ever see them for sure, those descendants of the very first humans to leave our mother rock. The ones the Captain calls gods, though they are no more gods than I am. Just other people from early colonies that got themselves lost out there.

Resolution blurs so the thing looks like any other rock. The Captain protests very rudely. Then I get the software going the other way, resolve, go past the point and blur again. And go back. At that single, easy to miss point where the image becomes sharp we can see it. Under the dirt markings, black and yellow, I note something regular etched out in distinct swirls.

Fins. Markings. The Old Man whistles.

A soft beep from my nav comp interrupted our reverie. "Lock," I say. "Set. Go."

Data first, the Old Man insists, and I agree. We aren't going into some unknown alien thing without a shrieking clue.

Bad news—it's Orris getting it. Orris is our systems ginny, and good at what he does, I'll give him that. But otherwise, a purer piece of jackassery never drew Guild papers. Cuddy tells me that he's not near so bad as I think, and Cuddy is lead ginny, but Cuddy's opinion of everyone is based on their competence, so I don't trust him as a judge of character.

Grove says it's because he reminds me of Walker, who happens to be one of my mistakes. I don't see it myself, but I listen to Grove's opinion. Grove and I go a long way back. At least Orris' station isn't near the bridge so I don't have to lay eyes on his satisfied mug as he hacks into whatever he can into the alien system.

"If he says a word you don't like, you call him an ass. If he flirts with Tas, you call him trash, even though he's not with anyone that we know and Tas makes big round eyes at him. Besides, I watch them together and I think he genuinely likes her," Grove says as I bristle while we wait for him to show. "He don't talk out of line to anyone. Why you hate him so?"

"That funny colored hair is all wrong," I grouse. "And too tall and he walks kind of stooped over. And he don't talk much except when it's systems and then he goes so way far off that no one else can follow him and no one cares." I take a breath. "And his skin is funny colored too, like the galley table. Looks half dead. Only his eyes are normal."

Grove snorts. "That funny colored hair is called ginger and you know it. So the poor guy got the short end of the recessive genes, so he reminds you of Walker. You used to think Walker was hot once upon a time."

"Once upon a time."

But Grove shakes his head and his forty-five (or forty-eight?) beads rattle. Damn beads weigh a whole lot when the gravity is always on. "You look at the honor beads and you think he's an ass because Walker was an ass. You look at that pale hair and paler skin and think he's like Walker because he's full of recessives."

"Recessives are weak. Walker is weak. Walker is the most crybaby crumple up and die tissue paper thin coward anyone ever met. But he's a damn smart ginny."

"And because Orris has recessive genes and is a damn smart ginny you're ready to call him weak and a crybaby and a coward. I'll bet you're willing to call him no good in bed, too. That's the most illogical crazy construction I have ever heard. Penna, get over it. Orris is not Walker. No fair to hate him because he reminds you of your ex, and your own bad judgment. That's your problem, Pen. You get all wrapped up in some idea or other and then you jump all in. And only find out after the fact that you were wrong."

So now I'm pissed at Grove, too. I wish he would shut up with his analysis of me. Sometimes he hits just a little too close to home.

We all wait to hear what Orris has found. The Commander lets Orris take the head of the table in the galley, the only space large enough to hold the whole crew. Spacers, soldiers, even apprentices like Tas, no one's going to miss this.

Orris sits in the best chair with his sleeves up to his elbows showing ink. "Not proper," I grouse to Tas, who sits next to me.

She only laughs softly. "Penna, I got ink. We all do, our gen. And it's okay to show, on special occasions. This is about as special as it gets around here. Manners have changed since your day."

That makes me even grumpier. Even Captain Barr has a rep for fancy proper dress and saying grace before meals.

Sounds like an Academy grad to me. Now the board behind Orris, usually dead blank, shows a whole lot of code that no one besides a systems ginny can read or cares about.

"Hacking an alien AI isn't trivial," Orris starts off. "The architecture isn't built according to human standards. If you look at the screen here, you'll notice that the pathways don't relate to anything any AI from any of our worlds would have done. But you'll notice here," and he changes the screen to something just as unintelligible, "that certain algorithms are more familiar than others. They follow structures we can identify, which gave me an opening to unravel the rest. Not that I could break the entire code in this little time." He smiles a bit, playing fake humble. I think. "But I was able to get some decent data at least. Of course, if we examine the actual hardware it would be useful to understand how the builders expected it to work. So far I'm not sure if it's meant to be mobile or fixed. But it appears, and I must stress appears from this vantage point, to be searching aggressively to defend itself.

"The good news is, I believe that I have discovered a weakness. From what records I have managed to decode in this very short time period, it appears that the AI believes that sentients appear either as other hard bodied metallic AIs, or biologicals with the following configuration and composition."

Now rough sketches that make some kind of sense appear on the screen. Buggy. With hard shells, either vacuum suits or exoskeletons, take your pick.

"Did it ask who you were?" the Commander asks, bringing the conversation back on point.

Orris smiles like he shits fresh ice cream. "Didn't catch me. Never knew I got in."

Yeah. Right. He sounds a lot like Walker, too, right now, ready to brag about his wizard code. And here's Tas on my left, hanging on to every word with her tongue just about rolling on the table, so bad is she into him. That worries me for her until I caught sight of the boss over by the back wall, looking all thoughtful like he has an idea or ten. Like he already has half a plan.

If he's maybe half as tricksy smart as he says, we might survive.

꽈 ꗝ ꗠ ꗡ

Twenty-seven hours later we enter synched trajectory with the Thing. Orris' deep scan indicates a hollow core with potential access at four specific coordinates. "How do you know that?" the Old Man asks.

"Do you see these internal structures?" Orris points to a tangle of shadows inside the bigger tangle of shadows that all look exactly the same to me. "That's a pressure lock. Not very different from ours."

"Air? Could they be human?" Tas asks. Tas can be dim on occasion, but works hard so I tend to be forgiving. People who do their job and don't whine are good in my book, definitely better than the ones who are smart and sit on their asses or gripe about everything. The ones like Orris, or Walker, who believe they're too smart for the rest of the crew and the rest of us aren't worth the time of day.

I happened to graduate at the top of my class at the Academy and was headed towards a Brilliant Career. Until I kicked some overly entitled dirtball Captain in the balls because he refused to back off and treat me with proper respect. Not a problem with spacers, but I got a bit of a rep with some of the big money clients.

"Naalaa," I cut in before Orris can say anything to Tas. Because he's always flirting with her and he don't care about her worth shit and she's so stuck on him, poor kid. "The signal is in base forty-seven. So—high probs not."

"Oh." Tas sounds disappointed. That's going to be the least of her disappointment I fear.

"But if they have airlocks, then they breathe some kind of gas," I point out.

"If they used air to breathe rather than for some other

reason," Orris interrupts, "then they're all dead because there's no atmosphere left in the vehicle."

"We don't know it's a vehicle," Brayley points out.

"If it looks like a quaghorn and it screams like a quaghorn and it gorges on human flesh like a quaghorn…" Grove says.

"Then it's a killer duck from Degga Quadrant," I finish the ancient third year joke. Orris looks at me like I grew a second head, like he never whispered kid humor behind his geology projects when he was in Baby Basic.

"Penna, Tas, Brayley, Cuddy, Lee and Sully are with me," the Captain says. "Orris, Grove, Nep, Sars, Aggie, Digna, and Dar, stay on board. Monitor us, anything happens get us out of there asap." Holy shit, he does know our names.

"Boss," Orris wheedles.

"You're the one who's in their system. You have to be here to watch if there's any trouble and let the escape team know immediately," the Old Man snaps and that closes Orris' trap pronto.

"Those of you coming with me, meet me at the main lock in twenty to suit up. And bring your pillows," the Old Man added.

"Pillows?" This is a new one on me.

"The soft thing on your bed. Most people put it under their heads, but with you lot…they come regulation. Soft, cushy," the Commander says very slowly, as if we're a class of foaming bingo brains.

I've been on plenty of expeditions and explorations, poked around plenty of places I was maybe not wanted. I've brought beer bottles and duster zaps, arse-ems (illegal) and mini lasers (seriously illegal) and old timey side arms to fights. Or just in case of fights. I never brought a pillow.

"Just bring it, Nav. That's an order. And rope. All of you."

The boss does not look like he's joking. So we show up with our bed pillows, some of them squishy and some of them puffy, most of them in white reg cases and one in a blue patterned thing with stars all over, but all of them out of place in the lock. Still, we suit up, buckle down, put our pillows in our laps, and Brayley flies the tiny shuttle down to the surface. We tether the shuttle to the thing's outer hull, turn on the magnetic boots, and link up. Then we shuffle over to the coordinates where Orris indicated an entrance.

Dark and stars surround us. No atmosphere softens the view. Does anyone wait below us, following our steps? So what if Orris says that no one can be alive inside. Do I look like a bingo brain?

Is this thing always sending out that signal in the hopes that it can draw in anything interesting wandering by? Or does our presence trigger it? Because I swear by the Holy Primes that I had no indication of any wacko regular base forty-seven signal when I got the comp unscrambled.

Cuddy steps forward to the hatch and studies the fastening for a moment. Even though Cuddy is a big man, he has more than a brain and a half in his head and on top of it he wears the red beads of a mechanic with yellow master ginny mixed in and seven galaxy-blown honor beads as well, not that I could see them stuffed in his helmet. So anyone who looks knows he's top of the line even if he takes half your life to answer a question. He looks at that latch and tries a few gentle tugs.

The Commander shoots off sparks of impatience. "Just open it," he mutters, but we hear it just fine on the comm channel.

"That would be unwise," Cuddy replies. "This lock is of unfamiliar manufacture. Now, I expect that any creature sophisticated enough to build this ship would do as we do, and not lock down the outer air lock against their own in case of emergency, but merely fasten it against debris. If we approach it incorrectly we could trigger a defensive reaction from the central AI…"

"Cut the lecture," the Old Man orders.

And so, in his utterly unruffled Cuddy fashion, he goes back to exploring that entry as if we have all the time in the world and he wants to write a journal article about the thing for tenure.

"It appears that some debris has sealed the segments," Cuddy says as he indicates a section of the seal.

Shaanaa, WD-40 to save the day—if we had any. We have ropes and toggles, lasers and grenades, switches and comp codes. We have all cursed-to-Prime bed pillows, as if that makes any sense since the Creation Bang. But do we have superglue or duct tape or good old WD-40 and a brush? Naalaalaa. Because why would we need to repair some derelict alien hulk with a functioning AI and maybe a persecution complex?

Leave it to Sully, who does the soldier thing, takes her laser to the latch and blows it wide in about the time it takes for Cuddy to finish a sentence.

"Great. Warn the enemy," the Commander says in the comm. But we're in. And Sully, just like the Old Man's heroes, goes down first. Because she's all soldier, full of the brave and getting killed and not so much on the caution and thinking through the many possible vectors. Makes me glad I'm too insubordinate for a military career.

"Hey, Orris, get us some lights down here," she yells as if he couldn't hear as well through the comm if she whispered. Except for blowing out all our eardrums, which must be her point since no light happens.

The rest of us make our way down the ladder in the blind dark, and totally fucked describes the exercise. The spacing of the rungs is too close, too wide, surely not made for human arms and legs. I want to turn off the mag on the boots and jump, but dirtballers hate when we do that. Besides, I have no idea how far the deep dark goes.

Someone gasps, someone thunks. Wanna bet someone misses a rung? Well, that gives me some idea how far to go, but I don't want to end up in a tangle of limbs and human mush, either, because dirtballers won't turn off their damn mags.

"Orris, you asshole, get us some light down here."

"You want me to announce your presence?" Orris finally replies, as if he has minutes of lag instead of microseconds.

"We're gonna announce our presence anyway when we crash into something it don't like," I say, and I guess that made some sense, because some low light begins to glow around the edges. Not much, all eerie with deep shadows, but enough that I can see that the entire interior is a single open space surrounded by a series of pods. Quarters? Bunks? Stations?

Where are the people? In the pods? Or somewhere else? Sleeping quarters in the bulkheads maybe? That'd be straight-up spacer design. Possibilities flash through my mind and they don't add up to aliens. Aliens might have come and might have died, but all abandon their ship like this? Not likely. And this signals the major "not legits" all over.

"Laashaa, here," someone yells, and I turn. A tube made of something transparent shows an entire terrarium, all alive. Plants grow, purple and bluish under a sickly light. Small animals scutter on the bottom. Tiny fliers flitter between leaves as anemic petals trap them.

"What the hell?"

"If we're taking this home we've got to lift the whole thing intact," Cuddy says. "The doc has to see this." He sounds as if he were in church and just saw a miracle.

"You think taking this home is a good idea?" Lee asks. "We don't know what's in there. Could contaminate the whole ship and kill us all."

Soldier thinking to the core. "Naalaa," Cuddy replies. "We can sterilize it before we bring it through the lock, and the doc has the isolation berth. We got to find out what this is. Alien or not." Yeah, Cuddy's onto the whole wrong in here. It ain't alien enough, but it's also too off to be full human.

"You don't think they had this to remind them of home?" I don't know who said that.

"Crazy waste of resources," I point out.

"Fresh food," the Commander says, and someone whistles. Fresh food? Who'd a thunk? I never heard of spacer craft with fresh food. I don't think I remember what that tastes like. "Don't get too excited," the Old Man says over the comm. "We can't eat this stuff."

Looking at the creepy crawlies, killer plants, the sickly light, and I know I don't want any. "But hey, how much worse than Chick-O Veg-O Ramen could it possibly be?" Tas asks. And she does have a point.

Cuddy studies the base of the pillar, Sully holding a utility light. Okay, so it isn't WD-40, but it's more useful than my ion wrench (which works quite well to hit an enemy over the head, as I have good reason to know).

"I think this was originally intended to be detachable," Cuddy says. "If you're ready to take it when I do the disconnect, I believe we may be able to acquire our specimen with little trouble. This outer ring was meant to unscrew, and the debris issue we had outside is irrelevant in here. I expect stabilizers and connections underneath, but those should be straightforward attachments if these were designed with the intention of being easily replaced. I wonder if we would find replacements, or spent tubes, if we searched…"

"Won't that be too heavy?" the Old Man asks.

No gravity, dirtballer. Which, I am grateful to say, Tas explains much more tactfully than I would. She don't make the Old Man mad. But just the fact it screws at all screams alarms to me. I wish I could catch Cuddy's eye, but the glare shield on the helmet gets in the way. Just like topside, righty tighty, lefty loosey.

Why the fucking hell would aliens use the same protocols we do?

Cuddy places his gloved hands around the ring and begins to turn. To the left. The little hairs on the back of my neck stand up at attention. This piece responds like it was oiled yesterday, smooth as silk.

And then all hell breaks loose. A siren pierces our ears through our helmets, a light blinds us through our visors. A great hulking thing of a thing bears down on us like a killer warbot with enemies in its scope. We hit the deck, all of us except the Old Man, who stands his ground. He may be crazy but he's crazy brave.

He yells something in a language I never heard before, his hand held out before him as if that will stop the screeching, shining attack that seems to come from all sides. But, strangely enough, the thing quiets, at least enough that we could see it.

It scans us and screens us like a Guild Medic after a disaster call. I know a scan when I feel one, and this is that and no kind of alien scan. No kind of alien anything, except I can't figure out what kind it is. Not quite human, but not quite alien enough for sure. Something strange and in between. Yet this warbot and these scans seem a little too familiar to be properly weird.

Besides, does that thing really respond to the Old Man? To his speech or gesture? Wrong, wrong, wrong.

Maybe this thing is some pirate lure. Now those I believe in. Pirates and lures both. Pirates are only greedy humans and they're all over land and space and everywhere in between. And using a derelict as a lure is one of their oldest tricks. Because humans are reliably two things; greedy and curious. Some are more one or less another, but the ones running around in space usually tilt toward curious. Even the pirates.

So shaalaa, lure 'em in, split the crew, pirates pounce and take the ship and either leave the landing crew (us!) to die, or take us when we return. And give us the choice to join them or get killed. In which case there is no choice at all. Even pirates respect navs. We're indispensable. Take a new ship and you need a new nav unless you've got a spare, and we are precious few. And I'm good. Very few spacers in the history of our Guild can boast eighteen platinum galaxy honor beads.

Shaalaa, I could believe this a pirate lure easy peasy scrunchie squeezy. But the Boss don't seem worried, which makes me double down scared.

"Take food," the thing bellows with an atrocious accent. Still I can make out what it said and it don't sound friendly.

"We didn't realize," the Commander replies, all diplomatic-like. "After all, we didn't read any life aboard. We didn't realize you need live food for sustenance. I see no evidence of other organic life."

"Take food," it repeats.

And it resumes battle mode, with a very unhealthy-looking

beam coming out of its single turret. Then the turret swings and things melt where that beam hits. We roll under what bits of cover we can find as it rotates quickly, searching us out. I grab one of the horizontal bars that cover the bulkhead and pull myself along the protuberances that look like work stations or entrances for racks. The horizontal bar rolls easily under my glove, and when I try to hook a boot through one it dislodges completely.

The Old Man, the only one who seems impervious to the robo's attack, pulls another long narrow horizontal bar out of the bulkhead setting. A lever? No, it looks more like a long mag grip for a series of stations. On short acquaintance, since I am just a bit busy avoiding that rotating beam as the warbot continues to shriek.

Then the Old Man throws that long spar overhand, easy as calculating a course home, straight at the angled edge of the melty beam and damn hot shit from hell if he don't hit it just from the side. So it only melts down when it hit the beam at the emission point, coating it over.

I think it will just give us a minute or two to hide better, then the robo will just melt it through. But instead it jams, shuts the beam down, and shrieks though the entire aural spectrum up and down, cycling as if it had been wounded bad.

"We are nobody," the Old Man said. "If anyone asks who hurt you, tell them Nobody hurt you." But the warbot don't stop. Instead, all the locks around us seal shut.

"Shit," Sully says.

"Now how do we get out, boss?" Tas asks.

And that's when the Old Man smiles. "Pillows," he tells us.

And Cuddy smiles, too. "Oh, indeed. Brilliant."

I don't like being behind the curve. Especially when it concerns the probability of my continued existence. "Pillows?"

The Old Man cackles, I swear. "I told you the story. I told you twenty times, you said. How I got us into the enemy stronghold and brought them down from within. How I cheated the sensors."

"Yeah," I say. "But you used a muon coil to do that. And all we've got are pillows?"

"We don't have any muon coils left," Cuddy informs us. "Or any other particle coils, for that matter." I know that. I burned them all to get out of the gravity well. "I'll go first," Cuddy volunteers. "And if it's not on their list of objects to watch, we'll pass straight through."

"And how do you know they're not watching for soft things?"

Now Cuddy laughs, but the Old Man answers. "Because in the entire history of warfare, no one has ever fought in something pillow-soft. Weapons are not soft, never have been. Soft things are—nonthreatening. Do you think you can get through that seal?" the Commander asks Cuddy.

Cuddy starts up the ladder hands only, mags off and no grav to slow him but cautious all the same. Then a flash hits and burns his gloves. He lets go and hooks a foot under a rung to propel him pronto back to the deck.

"Perimeter seal," he says. "If I can get to it, I can deactivate it easily enough. These things are pretty primitive as defensive tech goes. Besides, they rely too heavily on the perimeter sensors and the seals were never intended to hold anyone."

"They intended the warbot to eliminate any threat. Naïve. And stupid. The perimeter covers were only meant as a backup. But the makers never considered the robo being blind." The Old Man looks at all of us. "Put on the pillows."

We all look at each other like he is speaking alien. Put on the pillows. Like clothes? Where? With what? Cuddy, being a mechie, twigs first. He pulls out the rope the Commander had ordered us to bring and ties the pillow around his side so that it covered part of his chest and part of his back.

"That's weird," Lee says.

"If their recognition algorithms are anything like ours, and I suspect they are, we need only a small interrupted area to throw it off. Our suits read as a carapace, or a robo. But if their recognition software reads even a small soft area, it will fill in a much larger area as soft, which it shouldn't recognize as any kind of threat and should permit us to go through. It's one of the major difficulties with artificial identification. The warbot will still be using other means of identification along with the perimeter robos, which is why we need some pillow front and back. But even the small area will disguise us if the algorithm is even vaguely similar."

In Math there is truth. All that is Eternal and Holy is in the Numbers. No matter who or how, or how alien, they are always the same. Shaayaalaa, the Sacred Numbers bring us safely through danger; thank the All-Truthful Rigor of the Proof.

The Old Man smiles. "Exactly. The great weakness in the system."

Oh shaa, the story he told and told and told again, how he had tricked an entire regiment's way behind the lines in his great war. Maybe I shoulda paid more mind.

What the hell do I know about image recognition? Nothing, that's what. And yet here's the Commander, ancient of days with his dirtball war and his dirtball world. And he knows. He planned this from the first, from before Cuddy gave us the lecture, from before Orris said a word.

And why hadn't Orris said anything? Because Orris doesn't know? Or because Orris has another agenda? This thing smells of set-up and I was set up too recently. Grove says I'm paranoid, but I call it cautious. Comes with too much experience.

And my experience and my cautious together say this whole thing screams set-up. All the pseudo alien, those strange creatures in the tube, the base forty-seven, all that, was planted to throw us off. I know it's someone dealing a double cross and my stomach starts to feel very very cold. Because I don't know who. Pirates don't worry me; I have value to them.

Somebody not so alien wants something from us, and I don't know what that something is. That something is damn valuable to set up this whole lure.

The Old Man insists on going first, until Cuddy points out

that there is only room for one at the top of the ladder and that the Captain doesn't know how to unseal the lock.

"Then tell me how to unlock it," he grumbles, but Cuddy insists he couldn't explain it to someone without at least two years mechie training, and three would be better. And even then…

At which point the Old Man gives in. Because even as Commander, he knows that Cuddy's lecture will grow more and more abstruse until even Cuddy doesn't understand any more. And we need to scram. Pronto. Because that robo has more than the metal melty beam to cut us down and I, for one, do not want to face it. Take what we get and be grateful, shaalaa, but don't push too far or you risk backsnap from the slingshot. Once is a gift, twice don't happen. Not in hard vacuum.

Besides, who knows what's going on back on board? If this were a lure…I don't want to think of that. So before the Captain can get one more word out his mouth Cuddy jumps up to the top, with no interference from the perimeter dog while the Old Man climbs the slow way behind, Sully on his heels. Dirtballers. Can't turn off their mag settings when they need to move. Their need for local vertical slows them the hell down. Sully and then Lee follow the Captain, leaving me and Tas for last.

I wait until they are away and check Tas one last time before I go. Tas, being a young'un and all, seems way too calm once all the screeching is over, like that robo's a dead issue. Well, my job is to set a good example and I do, jumping the ladder with minimal effort and maximal speed. I use the attachment poles like Cuddy did, to stay on track after a good hard leap propels me upwards.

Tas tries to crouch a bit to add extra jazz to the jolt and springs upward. And falls to hell. Because that damn rope isn't tied right, not tight enough or the knot wasn't secure. Spacer should know how to tie a knot. But I am already at the lock and climbing out the hole when the robo starts shooting and Tas screams. Once.

I will never forget that scream or the silence that follows. Death it is and no mistaking. The warbot lives and rages and now the entire skin of this cursed craft crackles with living energy to fry us.

"Reverse the mag on the boots and turn on the gloves," I yell into the comm. I wonder whether the dirtballers have the sense to listen. I can already see a glint of silver on the horizon as Brayley brings our shuttle around. I slap off the boot mags and activate the gloves, then stretch my arms toward the growing shuttle in the sky. Cuddy is already rising upward, the powerful glove mags pushing to the red zone.

Under us, small irregularities that appear to be accumulated cruft begin firing projectiles. First rounds only hit a boot, a helmet, made to take it. Then a whir. Calibrating. More ports open. Projectiles and beams strafe the surface of the ship where we had been standing. I already nixed the mags in the boots and pushed my gloves to max, so I roll into a ball and shoot out flat toward the shuttle.

Sully imitates me. The Old Man manages to neg his boots out and pulls a roll, but he yaws wide and struggles with his gloves. Damn. Sully grabs him, hits a cuff and pushes him hard. Her energy propels him toward Brayley at high velocity, but equal and opposite reactions. She forgets how those work with no grav. Damn.

Physics pushes her backwards hard toward the abandoned ship with her gloves full mag and pointed toward the ship's surface. She panics and kicks out to reverse herself, but it only pushes her faster into danger. Lee, just under her, tries to turn her, but her thrashing only thrusts them back into enemy fire.

I turn away. I seen pain enough this day, and I don't need to carry more. Their names and cries will be in me forever, along with Tas' innocent smile and final piercing death wail.

I turn my visor and reach. I stretch out my fingers, my palms, gloves glowing. Gonna burn out this pair and they'll dock my pay for new, but I don't care. Fuck it. Then I feel the hard slam against the outer hull as I make it safe. Turn the gloves down to amber so I can crawl to the back hatch and wait for Brayley to cycle the airlock. Only then can I pull my carcass behind a bulkhead as Brayley cuts a cartwheel turn away and back to our own.

$$\text{⚇ ⚇ ⚇ ⚇}$$

Takes two days, silence and work, before we clear local space and know for sure that whoever, whatever, that thing is, it isn't coming after us. Orris doesn't show his face. Old Grove has the show, but sits around like always, no fuss, senior spacer and all.

"I blew its fuel main while it was distracted fighting you," Grove says in the access corridor when it looked like no one but the Old Man was around. "Caught and killed a signal, too. More than one. Human, nothing base forty-seven about it. And coming from us, not from that roboship."

He doesn't regale us with it like a story but tells the Captain alone. I just hear because I have long ears and happen to be hidden under the repair panel for the nav comp. Hey, not my fault that a few of those connections have come loose in the evasive maneuvers I take around the shit in the Belt to keep them from finding us. It's not like I exactly enjoy fixing computers.

Shaayaa, and who is them then? Not certain who, pirates maybe or Orris' kind. Whatever breed of humans they might be.

I catch the Captain on the way to the galley, first I see him since we returned. "Good job on that, Penna," he says.

"Got a question for you," I say. He nods and stops, leans a shoulder against the peeling bulkhead.

"What language was that you spoke to the warbot? How did you know, and did it really understand?"

The Captain closes his eyes for a moment, and I see pain along with memory flash across his face. "I told you, we fought the Children of the Gods. It was their language I used. The thing did understand, I think. When we looked over more information from the shell, I heard some phrases I recognized.

Not human, not alien. The Children of the Gods. They exist, Penna, they truly do. And sometimes we need to fight them because they do not negotiate with our kind."

"What do they want?"

He shrugs. "So many of our best died fighting that war. She stole it, that spy. Half goddess, half demon. They say we fought over her, but truth Penna? We fought over what she stole from us, and why. Why she didn't talk to us. She just became a goddess and disappeared. And died."

He walks off and I don't see him until we all meet in the galley to face the traitor.

⚏ ⚏ ⚏ ⚏

We all sit in our usual seats around the enamel table. This time the Old Man has the best chair, the one that doesn't wobble, and Grove is right next to him in the one that's second best. Everyone else is hard as stone, cold as vac. We all lost friends. We lost crewmates whether we knew them well or not, don't matter when we'd survived so much else.

Orris arrives calm, his hair unbraided hanging to his shoulders, shining clean and thick. He wears all his beads on a thread around his neck. Those honor beads from the Academy, when Tas had none, make me want to snatch them from him, but Cuddy puts a hand around my arm.

Something looks different about Orris now. His arrogance is gone and he appears—gathered. Relaxed even. As if he'd been waiting for now for a long long time.

The Old Man doesn't waste any time on formality. The whole meeting's a formality anyway. We know what's going to happen. Orris has got to know too, which is why I find his ease so strange.

"You led us in, you betrayed us, you got three of your shipmates killed. Anything you want to say in your defense?"

Orris looks to his feet and then looks at us, all of us one by one straight in the eye. "I never betrayed my own. I knew I was dead from the minute I agreed to the exchange, to get your eyes and give up my own. We got what we need and that's worth one life for us, that's all. If you care, we need you. We don't want to harm you but—there it is. The history between us. All living beings want to survive. So do we. We love our families, our worlds, and we'll do whatever we need to do to save them."

Shaalaa. First-Lost. But what did they get, what did they want?

Grove nods. "He deserves an honorable death. Not space him, but leave his people a body they can collect as they will." Because no one would let him live, and he accepts that clearly. But shaashaa, a clean death. That I can accept.

"The beads," Brayley says.

Orris takes the strand from around his neck and drops them onto the table in front of Grove and the Old Man. Grove takes them, studies them—the green systems beads with the yellow master's beads, the six Academy honor beads and the three he has earned since, the six mission beads, the three Guild rank beads—and hands them back to the First-Lost.

My colleagues start to protest but Grove glares with all the force of his age and his forty-seven beads. "He earned these. Earned. He won't wear them properly as a spacer in death, but they go with him all the same." No one is happy with Grove's decision, but no one challenges him either.

The Old Man stands. "You have proved yourself courageous, and while you have betrayed us you have never given any pledge of loyalty to any of us either, have you?"

"No, I have not," Orris says.

This we all know is true. Spacers do not require any oath, and whatever the Commander's people require was given long before any of us came aboard. Not that spacers give loyalty to any but our own.

"They you have deserved better than the dishonorable death of being thrown out the airlock. You have earned the respect of the death of an honorable enemy."

Orris dips his head. "That is far more generous than I expected."

"You have one last meal, which you may choose from among our stocks. And a large drink."

He chooses Vikram's Vindaloo with double chocolate squares. We all partake of the feast with him, though the rest of us have only a half square each, chocolate being the rarest substance aboard. Even more than fuel, though not so important.

We speak in far too much detail about systems engineering, since Orris sets the subject and tone of conversation. Even I join in, since I can talk my way through a navigational program or ten. It seems very odd to me, but the soldiers assure us that this is properly honorable among their people, and that Orris understands it as such. At one point he catches me in the ebb and flow of conversation. "I truly cared for her, you know. I would have saved her if I had been there. That is my only regret."

He is not Walker. I understand that in my head, but only in my head. The rest of me still believes otherwise, no matter what I saw. "Better this way. You would have broken her heart."

At the end of the evening he fingers the keyboard in front of him and calls up the most beautiful music I have ever heard. Something made of patterns and changes so elegant and pristine my whole soul quivers at the sheer magnificence of the score. Base forty-seven, I am certain of it.

I do not notice at first that Orris has taken the first sips from the goblet that has been placed before him. He leans back, smiles, as the glorious harmonies engulf us all, and then drinks deeply.

Before the final crescendo he is gone.

We eat only the good stuff as I tighten my calculations for a clear run straight home. Not a single round of Ramen, Mac N' Teeze Extra Spicee two nights in a row. But no matter how hot the spice, how rich the smell, how thick the cheesy sauce, it could be damned Chick-O Veg-O for all I care.

Tas' absence echoes in the lonely. Just a kid on a first outbound apprentice cruise. I never even knew apprentice to what, 'cause Tas always said she didn't know enough to not know anything.

"Tas died in space," Cuddy says when he catches me staring out the porthole after my shift. "None of us could ask more."

"Praise the Primes." But the formula don't comfort me, don't take the sting away from those missing innocent smiles.

"Holy Numbers see Tas to safe berth," Cuddy replies. But we both know Tas don't need it. All the matter and energy that had been Tas lives forever, which is exactly no comfort now. Still, a spacer's death. Better than burial on a dirtball, being consigned for eternity to a gravity well where no spacer belongs. Cuddy is right, Tas will become the stuff of the stars. From stardust we are made and to it we return.

"How long?" the Old Man asks. He sneaks up on us behind, as we mourn the kid who would never make apprentice second now.

"Should be there before we need to eat Ramen again," I reply.

"The things we brought back in the tube all died," he tells us. "But the doc saved DNA samples. Nothing she'd seen before, but mutated way off a human world. One of the earliest migrations, she thinks."

Yaashaalaa. The anomalies make sense. The very first of the First-Lost. But why couldn't Orris just tell us what they want? In the end, I have to accept that the real Orris was not the one I disliked so deep. And so I whisper a prayer for him, too. "Primes, see Orris safely to his own, that he may add his stardust into his own true star."

I can learn. I can change my mind.

Some say that there is only so much difference that can exist. The Sacred Numbers are universal, which is why we revere them. Not because they interfere with our lives or grant wishes true, but because by their own nature they are True, and Eternal, and Universal. And their Truth will be known to any sentient that has the desire to know.

Cuddy looks at me and I look at him and the Old Man smiles with far too many teeth. "He was one fine ginny," Cuddy gives him his due.

"We should have triple checked his bios," I say. "He swapped his eyes and got fake papers." What did they need so bad that Orris gave up his eyes? One thing to be willing to die, we all go through that stage young. But to lie down and let someone swap out your eyes—the very thought makes me want to puke on the deck. He had been one brave ginny and true to his own.

"You fought the First-Lost then?" Cuddy asks the Commander.

"Gods and the Children of the gods, no matter what you choose to call them," the Old Man said. "An ancient race, one of the first to leave. Legends, so different from us they are no longer truly humans as we are. But we defeated them."

"You defeated them." I acknowledge the truth of it. "You are a tricksy man sure."

He has the grace to look at the stars as a spacer would. "Shaalaa."

But as I look out towards the stars, I think of the beauty of the music we had heard, beauty that made me cry. Beauty founded bedrock on truth so that even the memory thrilled my soul.

Gods? First-Lost? Aliens? Surely whatever had made that signal had been something deeply different than we could understand. Something so beautiful that just the echo of the memory made my heart ache with the longing for it. How could Orris have been of the people who had made that warbot and that music too? Brave and loyal and so very human at the heart, and yet of a people who could create a such a bingo brained robo and a music beyond our deepest imaginings.

What we know is true is true, and all else is mystery.

Shaashaayaa.

The Sea of Stars

Genevieve Williams

K*yrenia* departed from Piraeus in haste, without even a token sacrificial libation. They had run into port ahead of the season's turn, only to discover that the summer's plague had not subsided with the onset of cooler weather. From the Long Walls to the Acropolis, people in Athens were dying in the streets.

Euphemus considered abandoning those of *Kyrenia*'s crew who had leapt ashore the moment the ship had touched dock. But the wind that had blown them into Piraeus could not blow them out again; when the sailors returned, unwilling to risk the brothels or the taverns with people groaning in the gutters outside, he took them back aboard and would not let them leave again. Tiphys, *Kyrenia*'s steersman, nodded approval, saying Athena would not look favorably on abandoning the crew.

"It looks to me as though she has abandoned her city," Euphemus replied. But quietly. He was not a superstitious man, but only a fool spoke ill of the gods.

As soon as the wind shifted, *Kyrenia* pulled away from the dock with the groans of the afflicted following them across the widening water. Euphemus hadn't worked out where they were going, but the wind drove them southwest. Past Salamis, where—as Euphemus well remembered—the people of Athens had taken refuge from the Persians. Athens had won that day in the end, turning the tide and sending Xerxes and his armies packing. But now Athens suffered an invasion no ship could defeat, and dark rumblings came from Sparta. Euphemus himself would not go ashore anywhere Sparta controlled—which limited their options.

"Get us on as southerly a course as possible," he said to Tiphys. "Keep us east off of Aegina."

Tiphys assented, not mentioning the other thing that was on both their minds. Water. The plague's persistence had left Euphemus dubious of Athenian wells. A fine thing, if they found themselves in the middle of the ocean, dying of thirst. Their lack of sacrifice before setting out nagged at him. The god of the sea could kill them any number of ways. Thirst would be among the worst. He contemplated the distance to the nearest fresh water, and closed his eyes. Kea. Or Naxos. Perhaps. Behind and to starboard, the land dropped away until all they saw in any direction was the sea.

Idomeneus came up from below and approached him, gray-faced. Euphemus's heart sank.

"It's Megakles," Idomeneus said. "He's sick."

Miasma. Euphemus thought the word before he could stop it. They had docked in a city infected with plague, they had set out without making the proper offerings, the wind and his own orders would take them deep into the open sea between the Peloponnese and the Cyclades, and they had a sick man with no way to keep him from the others. The gods had turned against them.

"Isolate him as best you can," he said, keeping voice and face as calm as possible. "Put a cloth over your face to keep from breathing his bad air. No one goes near him, understand?"

Idomeneus nodded, going back below with the air of a man going to his execution. Euphemus stared after him. What he ought to do was throw Megakles overboard. Up to a third of Athens was dead or dying.

He went to where Tiphys stood with a hand on the tiller. The steersman was squinting at the sun, his lips moving. Euphemus did not interrupt. At last Tiphys turned to him. "Sir?"

"Change of plans. We need to find a coast." If they left Megakles on a shore, his fate would be in the gods' hands. And they did need water.

"Even the land of the Spartans," Tiphys said.

"Even so. If there's anyone can find us a safe harbor, it'll be you."

"Maybe not," Tiphys said, and jerked his head to the northeast, where a haze obscured the horizon.

Euphemus had been going to sea long enough to know what that meant. "How long?"

"Before nightfall, if we're very unlucky. The wind's already picking up. We have no choice but to run ahead of it."

"Do the best you can," Euphemus said, and stumped off. He missed battles. There was no time to fret in a battle.

The wind rose, ice in its teeth. As the sun set, it seemed to glimmer off something high in the southwestern sky—a pinprick of red like the star of Ares, but brighter, and in the wrong position. Euphemus felt a thrill of fear. He was not given to omens, but...he glanced back at Tiphys, but said nothing. The steersman doubtless already knew. Beneath them the sea reflected the encroaching night, deep and dark as the sky above.

That night the storm came full force. They ran before the wind, Tiphys gripping the tiller with his eyes on the sails, until it grew too dark to see despite the ships' lanterns. The sea boiled around them. Clouds and lashing rain shrouded the sky. Euphemus prayed to whatever gods might be listening that they not be dashed to pieces by the storm. He told himself that attributing it to Poseidon's wrath was hubris. He was not Odysseus. Storms happened.

The ship creaked and groaned. Euphemus gripped the rail as if by that means he could hold *Kyrenia* together. A man, Polyas, risked a stumbling reel across the deck to grab a loose line. A great wave crashed over the starboard side, and when it receded, Polyas was gone.

At last, the wind lessened. Lashing needles of rain dwindled to cold pinpricks. The sky was still dark with clouds, *Kyrenia* sailing into a pitch darkness their lanterns could not pierce. Euphemus started to work his way aft.

An incredible jolt struck the ship. Even before the sound of splintering wood and the cries of the men reached his ears, Euphemus knew what had happened. He turned forward again, and peered into a darkness like the entrance to Erebus. Was that a shadow looming, a darker mass still within the shrouded night? Or did he only imagine it?

Xanthippos and Kallikrates came running from below. "Water coming in belowdecks and it's full of splintered wreckage."

Worse and worse. "Look to forward," he told them. "See if there's land. A rock. Anything." The deck was already listing, steep enough that he had trouble keeping his feet. Two sailors were busy tossing the aft stone anchor over the side. Crew poured onto the deck even as the ship listed further. Xanthippos came skidding back to him. "There's something like a shore, sir. Kallikrates was able to step off onto some rocks. It's quite steep."

"It's what we have," Euphemus replied. "Everyone ashore. Carry what stores you can. Especially water." His body had begun to shake. He forced himself into movement, clambering with the rest of the crew over the forward rail and onto the sea-washed rocks.

They spent the remainder of the night on what felt like a barren shore. Though the rain had stopped, there was just enough of a breeze to keep all of them good and chilled, no matter how they huddled together and wrapped themselves in their cloaks. Through all the dark hours Euphemus listened to the creaking of the ship and Megakles's harsh breathing. He imagined the man's breaths spreading over them all, infecting the air with miasma. The sailor next to him had taken one of the wine-jars out of the hold and was taking steady sips from it. Euphemus was not sure whether to admonish him or join him.

The darkness began to fade. A shadow of movement near the ship resolved itself into Tiphys, running his hands along splintered boards. Dawn streaked across a sky clearing of clouds, and they could see what had become of their ship.

Only the same jagged rocks that had torn open *Kyrenia*'s hull now kept her from slipping away and sinking. For a wonder, the sails were whole and the mast still straight. But there would be no patching that hole, not without a shipyard and a brace of shipwrights. By luck *Kyrenia* had caught a jutting shelf that had kept the ship from smashing to pieces—a little further to either side and they'd all have been taken by the sea-god last night, the waves washing over their graves. Before, above, and to either side of them stretched steep slopes of jagged rock, with nary a beach nor cove in sight.

He made his way over to Tiphys, who now sat staring at the ship, and rested his hand on his shoulder. Tiphys did not move, but relaxed beneath Euphemus's palm, his breathing slowing. Euphemus might own the ship, but *Kyrenia* had been Tiphys's since first he'd set foot aboard her.

"Do you know where we are?" Euphemus said at last.

Tiphys shook his head. "If I had to guess, we're somewhere on the Spartan coast."

Euphemus eyed the sun rising from the sea. They were on an eastern shore, somewhere. Anything beyond that might have to wait until they saw the stars again—and Tiphys had regained some of his equanimity. The man had seen more battles than his relative youth ought to account for, and he'd had two ships sink under him in those adventures.

"It may not be *Kyrenia*'s doom yet," he said, more to get Tiphys moving than anything else.

The sailors crawled and scrambled up the rocks. Megakles was still alive, but too sick to move, and no one wanted to touch him. They left him where he was, with some stores and blankets where he might reach them.

It was not a cliff that they had wrecked upon, but it was near as steep as the Acropolis, and before long the ship was looking small and vulnerable below them. The ground leveled out to a rough and stony surface, then sloped downward to the west. Here there was thin soil, grass and low shrubs, and even a few trees. Euphemus would not have been surprised to see goats. But it was deserted. Through the trees, he caught glimpses of water.

"I think," Tiphys said, as the rest of the sailors crested the ridge, "that we might be on an island."

Further exploration proved this to be the case. Not a large island, either. Just one of the many chunks of windswept rock that littered the seas. It was bad luck indeed that they'd had, and Euphemus recalled again their hasty departure from Piraeus. From the exchanged looks and murmured words among the men, at least some of them were thinking the same.

"Find water," he said, to keep them from stewing. "If there's any to be had. And get a lay of the land. See if there are any people here. If we can see any other land from the shores of this one. Let's not give ourselves up just yet." He rounded up the remaining sailors and put them to work unloading the ship, tossing cargo into the sea if it was ruined, bringing it up from the rocks if not. Megakles had lost consciousness and could not be roused; Euphemus forced himself to go and see to the man himself.

He lay sprawled, with his eyes half-closed. He had shoved away the blanket they had given him, and most of his clothes as well. His skin was an unhealthy red. By his head lay a small pool where he had vomited. Vomit likewise streaked his cheek and chin.

Despite his disgust at how the dying and the dead were treated in Athens, Euphemus could not make himself take a step closer. War and bloodshed, dangerous crossings and storming seas, all these and more he had faced with willingness and even relish, but Megakles's livid skin and bloodshot eyes unmanned him.

Those eyes opened, rolled toward him. "Water," Megakles croaked. Euphemus's gaze moved to the jar they'd left with him. It lay on its side, empty. No knowing whether Megakles had even drunk it, or spilled it in his sick delirium.

"Water," Megakles said again. One of the sailors, carrying a brace of water jars slung from a braid of leather cords across his shoulders, paused on his way from the ship up the rocks, uncertainty evident on his face.

In that moment, Euphemus made up his mind. "Give me one of those." It would be a waste, but he would not have the man go to Hades parched with thirst.

The sailor handed him the jar and hastened up the rocky slope without looking back. Euphemus unstoppered the jar and took a long drink, draining it more than halfway. Then he knelt on the rocky ground and poured some of what remained into Megakles's mouth. He had to get closer than he wanted to. Megakles swallowed some of the water; the rest spilled across his face, and he coughed. Euphemus reeled back, but caught a whiff of fetid breath.

Megakles relaxed and closed his eyes. Euphemus stood, and flung the water-jar as far from him as he could. It splashed into the sea. Then he drew his knife, knelt again, and slashed Megakles's throat.

He took the blanket and laid it over Megakles's face. Then he went down to the water, scrubbed his hands and arms up to the elbow, and poured more seawater over his head. He'd need to make reparation for that death, even though it was the plague that had killed Megakles. He'd have miasma until he was cleansed. He straightened and went to see what was happening with his *Kyrenia*.

She was listing worse now, and though removing cargo eased the pressure of her boards against the rocks, it also made her more liable to float off even on the gentlest lapping of the waves. Not that it mattered—the hole was so big that he could peer through it and see the men moving about inside.

The sun had slipped well to the west by the time they got everything that could be salvaged out of the ship: wine, oil, and grain. Few jars of the first two had been damaged in the crash. The grain was in worse case, much of it soaked and spoiled by seawater. And of fresh water they had little enough.

They made a camp of sorts just to the west of the top of

the ridge. As the air began to cool the sailors returned from their explorations of the island. He told them of Megakles's death, and did not stint in relating the manner of it. Those charged with handling the dead man's body would see the truth of it in any case. None voiced protest over what he'd done; people recovered from plague, sometimes, but far more often not. Still, he did not miss the sidelong glances, the slight hardening of expressions. Megakles had been dying anyway, but he'd still spilled the man's blood.

Nonetheless they all saw the necessity of consigning the dead man's body to the sea, and three of them agreed to help Euphemus do so. When they lifted his already cooling deadweight, translucent hair-like filaments running from his body to the stone beneath stretched and snapped. Euphemus and the others frowned, but no one said anything. They had enough worries.

The island, as it turned out, was small—and deserted. No shipyard, no village, not so much as an abandoned temple. Nor could they see any land from anywhere along its shore that they'd been able to get to. Aside from rainwater collected in depressions in the stone, there was no fresh water to be found.

"There's something else," Tiphys said, as Euphemus tried to absorb all this. "A very strange thing."

"What thing?" Euphemus said. Tiphys would not have mentioned it had he not thought it important, yet he seemed diffident.

"You'd better come and see," Tiphys said.

The sun was sinking fast. Euphemus thought about asking Tiphys if it could wait. But he'd known Tiphys since the helmsman was a lad and he, Euphemus, had still been young enough to believe that he might yet make himself a name worthy of the age of heroes. He knew when a matter that Tiphys brought to him was urgent, and when it was not. It was urgent now.

He tasked out several of the sailors with making camp and getting some sort of supper started. They had seen no animals at all, and of birds only gulls, so unpalatable as to be inedible. They might fish. He followed Tiphys northward, away from the camp.

Tiphys led him down a rocky hill punctuated by tufts of raggedy grass to a shallow hollow, like a mixing-bowl or a wine kylix. It was covered in gravel and fine dust. In the center stood an object so bewildering that Euphemus found it hard to look at.

It was gray, and angular not in the way that the rocks around it were angular, but as dressed stone or forged metal was angular. In fact it had the look of metal as well as the color. Its base was oblong, and then from its top extended a sort of stem, which broadened into curved shape something like a flowerhead. He was tempted to touch it to see if it *was* metal, except for its sheer unfamiliarity. The object was not large: it came up no higher than his knee. Of course he was presupposing that what he saw of it above ground was all of it that there was to see. It looked, in fact, as though it grew out of the ground, instead of merely resting upon it. He looked at Tiphys.

"It is passing strange, is it not?" Tiphys said. He looked around them as though expecting more strangeness to leap out of the scrubby grass.

"How did you find it?" Euphemus asked.

"I just came up from the hillside down there, and here it was. It is no natural thing. And how did it get here? There's no sign of habitation or human presence here, Euphemus. None."

Euphemus glanced back in the direction of the camp, then clapped Tiphys on the shoulder. "Let it remain a mystery for now, my friend. We will have time to investigate it further."

They found the camp well in order. Someone had started a fire and was preparing a sort of mash from the grain they'd had in the hold. Someone else had taken the ship's fishing nets down to a small beach on the island's southwestern side. The fish they caught were not as large as those they'd have netted in the open sea, but between that, the grain, and some of the wine—Euphemus insisted that it be properly mixed with water—they made a more comfortable meal than might have been expected.

Much of the conversation circled around topics bound to be fraught: the state of the ship, Megakles's death, where they were, and what might be done about any of it. Euphemus forestalled general discussion until the supper was done and everyone was feeling, if not relaxed, at least full-bellied. Then he stood up.

"My friends," he said. "We're in a bad position and no mistake. *Kyrenia* is damaged and we haven't the means to repair her. Megakles is dead and I account it the grace of the gods that we have lost no more." In case any gods might be listening. "We will make due obeisance for our survival thus far, but we all know that our chances are not good."

"Where *are* we, anyway?" someone asked. "I don't recognize this island at all." It was Iphitos, who was close to Euphemus's age and had been going to sea near as long.

Tiphys stood up. "I don't recognize this island either," he said, which yielded some exchanged glances among the sailors. A new oarsman on a war trireme might never have gone to sea before that day, but a helmsman was something else again. For Tiphys to admit that he didn't know where they were was tantamount to the Oracle at Delphi confessing to being unable to see the future. And Euphemus placed more faith in the helmsman. "Once the sun sets and the stars are out, I will be able to make a clearer determination." He sat down again.

"In the meantime, let us be careful with the water," Euphemus said. "We cannot be sure of more rain. Tomorrow we will look again for any sign that people come here."

They wrapped themselves in blankets, thankful that the weather was still clear and that the shape of the ridge sheltered them from the worst of the wind. Euphemus was exhausted enough to sleep.

Tiphys woke him with a hand on his shoulder. He came awake all in an instant, as he'd done since his days at war.

He rose without a word and followed Tiphys away from the camp. The sky remained clear aside from a few high wisps of cloud. It was late enough that the waxing gibbous moon had slid far to the west.

"I know where we are," Tiphys said, once they were out of earshot of the camp. Euphemus recognized the environs: they were close to that hollow in the bedrock, with the strange object at its center. "I've calculated and re-calculated, checked my observations and measurements many times." He sounded distressed.

"What's wrong?" Euphemus asked.

"That storm blew us well off any route regularly traveled by ships. We cannot hope that anyone will come close enough to see us, even if we burned everything on the island including the ship."

"Are you certain?" Helmsmen were the navigators—they knew more about the stars, the movement of sun and moon and planets, the tides and currents of the sea, and the winds than anyone. To even imply that Tiphys might not know what he was doing could be perceived as deeply insulting.

But Tiphys did not take offense. "As certain as I can be. I mapped out the stars again and again. Each time they say the same—though that red star, which brightens and dims and seems to hang right over this island, should not be there at all." He sounded frustrated, choking down the rising volume of his voice. "And there's something else."

"What?" Euphemus asked.

"That object." Tiphys paused. "Since this afternoon, it has moved."

Euphemus glanced in the direction of the strange object, though in the darkness he could make out no details. "What are you saying?"

"Not its position. But its topmost part, that curved disc. When I showed it to you this afternoon it was pointed toward the rising sun. Now it has turned south."

So small a thing. And yet. Euphemus shuddered.

Tiphys straightened, a shadow in the starlit night. "All my

life I have longed for wonders, such as in the ages you used to tell me of when I was a boy. You spoke of exploring distant seas and seeing great marvels that the gods performed in the sight of men in days long past. But Euphemus, I have never in my life actually seen such a thing as I might attribute to the work of the gods. Until the storm forced us onto this island."

"Do you think, then, that this object is the work of the gods?" The world seemed to sway about him. He prayed, he made sacrifices, his sister had been sworn to temple service, and ever since *Kyrenia* had parted company with the dock in Piraeus he had worried that neglecting the due offering to Poseidon had triggered their misfortunes. And yet he had never in his life seen anything that he could attribute, without question, to a divine hand. He glanced up at the red star that hung right over their heads like a warning too dire to ignore.

"Do the gods make machines?" Tiphys asked.

Euphemus frowned. "What makes you ask such a question?"

Tiphys raised a hand toward the object, the movement a bare shadow in the darkness. "That. I have been mulling it over since we found it. It is no natural object, yet I have never seen its like even when we journeyed to cities housing wonders of human invention." He turned back to Euphemus. "But I have never heard of a god making such a thing either, not even Hephaestus."

"Then you think it is man-made," Euphemus said, trying to follow Tiphys's thinking.

"I don't know what I think," Tiphys said. He gave a little laugh. "Perhaps I am trying to distract myself from our situation." He leaned closer. "I would not tell the men any of this, Euphemus, though of course that decision is yours."

Euphemus wondered whether, even with the knowledge of the stars to aid him, Tiphys could be as sure of their position as he said. The seas were wide, and much about them was unknown—just what lay west of the Pillars of Herakles, for instance. Euphemus had heard stories of mariners who had ventured that way, and continued west, rather than north or south along the coasts. Some came back, reporting only more sea. Others never came back at all.

The next morning, three of the men were sick with the plague. One of them was Idomeneus.

The sick were too ill to move, and nobody wanted to touch them. Euphemus ordered the camp moved instead. Some eyed their remaining supplies askance, particularly the water. Might the miasma of the ill have infested their provisions as well? Euphemus ordered it all moved anyway, deploying the leather-lunged bellow from his navy days. That would not work for much longer. Already the grumbles about angry gods had grown audible, which meant they'd been circulating out of his hearing before this. Now they meant for him to hear. From some of them he caught looks of resentment.

He couldn't blame them. Some of their disgruntlement was aimed at Tiphys, who didn't help matters by wandering off to look at the strange object every chance he got. Reportedly he was talking to it, too. Euphemus gathered an offering of wine, oil, and grain; a horse or bull was not possible, nor any incense or laurel for Apollo, but the priests said that absent the gods' preferred gifts, the best you could do was offer the best that you had. He made the offering from the shore near *Kyrenia*, which had settled and splintered further; even the small waves of the calmer sea ground her hull against the rocks.

He did it mostly to placate the men. He could not escape the notion that no offering he made now would be acceptable. Poseidon had harried Odysseus for years without ever letting him reach his home. Though Euphemus's warrior days were behind him and he was a merchant now, he had never lost the desire to explore, to find new and strange lands as Odysseus had, to live long enough to see a wonder. The gods had seen what was in his heart, and when he had allowed haste to overwhelm prudence, had punished him for it.

So he thought, and so the passing days seemed to confirm.

The three men who'd fallen ill died. When some of the sailors could finally be convinced to remove the bodies to the sea, they found them grown over with strange flexible fibers, their flesh itself gone to a strange petrifaction as though they had gazed upon Medusa. Nothing Euphemus said could persuade his men after that. Those posted to watch the sea for signs of other ships saw nothing. The weather continued dry.

The red star glowed at night, but its glow was intermittent, which if anything was more alarming. Tiphys studied the strange object but would say nothing about it, even when another object, like the top part of the first, appeared near their camp. The other men said that he'd gone mad, that the gods were displeased, that the offerings they had made were not enough. That was what they let Euphemus hear. Where he could not hear—yet—they might already have uttered the unspeakable. They moved camp again.

After an unsatisfactory breakfast—they'd gone to half rations, having for the last few days no luck with fish, and wood was getting scarce unless they burned the ship—he went to find Tiphys. As usual, the helmsman was in the crater, studying the object that had come to obsess him as much as getting off the island obsessed everyone else. He didn't even look up as Euphemus approached. He seemed to have shrunk, the long, corded muscle that was the hallmark of every sailor knotting in on itself. He sat on his heels with his knees drawn up. His gaze was fixed on the object, the disc of which was likewise turned toward him as though they regarded one another. It made Euphemus's flesh crawl.

"Tiphys," Euphemus said. The helmsman didn't respond. "I'm worried about you."

Tiphys turned his head slowly to look at him. They were all slower than they had been, clumsier, stupider. Sailors were not made for the shore. "Euphemus," he said. "It's doing something." He returned to his observation of the thing.

Euphemus looked from the object to his helmsman and back again. It looked the same as it had every other time he'd seen it: a smooth, angular gray object, with that curved disc on top. A third one had appeared near their new camp just that morning, surrounded by a net of fine filaments. "What do you mean, it's doing something?"

Tiphys gave a slow shrug. "A feeling I have, from watching it. It's not just sitting there. Sometimes I think I hear a sound. A kind of…humming, like a distant bee. I'm *not* imagining it. It happens when the red star shines its brightest."

"Tiphys," Euphemus said, refusing to look up at the sky. "I need your help. Sickness, short rations, little to no chance of rescue." As they drew toward winter, that chance, ever slim, would dwindle to nothing. The sea lanes grew less crowded with the onset of cold weather and storms. And with the plague not subsiding as it had in previous years, more ships would avoid Athens. And there were those rumors of Sparta. "We have near to mutiny on our hands. I need your help," he said again.

Tiphys nodded slowly. Euphemus could not be certain that the helmsman had really heard him. But then he said, "I can tell them where we are. But that will not help. I cannot make planks to fix the hole in *Kyrenia*. I cannot call for aid from the nearest harbors that I know of, though I could point to them from here." There was desolation in his gaze. "It was I who brought us to this disaster."

"The storm brought us to this disaster," Euphemus said. "I beg you, Tiphys, cease your obsession with this object. It is mysterious, I agree, but—"

"I think perhaps it is why we are here," Tiphys said. Euphemus wondered, with growing unease, whether the man was losing his wits. "And I cannot puzzle it out. It looks like a built thing, but like no built thing I have ever seen. It… interacts somehow with the red star. And it is changed in appearance as well as position from when we first saw it. I tell you, Euphemus, it is so beyond strange that in all the wide sea we should crash upon this tiny shore, I cannot help but wonder whether we were brought here. And then I wonder whether the gods do intervene in the world after all."

Tiphys paused, and Euphemus thought he would say

nothing more. Then he continued. "But for all our entreaties and prayers and offerings, they do not see fit to so intervene for our benefit." He moved, so suddenly that Euphemus started, but he was only standing up. "Maybe you should do as some of the men have been muttering, and make a… stronger offering. Maybe it should be me." And he walked off, upslope, in the general direction of the ship, on the circuit he had been walking between object and ship and camp for days.

Euphemus did not follow. Reassuring Tiphys that he would do no such thing, would allow no such desperate act by anyone on the crew—and he did not think any of them would really do it—would not help. Tiphys had been moved to despair, and against that Euphemus had few weapons.

His gaze fell on the object. The longer he looked, the stranger it seemed. Its shape was too regular to have come about by the natural forces of wind and water, nor even whatever forces beneath the earth churned ash, stone, and lava out of volcanoes, or raised new islands from beneath the sea. Yet what tools might have fashioned such a thing he had no notion. The facts of its movement, and of other objects like it appearing in places the crew frequented, were beyond disturbing.

So far as he knew, Tiphys had not touched it. Euphemus glanced all around, as though someone might be watching, though he did not know why it should matter whether anyone was or not. His feet crunched on the gravel as he crossed the shallow depression in which the object stood. He squatted in front of it.

It made no sound. Except, if he tilted his head just right, and held his breath, he thought he understood what Tiphys had meant. It was less a sound than a feeling, like when he put his ear to the ship's hull when out in the open sea. A sense of disturbance, of something out of tenor with the day. This thing did not belong here.

He stretched out one hand, and placed it on the object.

It was the same temperature as the surrounding air. Perhaps a little warmer on the sunward side. It was smooth but not slick. It was the dull gray of the gravel around it, but it felt like metal. The concave side of the disc had acquired a textured appearance, dimples and ridges that formed no discernable pattern and yet had a regularity to them.

Nothing happened. Euphemus felt a vague and inexplicable disappointment.

He ought to go back. Whatever authority he still had over his crew would vanish like snow in the sun if he stayed away too long. And yet he could hardly see the point. They could not survive for much longer. Not a ship had appeared on the horizon, and would not. *Kyrenia*'s crew would be presumed dead of the plague or lost at sea.

He found that he was speaking his concerns aloud. To the object, to the gods, to himself, it was all the same in the end. Yet his voice fell into the cadence of prayer, entreating whatever might be listening that some solution he hadn't thought of might occur to him. As well wish for Odysseus's cleverness—despite which, it had taken him ten years to return home, and then he had only succeeded with divine aid. Poseidon had been wrathful toward Odysseus, too, and the winds in a bag would do Euphemus no good with a broken ship.

"If I thought it the will of the gods that we should die, I would give up now," he wound up. "But I do not see how it is the will of the gods that we should live. Should there be any among the blessed immortals who hear my prayer, I entreat that we should make our escape from this island—or, if it be your will that it be not so, let our deaths be less ignominious than plague and starvation." He shuddered. "To Poseidon I vow to make the voyage to Sounion, and there offer a horse in thanks, and should I return home to my city and find it whole I will ascend the Acropolis every feastday of Athena and there make offerings. This I swear." He stopped, caught between the certainty that the gods were not there, or if they were, that they were not listening; and the knowledge that if they were, he would have to fulfill every promise that he made now.

"We are shipwrecked here, on this island with a mystery that we cannot explain, that seems to respond to our presence and yet chooses not to make its purpose known. I think we will die here unless some miracle occurs. I pray to gods whose existence I dare not doubt, and yet doubt gnaws at my heart, because I would rather doubt their existence than believe they have so turned against me. I can think only that they would not heed whatever promises I make, but would rather that I and all my men go to the shadowed lands below." At first he thought he was imagining the play of shadows across the object's disc. And then he wondered how long he had been staring at them without seeing them.

They rippled like waves, but so minute that he could not be sure he was seeing them. Then they resolved into a single oblong spot toward the disc's lower edge. There the surface seemed to vibrate, as though coated with hundreds of tiny insects.

"What are you?" he demanded. His gaze fixed on the object. "Be you some miracle of the gods or a working somehow contrived by human hands?"

Nothing happened.

"*Are* you a made thing?" he said then. "I think you must be." He felt a distant incredulity that he was talking to an object. No doubt the privation and stress were getting to him.

At first, the sound was so low that he could not be sure he heard it. Then he thought it must be what Tiphys had referred to, that sensation of activity without perceiving anything concrete. Then the hum was loud enough to be discernable.

It was coming from the disc. Euphemus frowned. "Are you...doing that?" That wasn't the right question. He didn't know what was the right question.

The sound ceased, long enough for him to wonder whether he'd heard it at all. Then it began again, a buzzing like a bee in a cup. Euphemus felt a trill of excitement. He cast about for another question. Something to which he already knew the answer. But he had no answers concerning the object. He glanced at the sky, which was a clear and brilliant blue. "Does it rain?"

Again, silence followed by sound. But this time, it did it twice. He wanted to dance like a bacchant. "What are you? The dramatists talk of the god in the machine, when they stage their plays where the mighty gods deign to intervene in the affairs of men. Yet this I have never seen in life. Is this the time when it occurs at last?"

The device went silent. Wrong question, then. Or, perhaps, too many questions. "Are you a thing made by a god?" Two buzzes. He found himself inexpressibly relieved—and yet also troubled, for he could not imagine the thing before him being fashioned by men.

And, if not made by the gods, then who was he talking to? He asked the next question with the greatest trepidation. "Were you...are you a thing made by men, then?"

Silence. Euphemus's frown deepened. "Have you something to do with the new star that shines at times in the night?"

A single buzz.

Asking his next question felt like stepping into empty air above a yawning chasm, like setting out on a journey without a helmsman, like the boards under his feet the day Athens had raised its wooden walls against the Persians. "Do you...do you, then, come from the sky?"

Once again, a single sound, followed by silence.

Euphemus expelled a breath. That last time, he'd almost thought he heard a word. He felt dizzy as he tried to compass what this meant. He had his answer, and yet it answered nothing. The stars and planets circled the world, or else all circled the Watchtower of Zeus. The gods had not made this object, and yet when he had asked if it had been fashioned by men it had given no response.

And why, he wondered, had it—or the powers behind it—chosen now to respond at all?

The mood in camp that night was sour, and though the men agreed to their duties as he assigned them, they did so with an ill grace that told him that he would not have command over them for much longer. He tried not to let what had happened with the object distract him. Whatever it was, it could not save him and his people from the disaster that had befallen them.

A few nights later, he woke to Tiphys shaking him by the shoulder. The helmsman was in such agitation that for several moments it was impossible to get anything coherent out of him. At last Euphemus agreed to follow him once again toward the object; on the way, he ascertained that Tiphys had spent much of the night questioning the object.

"But—Euphemus, I know not what to make of it. It says things about the stars and planets that I cannot believe, and yet are sound. It says that the stars are *not* fixed, and the planets are bigger than we can imagine and orbit the sun, which is also a star. It says that its makers are even farther from us than the gods, that though we are speaking with them *now*, they sent their devices here in a time longer ago than Herodotus or Thucydides ever dreamed, but that they only arrived this year. That—yes—they made this object, this *device*, and others like it, and they can make other things, too."

Euphemus did not miss the note of hope in Tiphys's voice, even as his own confusion grew. "It *says*?"

"Yes," Tiphys said. "Come and see."

Euphemus followed him to where the object lay. The moon and stars—imagine, that those stars might not be fixed in their courses, that planets might orbit them rather than the other way around!—provided enough light that he could see that it had changed, though not just how until he drew quite close. Above, the red star shone with livid intensity.

Once he did, he felt all the breath go out of his body. "Idomeneus." One of the men who had died, and been turned to stone before crumbling away. The disc had changed, and now wore the dead man's face.

He turned to Tiphys. "How—"

"We would have been faster, but even this much taxes

the limit of the power we can draw." The voice was strange, abrupt and somehow angular, as though unused to speech. Euphemus turned toward the device in shock. The mask had spoken. "We thought it would be easier this way."

"Easier," Euphemus repeated.

"Euphemus," Tiphys said. He sounded feverish. "They can help us. They come from the stars, and what they say of them—Euphemus, the world is other than we thought."

"Tiphys has told some of your stories," the device said. "At another time I would hear more of them, all the stories you could tell. But you are dying, and we are moved to intervene. There is help for you, if you will accept it."

Euphemus's gaze fixed on the mask. "Why?" Gods they might not be, but he knew something about power. There would be a price. There always was.

"We have been searching for curious beings for a very long time," the object said. "The device which speaks to you and which has explored every bit of this island grew from a seed, one of many generated from a stone floating in space, between the fourth planet distant from your star and the fifth, and sent to your planet. Those seeds in turn were planted by another that crossed distances vaster than any ocean to land upon that stone. We sent...millions of seeds. Your planet's is the first answer we have received."

Euphemus's mind reeled. He could imagine the wonders the object was telling him—but could not map them onto the world he knew. It was impossible. "How is it that you speak?"

"We have been listening to you," the mask said. "And to other beings like you, though the profusion of languages gave us some difficulty. We have other devices that have deciphered and learned your language. And we have discerned your distress and the reason for it. We are not gods. But we are builders. Our seeds contain instructions for building objects: instead of a plant, it built this device through which I am speaking to you, and other things besides. If you provide the necessary information, we can create another set of instructions for making your ship whole."

Euphemus felt reckless, like he was about to go into battle. He felt as he had with the deck under his feet at Salamis, the oars pushing through the water, the Persians ahead.

Because, if he said yes, then he would see a wonder, and have to make room within his understanding not only for godlike beings who claimed to be not gods, but for everything else that they said.

He looked up at the sky again. Above them arced the firmament, with its slow turning of the zodiac across the sky, the seasonal round of stars and constellations, so predictable that Tiphys could steer their ship by them.

The beings behind the device steered by the stars too, so they said. But they also said that there was no firmament, that the stars floated in empty space, and that their predictability was due to forces that Euphemus and Tiphys did not understand. Euphemus wondered whether he could.

If he accepted these beings' offer, he was accepting what they said about the cosmos, and that not only his own understanding, but that of the wisest people he knew of, was…incomplete. That was the price. Accepting that there was more to know. Accepting that he would never know the whole of it.

"You are most generous," he said. "We accept."

"We have been studying your ship," the device said. "It would help if you brought a piece here to seed our creation of the necessary material. And a description, as exact and detailed as you can, of what is needed."

Tiphys and Euphemus exchanged glances again. "Can't you…well, see the ship for yourself?" Euphemus asked. They had somehow, after all, perceived Idomeneus's face. He remembered the inexplicable petrifaction of the three dead men.

"We can, but it taxes the limit of the power we are capable of drawing. Your ship is neither something we made, nor is it alive in the way that a plant or an animal is alive. We cannot take a sample from it and determine from that what it is in its wholeness."

"But you can for the wood from which it is made," Euphemus said, frowning.

"Yes."

There was a mystery here. It tugged at him, in the same way that the horizon tugged at him, with the promise of the revelation of things unknown. But, as ever, he had more immediate concerns.

"I'll get some wood from the hull," Tiphys said, and headed up toward the ridge.

Euphemus rose to start back to the camp, trying to piece together how he would relay these new developments to the crew, all his understanding thrown into doubt by words he had limited means to verify. And yet he believed them. He wanted to.

If the powers behind that device made the ship whole, then he would. He felt that take hold of him, with the certainty of a vow made to the gods. And so perhaps it didn't matter whether these beings were gods or not.

The sky was growing light above the ridge. He wondered how long it would take the device's masters to do…whatever it was they were going to do. He had heard that everything was made up of tiny indivisible parts, but that had struck him as more of a philosopher's imaginative notion than anything that one might observe in the real world. And if the device's masters could make that device, why could they not make a ship? The device was no more alive than the ship was—it *was* a machine, he had concluded. And they could make wood, which was dead once it was harvested. He had a thousand questions.

Back at the camp the men were stirring. He nudged Kallikrates into getting a fire going with their dwindling wood, to draw the men together.

"I have good news," he said, as the men rose from their sleeping places and gravitated toward the fire. "We're getting off this island."

They looked at one another, and cast skeptical gazes in his direction. "And how's that?" Xanthippos asked at last.

"That object that we found, our first day. It's a device, capable of making things. It's going to repair the ship."

They were not persuaded, as well they might not be. Euphemus had to remind himself that he'd had some time to get used to the idea, as well as hearing the device's makers speak. Kallikrates said, "What manner of device?"

Euphemus shook his head. Now that he had to explain the whole thing, it seemed less likely than ever. "A marvelous one," he said, torn between trying to make a thorough and convincing explanation and offering no explanation at all. "Come and see for yourselves. Speak to the device, and it will speak to you. Tiphys is preparing—"

"Yes, Tiphys," Kallikrates interrupted. "It's from him that you have all this?"

"He has more experience with the device than I do," Euphemus admitted. "But I have spoken with it myself."

Kallikrates stood up. "And it's answered you? Made you promises?"

"Yes." Why did that feel like giving up ground?

"It strains credulity," Kallikrates said, "that you should try so hard to hold onto your authority, even now, when our disaster does not abate and in fact grows worse." He raised a hand toward the sky, where the red star shone bright as a burning coal. "We all recall the haste with which we departed from Athens, and will not say that it was not without cause. Yet since then we have experienced only ill fortune, and our hasty departure did not grant us safety from the plague." He waved toward two figures who had not stirred. "Eteokles and Axylus are ill, now, and who's to say that the sickness will not claim every one of us?" He was warming to his subject, as impassioned as any would-be orator who had ever claimed a square in the Agora. "And we may think them the fortunate ones, as winter sets in and food and water are gone."

"We'll be long gone from this island before that happens," Euphemus said, but he had lost the initiative. He'd bellowed at these men's fathers and uncles on the decks of warships in the midst of battle, and been obeyed without question even when an enemy ram stove in their side. He'd once captured an enemy warship that had sunk theirs, all his fighters and oarsmen making the leap to the other ship, slaughtering its crew and taking the vessel for their own.

But he'd never been stranded with his crew on an island with an object that had inexplicably grown a dead man's face, trying to persuade them that beings that he had never seen, that had powers akin to gods but were not gods, were willing to repair *Kyrenia* for reasons he feared to question lest they change their minds. He didn't even know how long the repair might take. Perhaps he should have told them that it was the gods after all. That, they might have been more willing to believe.

Tiphys appeared over the ridge, angling northward in the direction of the device. He was carrying something in his hand.

"You're just seeking to deflect blame from where it truly lies," Kallikrates said. "And that's with you, and with him." He pointed at Tiphys, who paused midstride and looked down at them. "You failed to make proper offerings before we set out—failed to know that the plague still infested Athens in the first place—and he failed to save our ship from being driven onto this rock."

"There was a storm," Euphemus pointed out.

"Which can be attributed to Poseidon's anger," Kallikrates replied. And Euphemus, who had thought along similar lines until just yesterday, could not say that he was wrong. "If we make him an offering, then perhaps he will send us salvation."

"We have made an offering, and salvation is already here," Euphemus insisted. "The ship will be repaired, and we will be able to depart."

"Even if you are right," Kallikrates said, "who's to say that the sea will treat us any more gently once we're afloat again?" That elicited some murmurs of agreement.

"I have already vowed to visit the sanctuary at Sounion, should our journey reach a safe conclusion," Euphemus said. "But first we have to get off this island."

"I heard Tiphys claim fault for our predicament," Kallikrates said. "Among us many believe that were he to make himself an offering to the god of the sea, the rest of us might yet see rescue."

"What do you think," Euphemus retorted, "that we are in the bad old days when men offered the blood of their daughters and sons? We do not live in that time, and I say we will not do that thing." He put as much insistence into his voice as he could. No matter how desperate their case, they could not seriously be considering such a drastic action.

"You are just one man," Kallikrates said, and his voice was dangerous and soft. Euphemus put a hand on his blade. He did not want to kill Kallikrates—it would make a mockery of his attempt to save them all—but if he did not put a stop to this now, they were all dead anyway. Kallikrates lifted his chin, daring him. Euphemus's weight shifted, in preparation to take a step forward.

A shout came from the direction of the object. Euphemus turned. He started walking, then he ran. The others came after, following or chasing he did not know, but he rushed pell-mell down the slope to the graveled bowl.

Tiphys was standing at the bowl's edge. On the ground in front of him lay a scrap of the ship's hull. He was speaking in a low voice. The fragment itself was moving—no, not moving, its surface mottled and writhed, as if crawling with thousands of tiny insects, hair-thin filaments running from it to the device, and before his eyes it grew. As he watched the fragment expanded, becoming a shape, he could see the curve of the hull beginning to grow, the piece that had been stove in and broken on the rocks.

The rest of the men came to a halt behind him. He turned to look at them. Their eyes were wide, their mouths silent. Even Kallikrates. The device stood quiescent in the middle of the bowl. For a brief instant the wind brought him Tiphys's words—"from there it flattens out a bit along the bottom, before curving downward again into the keel"—and they sounded like a prayer.

It looked like wood, and felt like wood, though heavier than it ought to be. It was all of a piece, as if it had grown that way.

"We need to get it to the ship right away," Tiphys said. "It has a lingering virtue to grow into the hole, but that will die before long." They did so, and watched as that crawling strangeness appeared around the edges of the new piece, which grew into place as though it had always been part of the ship. With exquisite care, the crew half-rolled, half-pushed *Kyrenia* afloat. "Get her bailed and loaded," Euphemus ordered.

On his own trip back up the ridge to help carry supplies, he diverted over to the object. It sat quiescent. "All goes well?" it said. Euphemus jumped.

"Yes," he said. "Yes, it does. Thank you." Something occurred to him. "You have been most generous with your gifts. We are in your debt."

"We have what we need from this world," the device replied. "It is what we came for. We wanted to know about this place, about its life. And that we have acquired."

"But why?" Euphemus asked.

"Because we are curious, but could not come there ourselves. Our machines have longer lives than we do, and travel faster. The best we can do is speak across the vast distances."

"That is a marvel indeed." Euphemus looked up at the sky, now masked with clouds. "Would that I could come to you, and see the beings who made such wonders."

"I understand," the device said. No. It was someone at the other end of a tube the length of which Euphemus could not even imagine, and the face which spoke to him only a mask. Behind that mask was someone who might look like a man, or like a monster. But either way, that being, or its ancestors, had done all of this, and Euphemus would no more inquire into its motives than he would into those of the gods. "This station will cease to exist once you are gone," the voice added. "As will all the others, in due time. Do not think to look for them, to show to your people."

"I would that it were otherwise," Euphemus said, thinking of what more he could learn from these…people? People. People who were not men, who lived among the stars.

"So would I, in your position," the device said, and then nothing more. Euphemus felt a deep regret, that he was no philosopher who might persuade that voice otherwise.

But they were getting off the island. They had a chance, where before they'd had none. And he had…what did he have? He was not sure. A broader horizon, perhaps.

"Thank you again," he said.

They managed to slip around the island's southern side before the wind picked up in earnest. After some debate with the crew, *Kyrenia* would continue west. Panormos, Euphemus thought. Maybe even Neapolis. After that…well, they'd see.

The island dropped astern. The sailors worked the sails, catching the wind like fish in a net.

There were winds between the stars. The device had told Tiphys that. Euphemus, watching the island slip away behind them, imagined the seed that had brought the device to earth as a tiny ship, sailing on those winds. Would that he could travel on such a ship.

They sailed into the sunset. The wind slackened to a gentle breeze that scrubbed the last of the clouds from the darkening sky. All around them the sea rolled away in every direction.

Euphemus walked over to where Tiphys still stood, his posture more relaxed but with no indication that he intended to leave his post. "All right?"

Tiphys's gaze flicked to him, then back to the western horizon. "Yes."

Euphemus wanted to talk further—about the extraordinary adventure they'd had, and why the makers of the device had chosen to help them, and most especially what they had learned about a universe that, for all that, looked just the same to him as it had before. Instead, he clapped Tiphys on the shoulder, and found a place to stretch out on the deck.

The stars had come out. He lay and watched them, framed by the mast, rigging, and sails. They still looked to him like pinpricks of light in a dark shell that encompassed the world.

He imagined instead looking down at the sea on an overcast day, when the clouds attenuated the sun's light and turned the water wine-dark. No knowing how deep the water really was on such days, nor how deep the glimpse you might catch of a fish, or a dolphin, or some other oceanic mystery. The firmament was likewise a sea, after all, its depths beyond plumbing.

He imagined sailing that sea, in a ship made to venture into such depths.

Between the Rivers

Judith Tarr

They tell this story among the tradeships of the time-between, when the people had gone out from Old Earth, but the worlds they found were few and poor. Any whirling rock with a scrap of atmosphere was contested bitterly; wars were fought over the rubble of moons.

The genship *Ninsun* had found a gift of the long-forgotten gods, a habitable planet orbiting a small yellow star. Its atmosphere, with encouragement, could support life as Old Earth knew it, and there were no sentient beings, either higher or lower, to complicate the matter. The ship settled on the largest continent between two rivers, and set about the creation of a world.

Negar stepped away from the ship's ramp onto this new world, her world, the world that *Ninsun* had made. She stretched and yawned and blinked in the light of a new sun. It was white and golden, and the fronds of the tree that whispered over her were deep green.

She smelled earth and water and something pungent that she could not quite find a name for. It was like Earth, but not. The sun almost but not quite. The gravity close but...different. A little less. Enough to give her a delightful sensation of lightness.

Ninsun laid it out before her: the planet, the continent, the city between the rivers. The walls were up, the people awake and populating the streets and the houses. Flocks of sheep and goats, fresh from their own stasis tanks, explored the newly green hillsides. There was even a boat on the river, a narrow construction of reeds with a brown canvas sail, pulling fish out of the deep clear water.

Negar laughed and stretched out her hands to gather it all in. "Mine," she said. "All mine."

Negar had waited all her life for this. She was not the youngest of the family, but there were so few habitable worlds, and so many aunts and sisters and cousins ready and eager to be the one, the representative, the family's voice and the ship's intermediary to the brave little people who allowed themselves to be loaded in boxes and cast into sleep.

For them it was a journey without return. Once they woke on the world to which the ship had taken them, they were bound to stay. Their children might leave, if a ship came and if there was space for them on it, but their own contract could not be broken. They belonged to the new world and to the ship and the family that had brought them there.

Negar had no such binding on her, but she was contracted for twenty Earthyears, renewable at the ship's discretion. That was the only absolute power the ship had. Everything else was hers. Her responsibility. Her world. Her people to care for, and her decisions to make.

She had so many plans. Building the city first, of course, and establishing an economy. Laying out the fields for planting and for livestock. Assuring that every being under her watch, human or otherwise, had what it needed to live and thrive.

But then, when all that was done, there was a whole world to explore. Resources to discover and exploit. New towns and cities to establish, as the population increased.

"First things first," *Ninsun* said. It spoke in the voice of Negar's biomother, through chips and relays directly into her mind. She would not have chosen that of all voices, but the ship's programming had not been hers to do. She had to endure the sparks of memory that woke every time the ship spoke to her, and determine that, however long it took, she was going to give the ship another voice.

In the meantime *Ninsun* spoke with quelling practicality, and Negar had no choice but to listen. Her duties were many. The sooner she began, the more quickly this one day's tasks would be done. She drew herself up. She was ready. The world was waiting for her to rule it.

"That is not exactly what you will be doing," said *Ninsun*.

Negar set her teeth, but she was strong. She ignored the provocation.

The little people were charming, so eager to work, and so adept with their hands. They had the pastures fenced and the fields plowed and planted while Negar was still sorting the threads of her duties. They had even established a government, with committees and duty rosters, and set up an economy that was mostly trade and barter, with the beginnings of a currency: iridescent shells from the rivers, and a particular kind of water-tumbled stone.

"We need you," the committee heads assured her. "To judge fairly and impartially, to settle disputes. And," their eldest added with a touch of diffidence, "perhaps to lend your physical strength, too?"

Negar looked down from her aristocratic height at these sturdy small people. "Of course," she said. "I'm here to serve." They nodded and smiled. Negar smiled in return. It was a most satisfactory meeting.

In the families, perfection was almost ordinary. Beauty and strength and long life were locked into the genes. Intelligence was a given.

No one went so far as to call herself a god. However true it might have been, it was just a little too grandiose. Simplicity was the fashion. Everyone cultivated modesty, and took quiet pride in the precision of one's understatement.

Negar had never lived below the heights, among the little people. She had always expected to, but all the training she had had was nothing like this reality.

They were old stock, unmodified, a mingling of languages and ethnicities, none so similar that they risked collapse of the gene pool, but like enough in their adaptation to the particular requisites of this world. Their bodies varied in ways that the family's never did; their faces were often asymmetrical, and many had allowed themselves to deteriorate with age or sickness.

"That is not a choice," *Ninsun* told her.

"But everyone chooses," she said.

"Only in the families," said *Ninsun*.

It still had her biomother's voice. She kept finding other things to do than dive down into the ship's programming.

She set herself to study the people for whose welfare she was responsible. She learned a little of their languages, though everyone spoke the standard speech of Centrum, and mostly used it outside of their own clans and families. She labored in their fields, herded their cattle, lent a hand with the building of houses and the grinding of grain. She learned to see past imperfection.

They had minds of their own, though they were happy enough to bring her their disputes and expect impartiality. She could do that. She was trained for it.

There were three sisters in the outermost village, who raised sheep and spun the wool into cloth which they dyed with roots and plants. Negar found herself visiting them often, at first out of fascination with their art, but that quickly transformed into fascination with the sisters themselves.

They were not beautiful as the families were beautiful. They were small and thickset. Their features were oddly balanced—broad cheeks, narrow chins, eyes set slightly out of true. Their skin was neither perfectly dark nor perfect ivory, but somewhere in between, and one had a patch of pinkish-white staining her neck and part of her cheek.

And yet Negar could not stay away. Their wit was quick, their facility with both words and colors unlike any Negar had met even in the salons of Centrum. But most of all, they showed neither fear nor awe of her. They accepted her as they did anyone else who happened by their village.

"I am going to build a house," Negar told *Ninsun* on return from her latest visit. The idea had come to her while she was walking through the fields, striding long-legged over the furrows and fording the little rivers. She had mud on her feet and a string of weed in her hair, and she was incandescent with joy.

"You already have a house," *Ninsun* said.

Negar had expected that. "Not like this," she said. "A house to contain you, and me, and the great talents I mean to bring together. A palace, a university, a house of wonders. A place for all the people to gather and make beautiful things."

"A palace," *Ninsun* said. Its voice was usually as bright and varied as a living woman's, but for once it sounded perfectly flat.

"For everyone!" Negar cried. And, she added in her secret self, for the three beautiful sisters who dominated her dreams.

It was a good thing she was doing. A world needed more than plain practical shelter. It needed beauty.

"And how will you pay for it?" *Ninsun* inquired.

Negar had been prepared for that, too. "The people will help. It's their house, after all."

"Have you asked them?"

"I will," Negar promised.

꛰ ꛭ ꛬ ꛮ

The people did not argue with Negar when she asked them to contribute to the building of the great house. Some of them did not look altogether happy, but they gave their portion. It was for them, she told them through her gatherers of the gifts, people who came to her call and professed themselves delighted to help.

The great house grew on a long hill above the river. She had designed it herself, to look somewhat like the cloud mansions of her homeworld, and a little like the mud-and-wattle huts of this one, but mostly like a dream she had had of a boat that sailed the sea of stars. It stretched long like the hill it sat on, with a courtyard in the center and a pool in the center of that, reflecting the sky. All around the edges, inside a wall of mud brick, were clusters of lesser houses, some to live in, some to work in, and a whole long course that would be a library, and on the roof an observatory, because the people should never forget where they had come from.

Ninsun had a house, too, dug deep into the hill, with a gate that opened on the river, and a roof that would slide back if there was ever need for the ship to take to the air. That was a great work, and difficult, and almost more than the people could manage with what technology they had.

They did manage it, eventually. By then the gifts that Negar had gathered were all spent. She had had to ask again, and yet again, then wait for a harvest to be gathered in. Her gatherers took what they were calling the royal share of that; even so, it was barely enough. She would need more all too soon, if she was to finish the work: to glaze the walls as she had envisioned, and ornament them with a frieze celebrating the people who had built this wonder of the world.

But that could wait a while. What could not wait was the arrival of the three sisters for whom Negar had built it all. She had kept this from them, to make a gift of it; to give them joy as they had given it to her.

She had hoped to go to them herself and see firsthand the delight in their faces, but some necessary nonsense of her position kept her away. She sent some of her gatherers instead, with a gilded oxcart for the sisters to ride in, and an honor guard of handsome young people.

The cart came back empty. "They said, 'Please thank the great one, but we're content where we are,'" the chief of the gatherers said.

Negar had not understood before what it meant to be stunned. It truly was like a blow to the head, or more properly to the heart. "Are you sure?" she demanded. "Did you speak to the right people? Did you say exactly what I told you to say?"

The gatherer flinched. Negar's voice was barely raised, but the heat of her temper was enough to singe one of these fragile little people. He was brave, even so. He said, "I spoke to the sisters Eloisa and Eriol and Elumi, just as you instructed. They replied exactly as I have said." He paused, then after a moment added, "Great one."

Negar took time to breathe. She counted each breath. At forty, she was calm enough to say, "Thank you. You may go."

He wasted no time in escaping. She had already forgotten him. The sisters obviously were overwhelmed by the shock of her generosity. She would send another party of gatherers, larger and even more imposing, and this time they would not ask. They would simply take.

"After all," she said to the beautiful rooms she had made for them, to the looms and the spinning wheels and the dyeing vats, "they're simple people. They won't believe it until they see it. Then they'll dare to be overjoyed."

She hugged herself at the thought. They would make such beauty here, and be so happy. And she would be able to visit them every day.

The second party came back empty-handed, too, and without the courage to face Negar directly. They sent a written message instead through one of the people who tended the palace.

Great one, it said in careful calligraphy, *we beg your forgiveness, but the sisters Eloisa and Eriol and Elumi decline to be taken into custody. They have too much to do at home, they tell us, and they have entered into a spousal contract with a family in the next village. They thank you for your kindness; they ask you please to let them celebrate their union in peace. Also,* the letter added, *they send a peace offering, this fine coverlet for the great one's bed.*

It was more than fine. It was exquisite. It was glorious. Its colors were the colors of the earth and the river and the sky, embroidered with bits of brightness: fish dancing in the river, birds spiraling in the sky. There were herds of cattle in fields of flowers, and oxen plowing furrows in black earth, and a skein of dancers in the middle, circling a quite remarkable likeness of Negar robed in stars and crowned with the sun.

It was not the sisters. "How dare they?" Negar cried. "How can they?" And then she stopped, because she knew exactly what to do.

A decree first. She had her lawyers write it up in proper form. When it was written, she took a copy of it, pendant seals and fluttering ribbons and all, and called for the same splendid cart in which she had meant the sisters to ride, and rode in it, accompanied by the by now rather weary honor guard, all the way to the sisters' door.

She could have walked there faster, but she had a point to make. This was a mighty concession. It was, above all, sincere. She truly loved the sisters, and was willing to make a sacrifice, with but one small condition.

"One night," she said after she strode into the meeting place where the sisters and their new spouses and all their families were gathered. She said it in their odd, rare, complicated language, with its rhythm almost like a song. "A few brief hours when I may honor you."

The spouses stood shocked into stillness. The families had flung themselves on their faces. Eloisa stood perfectly still. Elumi opened her mouth but seemed bereft of words. It was Eriol who said in standard, "One night? That's all? Then you'll leave us alone?"

Negar forbore to feel the sting of that, either the words or the choice of language. "One night only," she said, forsaking their lilting speech for flat mundanity.

"And leave and never come back?"

Elumi hissed and jabbed Eriol with her elbow. Negar forbore to acknowledge that, too. "Never," she agreed, though her heart died a little with the word.

"Right, then," said Elumi. "Let's get it over with."

That was one sting too many. Negar held her anger in check, but even while she bent her head and allowed them to lead her into the marriage chamber, she made a decision. She had meant to rescind the law after this; it was only intended for a single use.

No longer. This would be her firm decree. It was Elumi's fault. If she had only held her tongue, if she had but recognized the honor...

They were little people after all, however beautiful they seemed. Their minds were small and their understanding weak. Negar would teach them to respect their betters.

𒌷 𒐕 𒋾 𒁹

N*insun*'s powers on-planet were considerably restricted, but nothing prevented it from gathering data and observing the people it had transported here. All of them, including the family's representative. She was not the worst that *Ninsun* had seen, either for itself or through a deep scan of the archives. Nevertheless, the trajectory of her behavior triggered certain alarms, which activated a particular subroutine.

Ninsun was not subject to emotions as humans knew them, but it might define its response to the subroutine as bemusement. That one had not been triggered before in the history of the genships. It was almost a jest, a bit of whimsy on the part of the programming.

Other options presented themselves, but the data kept returning the same conclusion: of all the probabilities, this was the least likely to fail. Although its chances of success were barely statistically significant, the rest were worse. If *Ninsun* had had a body capable of the motion, it would have shrugged. It allowed the subroutine to proceed.

𒀭 𒐀 𒁀 𒉌

Her name was Anneki. Mother Ninsun had given her names to choose from, in among the rest of the things she was born knowing. She liked the sound of that one.

She came out of the womb whole and perfect and only a little weak, weakness that passed as she taught herself to stand and walk and, in short order, to run through the Mother's corridors. She was fast and light, and running filled her with something that, from the knowledge unspooling inside her, she learned to call joy.

A cord bound her to the Mother, stretching as she ran. The knowledge came from it, the words and the names, the shapes and colors of things. There were so many, spinning so fast. They made her head hurt.

She ran faster and faster, stretching the cord ever thinner, fleeing toward the edges of the Mother, away from the pain of too much knowing. Where the corridor ended, where the airlock began, the cord snapped. She tumbled out into wet and cold and tumult. She fell down the mountainside, long limbs flailing, lashed with wind and rain and terrorized with thunder.

𒀭 𒐀 𒁀 𒉌

Ninsun had made a thing out of Negar's own cells, cloned it deep in the ship and begun to program it as a counter to her rising tyranny. But it had miscalculated the clone's rate of growth; allowed too little time for mental programming and too much for physical. The body, fully mature and unexpectedly strong, had escaped while the mind was still only partially formed.

And now it was gone, fallen out of the ship's forward

hatch, down the mountain in a storm as furious as this world had seen. *Ninsun* had no resources to follow it or to repeat the experiment. It could only wait and record, and continue the report it had begun when it came to this world, for the family's review—whenever that would be. Twenty Earthyears, Negar's contract said, but contracts were no more or less flexible than the cord that should have bound the clone, out here among the stars.

Ninsun was not constructed to feel, or to despair. But it recognized failure. There would be no check on Negar unless or until the family should send a new representative. The ship powered itself down, maintaining only essential processes. The intelligence that was *Ninsun* slept.

The world spun through its cycles. Negar did whatever Negar chose to do, and no one dared speak against her. The people were worshipping her as a god now, swearing their lives and loyalty to her and to the ship. The ship recorded but did not wake. There was nothing to wake for.

𒀭 𒀀 𒀀 𒀀

Anneki fell far and long and hard, straight out of memory into a turbulent darkness. When she could feel her body around her again, all the knowing inside her was jumbled together. The only clear thing was her name, and the conviction that she must run.

She ran out of the night into the hard light of day, and back into night again. Sometimes she fell. More than once something chased her, but she did not look to see what it was.

She ran until every part of her was a stabbing ache, until her eyes darkened even in the sunlight, and her knees wobbled and her chest heaved and the taste of blood was in her throat. When her knees would not hold her, she crawled. When that failed, she lay on her face and groped for a word.

Death. That was the word. Her lips shaped it, but her voice was gone. So was the rest of her, after a while.

She was warm, and wrapped in light. Something large and bristly-soft was prodding her. She looked up into a long pale-brown face and the wide twin arcs of horns.

She was empty of both words and fear. The large sweet-smelling brown thing cropped the fragrant green beside her. She tried to do the same, though her face was too flat to be really comfortable. She bit, chewed. It tasted the way it looked. Green.

A smaller brown thing tucked itself up under the large one, latched on to a dangling part and sucked eagerly. She smelled warmth and richness and a hint of sweet. She crawled up beside the little one and studied what it did. That was easier than trying to eat from the ground. It filled her mouth with warm wonderfulness, spilled over till she understood how to swallow.

When she had drunk all she could hold, she sprawled with the little one, while the large one grazed peacefully beside them. Others wandered past, some with little ones, others alone. If she had had words inside her, one of them would have been contentment.

The village of Three Cows would have been rich with cattle if the tyrant's taxes had not taken most of the milk and cheese and so many of the young stock that there were barely enough left for a proper breeding herd. She was building her useless hulk of a palace again, and stripping the country bare to pay for it. It was little comfort that the grass was rich this season and the cows were still, by some miracle, both fat and fecund. The bulls had done their duty nobly; there would be a new crop of calves in the spring for the tyrant to take.

The one small herd that been allowed to keep its calves was pastured down near the orchards, where the cows could feed on windfalls. The town had come to a tacit agreement, almost a superstition, that if nobody talked about the herd, the tax collectors would not think to look for it.

That translated, one way and another, into the cows being mostly left alone. There were no large predators in these parts, aside from the tax collectors. All the herdsfolk had to do was wander by once in a while, count heads both large and small, and make sure everyone was healthy.

The person sent on one particular day to look in on the cattle was young and inexperienced and more than a little sulky. She would much rather have been fishing in the river. Which, she swore to herself, she would do as soon as she had counted all the stupid animals and their stupid young.

She counted twice, because she might be sulky but she was not irresponsible. The second time, as her eye ran past the big brown cow with the crooked horn, something stirred in the grass beside it. It was a calf, brown like its mother, but with an odd black patch on its back.

The patch separated itself from the smooth brown hide. It resolved into a mat of hair on a human head, but such a human as she had never seen: filthy, naked, and staring at her with wide wild eyes.

She was not the kind of person to screech and run, though she seriously considered it. She backed away cautiously instead, and went to fetch someone who could do something about this intruder in the cow pasture.

Again Anneki woke knowing her name, and this time knowing she had done so before. The rest was different: the sense of emerging from a long siege of shadows, and the voice speaking at a distance rather than inside her. She had a sense that time had passed, but not how much, or where she was or had been.

Words came back slowly, too few at first for use. She listened to the voices and marked out the perimeter of her body and let the light break over her. She was wrapped and bound and lying on something not particularly comfortable.

She had been fighting, she thought. She had aches, and parts of her stung. Her heart still beat hard; her legs wanted to run, but could not move.

She brought body and mind together carefully, no faster or more slowly than the task needed. By then her body was calm, and the words spoken above her had begun to make sense.

"What do we do with it?"

"You're asking me? I'm the one who got the fist in the face. I'd like to truss it up tighter and toss it in the river."

"It's not an it. It's a person."

"Does it know that? It looks completely feral to me."

Something prodded her side. "You. Do you have a name?"

She did, but her tongue did not want to answer. She stared up at two people who stared down. They were of a size and a shape, but their expressions, as she found the knowledge in her to recognize them, were distinct. One was scowling; that one's nose was oddly flat and distinctly red and blue. The other stood with head tilted, studying her, and said, "We'll take her to the common house, clean her up, see what we've got."

"*You're* taking her," said the one with the multicolored nose.

That was fair, she thought, somewhat distantly. Her mind and body were still having difficulty meeting.

She was filthy and wild and showed no sign of ability to speak, but her shape was human. She lay in the common house, wrapped in the net with which the hunters had caught her, staring at them all with eyes as wide and dark and liquid as a cow's.

"Cows are smarter than they look," Rani said. She always wanted to rescue wolf cubs and bottle-raise orphaned calves and throw hooked fish back into the river. If they grew up to bite or gore her, she never blamed them. Their nature was their nature.

A feral human was a new challenge. The elders eyed it sidelong and muttered. "That's not planet-bonded stock," they said. "We don't grow like that. This thing came from the cloud cities. See how long and narrow it is. And that face. It looks just like—"

"*That* one has never come anywhere near Three Cows," Rani said, "and please the stars she never will. I'll take this wild thing in. If it's possible to tame her, I'll find a way to do it."

"And if not?" asked her sister Peret, whose nose would never be the same after the wild thing's fist had flattened it.

"That will come when it comes," said Rani.

The words were present inside long before they allowed themselves to slip past her tongue. She was able to give Rani her name not too long after she was let out of the net, but before they stopped keeping her in a cage. "Anneki," she said. "I am Anneki."

Rani accepted that with a nod. Peret grunted and dragged Anneki to the public baths with a rope wound around her wrists. The baths had been cleared for that hour, also for safety, though Anneki would not have done anything to anyone. She suffered the daily scrubbing of her body and the ungentle tending of her hair. "We should cut it off," Peret said.

"I don't like to," said Rani.

"It can't be comfortable," Peret pointed out, craftily. Anneki truly was waking to herself, that she could perceive that. "It's all a mat. It must hurt when she moves." Rani made small distressed noises, but did not stop Peret when she advanced with the set of shears.

Anneki recoiled. Peret was ready for it: she sprang in to truss Anneki hand to foot, just like a sheep for the shearing. And shorn she was, in quick strokes that were not quite as rough as they might have been.

It was a relief, that was true: all that heavy weight gone, and the air cool on the tight curls that were left. She looked

Peret in the eye and smiled. Peret shied, but Rani smiled back. "I feel better," Anneki said to her. "It's good."

Both of them blinked. "Not so feral after all," Rani said. "Are you?"

Anneki had no answer for that. Nor did they let her off her tether, not that day or for a solid count of days after, until she had proved that she would not either attack or run. Even then, she still was shut in the cage at night and when the sisters had to be elsewhere.

Trust had to be earned. That was one of the things she had known, in the time before she became a beast of the field. She did not want to run away and she did not want to hurt anyone. She wanted to live, that was all, and learn how people lived here, what they did every day, what dreams they had at night.

She could sit in the sun when it shone or in the common space when the rain fell, and people would come and go, and they would talk. People talked; that was what made them people instead of cows. Not that cows lacked for ways of sharing how they felt or what they knew, but words were a human affectation.

Little by little the talkers learned that the strange tall one would listen when they spoke. Really listen: not grow bored or wander off or fall asleep. She never said much in response, but that was not what most of them were looking for. They just wanted to be heard, and if possible understood.

She did understand, they were sure. Maybe not so much at first. But the more she listened, the more she learned, and the better she became at nodding in the right places and inserting the right sound.

In that way she learned what people wanted and did not want. What they needed. How and why they did what they did. She learned songs, which she would sing to herself when she was sitting alone or sitting with the cows or, as time went on and she was let off her leash, working in the fields. But not when she was hunting in the woods. She was good at hunting, though she always apologized to the prey, and thanked it for its sacrifice.

Most of what people talked about was the life of the town, the weather, the state of the crops and the herds. No one had time to spare for things and people outside of Three Cows, except one thing.

"Taxes." Rani spat. That was so unlike her that Anneki started and nearly dropped the harness she was mending. For once it was Peret who rolled her eyes and forbore to argue. The rest of the circle around the evening fire muttered and growled.

Anneki knew about taxes. The order for them came from outside, and people from outside came with wagons to take the best of everything and leave just enough for people to go on with, if they were clever and hid some of it from the collectors. Seed, cattle, fish from the river, all went on or beside the wagons and rumbled away down the road.

"Where does it go?" she asked now, having recovered the dropped stitch and fallen back into the rhythm of her mending. "Who wants our calves and our salt fish? What do they do with it?"

"Does it matter?" Peret muttered.

"I want to know," Anneki said.

Everyone glanced at everyone else. She knew those looks. She had asked an unanswerable question. Or one with so many answers there was no way to explain them all before the night rolled into dawn.

Rani had begun this. She sighed and took on the responsibility. "They go to the great city, the biggest of all, where the tyrant is building a palace."

"A palace," said Anneki. The sound of the word in her own head gave her one of her flashes of knowing. She saw a high ridge and an undulating wall and a swarm of people hammering and grinding and piling stone on stone.

"A place for a tyrant to live in," Peret said.

"Only a tyrant?"

"She says it's for everyone," said Rani, "but the only people who live there are the tyrant and the people who do what she tells them."

"That's not fair," said Anneki.

"No, it's not," Rani said.

"Then we should stop giving everything to the collectors."

"Oh, no," just about everyone said, a choir of denial.

Peret explained it for them. "Then they'll come and take everything they haven't already taken, and drag off our strongest people to build the palace."

"Punishment," Anneki said as the word came to her. "Obey or be punished. But why? What gives her the right?"

That truly seemed to be unanswerable. It ended the night's gathering, and left Anneki alone by the fire, gathering the scattered remnants of knowledge into a heap of gaps and confusion.

One person was still there, quiet in the shadows. Lakshmi was Rani's grandmother. She was the oldest person in Three Cows, and one of the most silent. She spoke so seldom that some of the youngers told one another she could not speak at all. But Anneki knew she simply did not like to waste words.

She spoke slowly, not particularly loudly, but clear enough. "It's not that taxes are bad," she said, "but what they're wanted for—that's different. If it really is for the people, and everybody shares the burden, and everyone gets something from it, then that's fair. When it's for one person's whim, and everybody else has to give but no one gets, well, you see."

"I do see," Anneki said. "What I don't see—"

"You will," said Lakshmi, rising stiffly and wrapping her shawl around her. Anneki half rose to help, but Lakshmi stilled her with a glance.

Long after she was gone, Anneki sat staring at the embers, as they died one by one, and faded into the last of the night.

⸱⸱⸱

"You look like her."

Some of the herdsfolk had gone to the city with the taxes, to help with the oxen and the loose cattle. Not all of them came back. Some, the largest and strongest, had been taken for the palace.

Peret, who was amazingly strong, was also small and wiry. She had escaped the takers. For three days after the few remaining herdsfolk had come back, she stayed in the far pasture and would not speak to anyone, even her sister.

On the fourth day she stood across Anneki's path as she came back from a hunt. Anneki stopped. Peret's hot stare raked her up and down, from wild half-unbraided hair to booted feet, with a brief pause at the fat stag draped over her shoulders. "You look just like her."

Anneki shifted her feet but otherwise stood still. The stag was heavy and she had carried it far. She would be glad to set it down in the cooks' house.

"I don't look like anyone here," she said.

"No, you don't."

"Then who—"

Peret hissed and spat and spun on her heel and ran away. Anneki stared after her, puzzled and obscurely hurt.

"You really do, you know."

Anneki had not noticed Udo till he spoke. Udo was even smaller than Peret, and really was as weak as he looked. He was wonderful with animals, which was why he had gone to the city, too, but with people he was not so adept. That he had said anything at all was remarkable. He was usually even more silent than Lakshmi.

"I don't know what you mean," Anneki said.

"I'm sure," said Udo. "Go look in the library. Ask it to show you the tyrant."

"I'm not—"

"Just look," Udo said.

Most of the houses in Three Cows were built of mud brick and painted in colors that marked the families inside. The community house was different. It was built of reeds from the river, bound tight and curved into arches high over even Anneki's head. Wind blew through it in hot weather, cooling it miraculously, but when the air grew cold, people hung doors of woven reeds at either end, and the spaces inside were warm.

The library occupied a smallish room behind the large central one where the elders met. It was mostly books on rolls and bound in leaves, but in a far corner was a relic of the times before people came to this world. It ran on sunlight, and it talked, though one had to ask it in exactly the right way and with exactly the right accent. It did not speak the language people spoke in their houses, but the one they used outside, to people who were not family.

Anneki could speak to it with the words she had known before she came to Three Cows. She had not done it often: living words and people's faces were the best way to learn, and gave her more satisfying answers to her questions.

Still, she sat down in the corner and spoke the word that woke the machine. Its screen blinked to life. "Show me the tyrant," she said.

"Specify," the machine replied.

Anneki's brows rose. "There's more than one?"

"Tyrant," the machine said. "Tyranny. Rule that exceeds its proper and legal bounds."

"Yes," said Anneki. "I want to see the tyrant people talk about. The one in the city, building the palace. The one who takes all our taxes."

"Negar," said the library, "of House Innunakil. Delegated by the family to oversee the settlement of this world."

"Negar," Anneki said. "Show me Negar."

The screen had been reflecting Anneki's face, the long oval of it, the high cheeks, the wide dark eyes. Suddenly that face was perfectly clear, as if the screen had brightened into a mirror.

Through the shock of startlement, somewhat slowly, Anneki recognized differences. The hair was longer, the braids notably tidier. Pendant jewels hung from the ears, glowing deep red. Anneki brushed one of them with a finger. The screen was flat and cool, the image perfectly still.

"She does look like me," Anneki said.

She turned on the stool to face the one who had come up behind her. Peret looked ready to scream or cry or kill, or maybe all three.

"You came to spy on us," Peret said.

"No," said Anneki.

"Then why? You're not one of us. You're one of them. The high and mighty. The family. Do you laugh at us? Do you find us entertaining? Are we quaint?"

"No," Anneki said again. "I don't know anything about family, except the ones here. And the cows. The cows have families."

"Herd," Peret said with tired annoyance. "Cows have a herd. Humans have families. Humans in the cloud cities, altered humans, have the family. The one that rules us all."

"I don't rule anybody," Anneki said.

Peret walked out on her. That was not unusual, but it felt worse this time. As if Anneki had done something terrible.

If she had, she did not remember it at all. She could, if she tried very hard, remember something before the cows and the village. A long dark time, and a glimmer of light. Corridors that went on and on. A voice whispering, like a woman's but not quite. Giving her words in every language that people spoke in this world. Filling her full of knowledge.

She sat up straight. "I am not a spy. I never wanted to rule anyone, or hurt anyone, or betray anyone at all. The only family I know is here."

No one was there to argue with her. She shut down the library but stayed in front of it, stiff-backed, unable to move.

She could not go back to the house Peret shared with her, even with Rani to smooth the raw edges between them. She might sleep with the cows, but she had changed too much. She was human now.

She stood up slowly. There was a thing she could do. She had to think about it first, and plumb the knowledge that was in her. But she would do it.

While Anneki was thinking, some of the young hunters started talking about getting married. Marriage, she understood, was a contract to share a house and a plot of land and a share of the sheep and cattle, as well as a blending of families and, best of all for everyone else, an opportunity for a festival. Usually it was two people, but sometimes three or four or even more.

This time it was three, and they were in a fret over it. They all wanted it. Their families wanted it. It was good business as well as good politics. But for one thing.

"The tyrant," Rani said with completely uncharacteristic venom. "Anyone who wants to get married has to go to her or suffer her coming to them, and she gets the right of the first night."

"What does she do to them?" Anneki wanted to know.

"That's not what matters," Rani said. "She has no right. They belong to each other. She acts as if we all belong to her."

Anneki sat back on her heels, in between turns of the bread she was kneading. She had heard words like that before, but here and now, they made more sense than they ever had. They showed her the way. She knew what to do.

ᚠ ᚦ ᛏ ᛒ

When she left it was still night, and everyone was asleep, even the three lovers who had been arguing for hours over the law they all hated. Two declared they could stand it for one night in return for a lifetime together. Shura, who was soft and kind and utterly gentle, had turned to stone. "I will not," she said, hour after hour. "I cannot. I refuse."

Anneki put on her hunting clothes, took her bow and a quiver of arrows, and filled the rest of her bag with bread and hard cheese and odd bits of fruit and dried meat from the communal stores. She was not sure exactly how far she had to go, but she was as well prepared as she could be.

She did not look back once she had begun. If she saw this place again she would be glad. If she did not, then so be it.

What she did, if she succeeded, would make everyone's life better. That was the only thing that mattered.

She set a good pace, neither too fast nor too slow, alternating running and walking with long-legged ease. The sun rose in front of her, climbed to the summit of the sky, and sank into the low rolling hills at her back. At more or less regular intervals she skirted a village, and once a town of fair size, with traffic crowding in and streaming out. It was market day, but she had nothing to buy or sell. She had somewhere else to go.

Nine days' walking, with intervals to rest and eat and, toward the end, hunt or trade for sustenance, and one of the days shut in a herdsfolk's hut with torrents of rain, brought Anneki at last within sight of the city. She trod the last of it on a wide road beside the river, looking up at the palace gleaming on the spine of its ridge.

She was dusty and footsore and tired, and something about that blaze of color and light made her inexplicably sad. It was beautiful, she supposed, but it had no sensible reason to exist. Nobody she had heard or talked to had any love for it. They all hated what it stood for. None of them saw any way to stop it or the one who had built it.

They were afraid of the tyrant. The closer she came to the city, the more afraid they were. People whispered about friends of friends taken away and not seen again. Some had seen things. The tyrant's gatherers taking whatever they pleased, and beating anyone who objected.

"If you argue, they take you," Anneki heard over and over. "If you fight, they take your family, and then they break you."

Anneki supposed she should be afraid. All she felt was anger, a long slow burn that set itself deeper with every story she heard.

She had seen the gatherers now and then on her way to the city, but only at a distance. The first time or two she had thought about intercepting them. But they were only doing what the tyrant wanted. If she was going to stop them, she had to stop the one whose orders they followed.

Now she stood in front of the west gate, which was open from sunrise to sunset. The sun was just beginning its climb, casting long light over the plain brown stone of the walls and striking fire in the ornaments of the tyrant's palace.

Crowds of people were already streaming out and jostling their way in. Guards in tall helmets kept the streams separate, wielding long poles like the staffs shepherds carried to herd their sheep.

That was insulting. People were not sheep.

"You! You there!" Anneki looked down at a guard whose head came just to her shoulder. He had a bristling beard and a booming voice, and he liked to wave his staff about. Probably he liked to hit people with it, too.

She caught it as it swung toward her. His face went from dark brown to deep purple as he realized how easily she was holding it and how hard he was trying to wrench it free. "I'm here to see Negar," she said.

Even struggling and cursing, he laughed at her. "Her mightiness won't even clean her shoe with a raggedy thing like you."

Anneki lifted him, staff and all, and set him down out of her way. He yowled and sprang at her. So did the guard on the other side, though impeded by staring, gaping people. Others sprinted toward them.

They were quick. She was almost impressed. While they converged on her, she raised her voice. "Negar! *Negar*! Come out and answer for your sins!"

꜒ ꜕ ꜖ ꜔

Negar's life had grown sour. It came on gradually: a dimming of the light that surrounded her, a dulling of the joy with which she had greeted each new morning. She had lived for her people, and they had given nothing back.

She heard what they muttered to one another when she walked among them, either not knowing or not troubling that she could hear, until she did so less and less, and finally not at all. They hated her. All she gave or tried to give them was nothing to them. None of them understood. None of them cared.

Her beautiful palace, her house that she had built for the people, was empty. Workers came because she commanded them, but none would stay. No one wanted to live so close to her. Where she could spy on them, they said. She had tried to talk to *Ninsun*, to ask what she had done wrong. But *Ninsun* had gone silent. She was all alone.

She sat in the hall of judgment, though there were no petitions to consider. People had stopped coming with those. They still came to judges outside of the city, but not here. There was no one else in that wide high space hung with banners from each of the towns and villages, and its floor that was a map of the world. It was only she, in a bubble of silence.

Maybe she would go hunting. Or walk out at least. She would be safe. Who would dare threaten her?

Someone had, the last time. A stone flying, a hail of curses. Her guards had not found the perpetrator. She wondered, in the darkness of her solitude, if they had tried particularly hard.

She rose abruptly, let fall the robes of judgment, strode into the harsh glare of the sun.

⁂

"Negar!" a clarion voice was calling. "*Negar*! Come out and answer for your sins!"

No human here had ever called her by her name. Only *Ninsun*, and only rarely. She could be afraid, she supposed. Apprehensive, at least. What she felt, instead, was a kind of hectic glee. It had been too long since she stretched her legs and ran. She felt it quickly: breath coming short, stitch in her side. She did not care.

She came out of the empty halls onto the road that wound down from the palace. People avoided that, too, but the city below was as crowded as ever. She skirted it along the wall that had been built not to keep anyone in or out, but simply to contain the city's sprawl.

The strong voice that had reached even into the palace was still calling, lifted above a tumult of lesser voices. She had never heard the noise of a riot in this world, but she knew the sound of it. Every member of the family was taught to recognize it.

The western gate was in uproar. Traffic had snarled hopelessly. Guards had gathered, shields upraised that had never been in use before. The center of it was a figure that towered over the rest. Wild hair, rough clothes stained with travel. Weapons meant for hunting: bow and quiver, short spear. The voice was unmistakable. It rang like trumpets.

"Negar! *Negar!*"

Rage gusted through her. How dare this wild thing—how *dare*— But then, out of nowhere, she laughed. "I am here!" she called down from the wall. "Who are you? What do you want with me?"

"Come out and face me!" the wild one called back. She had power in her lungs, that one. As if she were one of the family.

That was not possible. Negar was the only one here. All the other people were little people, short-statured and short-lived, unaltered from the stock of Old Terra. There could not be a sister on this world, or a cousin. Negar would have known.

"Why should I listen to you?" she demanded.

"Certainly," said the stranger, "it seems as if you've listened to no one else. Don't you know what everybody says about you?"

"Nobody understands," Negar said. She heard the whine in it. She hoped no one else did.

"Oh, we understand," the stranger said. "It's you who understand nothing about us. No one wants to marry because of that terrible law you made. Why did you do that? What possible use do you make of it?"

"It's only a single night," Negar said. "It's an honor I do them. A gift of my self."

The stranger's laughter ripped like claws at Negar's vitals. "That's not how they see it."

"They know no better," she said.

"You really think that?"

Negar looked down into that face. Dirt and dust and hair matted half out of its braids—it was disgraceful. "Who are you? Where do you come from?"

"I don't actually know," the wild thing said. "But I do know what I came here for. You are a tyrant, and it's time someone stopped you."

"You are an outrage," Negar said through clenched teeth.

"That's two of us, then," said that appalling person.

Negar had never had anyone killed. It was not even supposed to be a last resort. People did it nonetheless, and if they were family they seldom suffered for it, though they might lose the world they ruled and be forced to go back to the cities.

She might be able to live with that.

"Come down," said the person in the road. "Look me in the face and tell me what a kind and benevolent ruler you are."

All the people who had been swarming around her had stopped. The guards stood flat-footed. None of them touched her. There was a clear space all around her, a zone of empty air and expressionless stares.

Were they expecting Negar to blast her for them? She had no such weapon here. *Ninsun* did, but the locker was sealed. She could only access it under specific and dire conditions. This was not one. Yet.

Negar shot a glare at the guard nearest the wild thing. "Seize her," she commanded. The woman did not move. Her fingers clenched and unclenched on her staff, but she held it still, grounded in the dust.

"I don't think anyone wants to do what you tell them," the wild thing said.

"These are my people," said Negar. "This is my city and my world. All I do, I do for them."

"You do not," the wild thing said.

It was not that relentless, needling voice, or that dirt-stained face, or even that insolent stance. It was the utter silence of the people who surrounded her. Hundreds now, lining the walls—but not where Negar was—and hanging out of windows as well as standing in the road. They should have been raging at the insult.

They loved her. She lived for them. She had never done anything except on their behalf.

The wild thing stood towering above the tallest, head thrown back, and dropped her weapons. "Here. Hand to hand, tyrant. Show me how much better you are than any of us."

Negar's lip twisted. "How primitive do you think I am?"

"You're afraid," said that voice of torment.

"*Take her!*" Negar bellowed at the lot of them, all those still and staring people. The stare shifted and rose. It fixed on her. Flat. Hard. Cold. Hundreds of them. One of her. But one of that other, too, and she was as free as ever.

Negar leaped down from the wall. It had been a long time since she used her body so, but the muscles remembered. She landed only a little hard, only a little off balance, and directly in front of the one who dared challenge her.

They were exactly of a height. She braced for a rank animal reek, but the wild thing's scent though pungent was more pleasant than not, like a cow in a field. The skin under her hands was smooth, the muscles solid beneath, and strong. As strong as she was herself.

"Who are you?" she spat into that grinning, straining face.

"Anneki," the wild one answered. They grappled. Primitive, oh so primitive, but unexpectedly satisfying. Body to body. Breath to breath. Strength to strength.

She had no art. Neither did the other. It did not matter. They rolled in the dust. Now one pinning the other to the earth. Now the other. Gripping. Kneeing. Biting—Negar yowled. Blood ran down from her torn ear. It slicked her skin, and slid between them, smelling of iron and of life.

She clamped her hands around the strong and straining throat. Fingers clamped around her own. Darkness hovered. There had been pain, but it was lost somewhere, forgotten. The body beneath her bucked, rolled, twisted. Her hands tore free. Anneki's held. Negar lay still. Waited.

"Oh, no," said Anneki. "Not that game." She surged up, hauling Negar with her, holding her upright though her knees buckled. "Not that, either," said Anneki. Her voice was raw. Negar's doing.

She let go Negar's neck and caught her wrists, spun and twisted, and bound her arms behind her. Negar's mind woke from its shock. She kicked and thrashed. Anneki evaded her easily. A sharp tug, a wrench of pain in her shoulders: she staggered forward.

The people stared. None of them moved. Not one hand lifted. Not one voice spoke. They watched as Anneki half dragged, half pushed her toward the guards' station, the high platform with its awning, from which one or more of the guards could survey the road and the gate. Anneki set her firmly in the middle of that, still bound, and hobbled her for good measure.

She tried to bolt, but Anneki had anticipated that, too. She tripped Negar and sat on her, and snubbed her head to heels like a rebellious calf. Then she stood up, looming impossibly tall, and said in her voice that carried so easily above the hum and the muted roar of the city, "So then, people of the world. What shall I do with her?"

It came up out of the earth, a deep rumble, as if the stones themselves had shifted. That was not love. Nothing remotely resembling it. They hated her. After all she had done, all she had tried to do—

She read it in those eyes that looked down on her, dark and wide and terribly, brutally clear. She had told herself a story. That story was a lie. They wanted her dead.

She lay helpless, waiting for it. That was what happened to the calf, after all, or the lamb. One quick stroke, a gush of blood. She tilted her head back, to make it easier.

A voice spoke out of the crowd. It had no particular timbre to it; it might have been a distillation of them all. "She owes us for what she's done. Let her pay with the rest of her life. Let her serve where she lorded it over us. Let her do our will instead of her shifting whim."

"I like that," Anneki said. "No more first night. No more taxes for her palace. No more laws that break our backs while she sits in her big house. No more takers."

The rumble rose with each word spoken, till even Anneki had to raise her voice to be heard. Negar's skin prickled; the hair rose on the back of her neck. She was not safe, no matter what the speakers said. She could still die.

"No more ruler in the high house," said the voice of the crowd. "We rule ourselves now."

"Isn't that how it's supposed to be?" Anneki asked.

"*Yes!*"

Negar's ears rang. Dimly through the hum and buzz inside her skull, Anneki said, "I'll take this one, then. Unless you want her?"

Silence, again. Cold on her skin in the sun's heat. Anneki hauled her up again, cut the cord that tied feet to head and hobbled her ankles, but kept the halter around her neck. When she walked forward, Negar followed before the rope could tighten.

𒀭 𒂍 𒁇 𒆠

Negar was not broken. She told herself that. It was not a story, not like the ones that had gone before. This one was true. It was also true that she had stopped trying to fight. The deep growl of the people's hate had taught her one thing, and their silence at the end had taught her another.

Anneki led her away from the city, walking as docile as a cow on a lead. She was deep inside herself. When they stopped, at first she was hardly aware of it. Anneki's voice penetrated the darkness she walked in, bringing a slow glimmer of light. "I hope you're not willing yourself to death."

Negar blinked and shook herself. "What? No. No, I'm not doing that."

"Good," said Anneki. She sat on close-cropped grass beside a bright bubble of stream, bathing her feet. Something huge and brown loomed over her.

Negar scrambled backward, stumbling, falling, rolling till she fetched up against something hard that suddenly yielded. Another long brown nose looked down at her, blowing sweet breath in her face.

The one over her was much smaller than the one who stood beside Negar. It must be a young one. Or a female. The big one—

"That's a bull!"

"Yes," Anneki said serenely. "Isn't he beautiful?" She reached up to rub an enormous ear, scratching the base of a horn as long as she was tall. The bull moaned and leaned into her fingers.

Negar gasped. Words had abandoned her.

"You have so much to learn," said Anneki.

Negar got her feet under her and stood. The cow helped. It, or she, regarded her with a big round empty eye. "I have to go back," she said.

"You can't."

"I have to. No matter what they think of me. Someone has to take care of them. Someone has to—"

"They'll do it themselves."

"They don't know how."

"You don't know them at all."

Negar reared up, though she nearly pitched over backward. "No one knows them better. They belong to me!"

Anneki tugged on the halter. Negar fell flat, and lay winded. The cow cropped a tuft of grass beside her ear. The sound was deafeningly loud.

"No one belongs to you," Anneki said. "No living thing. Nothing unliving, either. Not even the earth under you. All you own is your small and foolish self."

"But who will take care of the people?" Negar cried.

"Not you."

Negar lay still. Of all the words that anyone had said, including herself, those two struck deepest.

Anneki went back to her bathing. Negar lay in the grass. The bull lay down to chew his cud. The cow wandered off. The sun transcribed its slow arc, up to the zenith and then, by degrees, down to the horizon. Negar stared into the vault of heaven and knew herself for an utter, perfect, oblivious fool.

When the shadows began to lengthen, Anneki tugged Negar to her feet. "It's time to go," she said.

Negar stared at her. Anneki grinned, baring strong white teeth. Negar said it, because Anneki dared her to. "Why?"

That was not quite what Anneki had been waiting for. She laughed. "Because it's time. And because you need to see the world."

"I already—" Negar bit her tongue.

"The world as it really is," said Anneki. "Not the one you looked down your nose on from your gaudy palace."

"How do you know it's gaudy? You've never seen it!"

Anneki sighed. "It's going to be a long walk," she said to the bull.

The bull sighed even more deeply and shut his eyes as if in agreement. His jaws worked. Back and forth. Back and forth.

Negar caught herself staring, transfixed. The halter tightened around her neck, a brief tug, quickly released. She was walking before she knew it.

She looked back once. The bull was asleep. His horns stretched as wide as the arms of the world.

She turned away from him and focused on the figure in front of her. It was exactly as tall and exactly as wide and, by then, somewhat cleaner and not much less tidy than she was herself. It was her image, as she was the image of it.

There was a truth in that, as in everything else that Anneki was and did. Negar walked in her lengthening shadow. Her mind was as empty as the sky, and as full of possibilities.

Calando

James L. Cambias

Twenty thousand kilometers to fall. The thought made Ari chuckle. "It's not the fall that kills you, it's the landing." Though in his case, there would never be a landing. Somewhere in Neptune's upper atmosphere his suit would get hot enough to kill him. With luck he'd miss the part where he turned into a bright streak of plasma and then dissipated into the wind.

He could almost write a song about that. Some nice imagery, build to a crescendo as the air turns to fire. End with (of course) a dying fall. Heh.

Well, there was plenty of time. He had four hours before he reached the cloud tops. He'd written songs in less time. His signature piece, "Immortal Affair", had come to him while eating breakfast, and he'd recorded the first rough version before lunch.

ᚊ ᚕ ᚈ ᚐ

"How many times am I going to have to sing that damned song?" Ari was tired and sweaty and hungry, as he always was after performing. That night he was out of sorts, too. The crowd had demanded "Immortal Affair" as they always did, and he'd sung it so contemptuously that they started booing.

"How long are you planning to live?" his daughter Oni replied. "Figure a hundred times a year, maybe more. Just add two zeroes to your lifespan."

They were having dinner on the balcony of his apartment, on a tower with a view down the center of the Nysa-4 habitat, at the inner edge of the Belt. Oni had made an excellent meal of grilled fish, chickpea puffs, and a big salad. All grown in the hab rather than printed.

Ari was too annoyed to pay attention to his dinner. "It's boring," he said. "I've explored that piece until I'm tired of every note."

"Write something new."

"I've *done* that. A hundred songs, and nobody wants to hear them. I even got an AI to write me some tunes, optimized for emotional effect. Nobody cares."

"It's not the songs people care about," said Oni. "They've got ten thousand years of music to listen to, and algorithms to pick out exactly what suits the moment. They want to see a performance."

"Well, I perform," he said, refilling his wineglass. "My voice is as good as it's ever been."

She shrugged. "There's a billion singers with better voices than yours right now, and a hundred billion dead ones on recordings. It's the whole experience that matters. People want to hear you sing something you wrote. They want something authentic. If *you* don't like what you're singing, how can they?"

"Maybe I need a new audience," he said, picking at his salad.

"A tour? That's an idea," she said. "We'd have to figure some way to cover your travel costs."

"Juren! Or Deimos!" said Ari. "Maybe Earth as well."

Oni looked skeptical. "You've never had much luck breaking into those markets. What about the outer system?"

"Long travel times. I'd be gone for a decade."

"Longer than that," she said. "You can't afford a fast ship to anywhere. It's either working your way aboard a cycler, or hibernating in a cargo pod flying minimum-energy routes."

The idea of spending years aboard a cycler station, singing "Immortal Affair" every damned night, made Ari feel sick. A long sleep in hibernation was much more appealing.

In the end, they settled on the Neptune system. Ten years in hibernation, then five years touring all the moons and habitats circling the blue planet, including a year making the circuit of the Great Ring of linked habs around Neptune's equator.

He sang, he rode shuttles and travel pods, he learned the etiquette of the Great Ring and which local specialties he liked. He spent a lot of nights alone in rented rooms.

Receipts hovered right around the break-even point. Ari came to resent the people who did show up more than the ones who didn't want to hear him. If they all stayed away he could write the whole tour off as a bad idea, quit and go home and think of something else. But there were just enough to keep him trying to figure out how to attract more.

He studied the demographics. Who was coming to his performances, and how could he broaden that category? What styles and lyrics would attract more listeners? Nothing seemed to work. They applauded politely after every number, but that was all.

⚏ ⚏ ⚏ ⚏

The final set of performances was on Ephyra, one of the low-orbit habs, where skimmer pilots amassed fortunes in helium-3 and deuterium, or died when Neptune's fierce winds shifted without warning. To get there from the Great Ring Ari flew aboard a cargo shuttle. The hold was full of luxury goods, but the passenger deck was almost empty.

"Looks like it's just the five of us," said the only other human passenger on the shuttle, a woman with thumbs on her feet and skin which lit up in a pattern of glowing blue photophores. "Mind if I join you?" She buckled into the seat across the aisle from Ari. "They don't want to socialize," she added, with a nod of her head at the three spider-shaped mechs sitting together in silence at the rear of the compartment. "My name's Panna."

"Ari." They touched palms.

"So," she said after the shuttle undocked and fired thrusters to drop away from the Great Ring, "Why are you heading for Ephyra? Family? Looking for work?"

"I've got work. I'm a singer. Ari Akorin Jilqi Nysa-dan." He didn't bother to ask if she'd heard of him. "I'm performing there—Treva Auditorium, about fifty hours from now. You can still get a seat."

"Maybe I will," she said, in that tone people used when they almost certainly wouldn't. "And after that?"

"More work. Two private performances and six classes, a final appearance at a restaurant called Quedal, and then I go back up to the Great Ring and catch a ship to Laomedeia."

"And nobody goes to Lao unless they're leaving for good." Neptune's outermost moon was home to a fuel depot, a hundred-gigawatt laser-launch array, and not much else.

The shuttle fired its main engine to shift into the aerobraking course through Neptune's upper atmosphere. It would shed just enough speed to put it in the right orbit to meet Ephyra, using almost no fuel. Spacecraft always obsessed over saving fuel.

"What about you?" he asked when the shuttle had finished its burn and rotated to glide position. "What will you be doing in Ephyra?"

"Well, you could call it work, but that's only because I fool people into paying me. I'm studying the feral bioships." She smiled at his expression. "Sorry, forgot you're from down in the Swarm. Back in the Sixth Millennium some bright girls and boys and AIs in the Great Ring around Neptune got the idea to create living spacecraft—not just cyberships but actual organisms which could heal, grow, and reproduce."

"That sounds amazing! Why haven't I seen them?"

She chuckled. "Well, part of the idea wasn't so bright. Most regular ships have Baseline-Equivalent minds installed when they're built. They're as smart as anyone else, maybe smarter. But of course that gives them the same legal rights as other people. Evidently our bright designers four thousand years ago thought that was a problem, so the bioships were designed to push right up to the limit of Baseline intelligence without going over. The creators really should have talked to someone from Earth about that."

Ari puzzled over that for a moment. "Because...natural biosphere?"

"Right. Earth still has unmodified animals with near-Baseline minds. You don't see them most other places. Turns out it's not a bright line, it's kind of a huge gray area. They may not have been able to pass a Turing test, but the bioships were smart enough to run away and survive on their own. There's a population of them in low Neptune orbit, and another bunch living around Triton. I'm part of a group doing research on them."

"Do you go out and catch them? Like Sky-ray hunters?"

"No, no. Just tag them with trackers and probes. My team is studying their genetics—how they've diverged from the original genome over the past four millennia, and how the low-orbit school differs from the Triton group. There's another research team trying to learn about their social structures and behavioral patterns. They've got some great data on how bioships look for storms in Neptune's atmosphere for gas-scooping runs, because they get a higher proportion of carbon compounds that way. The commercial scoopships out of Ephyra follow the bioships now."

She stopped and looked around. "Where did those other guys go? The mechs?"

Ari looked back. The rear seat was empty. "The bathroom?" He looked forward and saw the door partly open.

"Why would mechs go to the bathroom?" Panna mused.

"Maybe they need help." He unbuckled and floated forward.

Just then he heard a muffled bang from the direction of the command module, and the lights flickered.

"Shuttle? Hello? What's going on?" Ari called out. No reply. He felt a stab of panic. When you talked to the air and got no answer, that meant something seriously bad was happening.

Two of the mechs came back into the passenger compartment. Behind them Ari glimpsed a hole in the bathroom wall, and a crawlspace beyond. "This vehicle is under new control," said the shuttle's voice from the air. "Cooperate and you will not be injured."

The two mechs didn't say anything. They just grabbed Ari and Panna with superhumanly strong hands and dragged them forward—toward the airlock. Both humans realized what was happening in the same instant, and both of them activated their suits. Ari wore his as an inconspicuous body-stocking under his clothes. In less time than it took him to take a breath the hood shot up over his head, the gloves flowed over his hands, and he felt it tighten to give counter-pressure.

"No, no, please!" he shouted. "I've got money. I'm a famous singer. People will pay ransom for me. For both of us! Lots of money! Please, don't—!" And then he was outside the hull, tumbling slowly as he drifted away from the shuttle. Panna followed a couple of seconds later, struggling as the mech tossed her out. She hit the edge of the hatch as she went out and spun off in a different direction, no longer struggling.

"Panna! Can you hear me? Panna?"

She didn't answer, but her suit did. "Medical emergency! Injured human! Medical emergency!"

The sun was just rising over the limb of Neptune, a yellow dot in a smear of red. Ari could just make out the shuttle as a faint shape against the stars. Beyond the shuttle the Great Ring was a string of little beads overhead, ten thousand kilometers away. Below, Neptune was a dark disk spanning a sixth of the sky, with a hair-thin crescent of blue at one edge. As he turned, it gradually filled his field of view.

Ari looked down into that black disk, hoping to see lights, fusion flares—any hope of rescue. A couple of tiny sparks flashed, and for a moment Ari almost hoped. Then he realized he was seeing vast lightning storms down in Neptune's atmosphere, twenty thousand kilometers away.

Ari tried to call the Great Ring, or Ephyra, or anyplace, and spent ten minutes shouting inside his hood before he remembered that all comms would be relayed through the shuttle, and any sensible space pirate would shut that down right away. He called up an instruction display and painstakingly switched his suit to general-broadcast, then tried again. And again.

His slow rotation brought the shuttle back into view. The mechs were jettisoning all the passenger seats, the luggage, even some of the deck panels. His own bag caught the faint sunlight a hundred meters away, and Ari felt an illogical pang of worry.

He guessed the hijackers were lightening the ship. Maybe it wasn't anything on board they were stealing, but the shuttle itself. When he had turned around twice more, he saw the shuttle's nose swing upward, at an angle to its orbital path. Then the engines flared and it fell away from Neptune, on a new trajectory to…somewhere. Wherever the mech hijackers planned to dispose of a stolen shuttle. Ari had heard about dark habs out in the Kuiper Belt. A shuttle could get to one of them from Neptune on a slow minimum-energy trajectory; mechs wouldn't mind spending a decade or two in vacuum. He turned back to Neptune, and by the time he was facing outward again the shuttle was gone.

He thought of Panna again and felt pure horror at what had happened. They'd barely met, and likely would never have seen each other again after docking at Ephyra. But even if they'd never spoken the sight of her spinning lifeless against the stars would still be awful.

Was she still alive?

And would it matter much if she was? The shuttle had been diving into Neptune's upper atmosphere in order to slow to a rendezvous with Ephyra in low orbit. A suited human wasn't a sleek spacecraft, massive and aerodynamic and heat-proof. Ari wouldn't just slip through the upper atmosphere and emerge. He'd slow, and drop deeper, and burn up. So would Panna.

Had anyone seen the shuttle change course? Could they deduce that Ari and Panna had been thrown out, and launch a rescue in time? Did anyone care? His suit radio calls brought no reply. Probably too far away for anyone to hear.

All right, then. He was going to die. He could just override his suit, open the hood, and go out quickly. Or wait until the end, and feel the air turn to plasma around him. The suit's recycling system could keep him supplied with oxygen long enough for that.

He wasn't afraid. Some of that was probably the suit's medical pack, lacing his bloodstream with tranquilizers. Don't want all that stress. It could take years off your life.

To distract himself, he started to sing. He had hours of free time, and nobody was listening. No audience but himself. It was comforting, and it gave him something to do besides fret about what was going to happen in a few hours.

He ran through some favorites, and eventually started "Immortal Affair". He thought he had done all possible variations on it, but this time it was almost like that first morning, when he'd been so happy and excited at this new song pouring out of his head. Now, ten thousand kilometers above Neptune he tried to recapture that feeling.

But of course the song had to include some of his own sadness and regret, that he'd reached his own limits and stayed comfortably stuck for so long, the frustration and disappointment when you got what you thought you wanted and realized the wanting didn't go away. And underlying it all was the knowledge that he only had an hour left. The old subtext of the song, which he thought he'd been so clever to come up with, all about love and loss, now felt very immediate.

Neptune took up a quarter of the sky, a bright blue crescent holding a black disk. He couldn't see Panna any more. The Great Ring was unattainably high overhead. And somewhere in that dusty red smudge around the Sun was the asteroid

Nysa, and his daughter.

He wondered briefly if she ever listened to recordings of him singing. How did Ari in performance reflect her real father? He wished he'd asked her. No chance now.

Just then Ari became aware that something was moving toward him—no, several somethings, below and ahead of him, rising to meet him, suddenly shining in the sunlight against the dark clouds below as they caught the sunlight. They looked like winged goblets, or maybe dragonflies wearing hoop skirts. He couldn't judge size and distance. Were they small, approaching slowly?

No. They were big. *Very* big. Much bigger than the shuttle. Almost the size of a small habitat. A kilometer across, at least. They had no running lights, no insignia, no windows. What ships were these? Panna's bioships?

The closest one turned to point its skirt away from Neptune. The skirt flexed and glowed blue-white, then spat out an incandescent smoke ring, then another and another, and Ari could see that the strange ship was matching speeds with him. The wings pulsed bright yellow with each new ring.

"Hello! I'm here!" he shouted. "Mayday mayday mayday! Please help me!" Tears pooled in his eyes and he had to shake his head to get rid of them. The sense of hope, of relief, was so strong he could scarcely breathe.

The reply was hard to make out, as each smoke ring was accompanied by a burst of loud static. Only when it stopped pulsing and hung a kilometer or so below him could he make out what it was sending.

The words were gibberish but the tune was clear. It was singing "Immortal Affair".

Stifling a laugh, he sang it back. The ship responded. Again, the melody and rhythm were flawless but the lyrics were random syllables. Ari took a couple of breaths, then sang again, filling it with pure joy and hope this time. No tinges of regret, no ironies. A song of life and imperishable love.

Through the blinding tears he could make out the ship as it closed. The great fragile wing slid past and he saw long flexible limbs reaching out from the tiny core of the ship. They cradled him, and he sang. The bioship rotated slowly, pointing its skirts down toward Neptune. Static buzzed and he slammed against the limbs as the bioship boosted him, then gave him a shove for good measure.

They flew together, Ari and four of the bioships, and sang together, jamming and improvising and doing call-and-response and five-part harmony, until finally he was so hoarse he could only manage a bluesy croak. It occurred to him that he hadn't had this much *fun* performing in decades.

The ship which had shifted Ari's orbit let him drift a few hundred meters away, then the four bioships turned together, nose down to Neptune, and puffed out a few more blazing smoke rings. The ships dropped away quickly while Ari rose toward the arc of the Great Ring overhead. He was going to live.

His suit stopped listening to his overrides and knocked him out to save oxygen, so he missed the rescue shuttle and the team of suited chimps who brought him aboard. When he woke he was in a clinic in the Great Ring.

He insisted on doing the Ephyra performances, despite a little delay. When he stepped on stage at the auditorium he made sure the whole thing would be beamed out into Neptune's upper atmosphere.

A gift to his fans.

One Box too Many

Christine Lucas

"Perhaps we should stop poking it?" Penelope asked Sophia across the narrow stainless steel table, then poked the alien box again.

"You think?" Brian grunted from across the room. He wouldn't approach the halted conveyor belt. Instead, he glared at them, squirming to settle his skinny ass on the unprocessed sample crate by the wall. His pale complexion had an almost waxy shade under the full spectrum lights of the screening area.

"But it's fun," Penelope said and poked the artifact yet again.

Roughly the size of the ancient Rubik's cube, this little piece of crap had sealed them in this tin can of a station. No false alarm this time. No fossils of extinct starfish from long-dead seas. No bent, rusted, charred junk from millennia-old crash sites. The real deal. Yet nothing happened when they poked it. No jolt of static, no illumination of the intricate golden patterns of its copper-colored surface. Perhaps it was some alien paperweight, or something equally useless? *How disappointing.* Penelope traced a pattern of spirals and entwined vines, and this gave her the slightest tingle on her fingertip that roused a shudder in the nanobots inside her head.

She bent over the artifact, pretending to study the little slits at the edges of the engraved patterns, and that circular section that could be clickable. Had the others noticed? Had her face reflected her bots' terror? Was it just her, or did the others sense it too?

Hearing voices was never good—or, worse, seeing things to match those voices. Not now, after the Panacea code, not ever. And certainly not for those stationed in Mars and handling potentially hazardous samples from every mining site across the solar system. Crates on top of crates from Europa, the latest shipment of a Russian harvester ship, awaited their turn to be screened all around them. The mechanical arms that usually handled the samples now hung limp from the low ceiling. Penelope had never known this part of the station to be this quiet in the two years of her confinement there. Now nothing moved around them but specs of dust and the ever-present red sand that crept everywhere.

With one crate from Europa, the center of the Universe—*their* Universe—had shifted to that damned box on the belt.

Sophia poked it again and chuckled. More stress than mirth, but her brown eyes did light up. These incidents were rare, and they reminded Penelope of better times—carefree, even happy times, before her own sister had ratted on her and had her sentenced to three years of hard labor on Mars. It could have been worse: she could have been sent to any other possessing spot across the Solar System or—gods forbid— the algae farms. At least here she didn't smell like fish and Sophia was in charge of things. She'd never admitted to it, but Penelope always suspected that Sophia had called in too many favors to arrange this particular deployment. And she hated and loved her big sister in equal parts for this.

"Will you stop doing that, you illiterate heathens? Why can't your thick heads grasp that we're all going to die?" Brian slammed his hand against the steel wall of the cargo bay. "Just stop it!"

Penelope opened her mouth to respond with some witty retort, but a swarm of nodding nanobots—cartoonish little critters, like metal scarabs with huge, beady eyes and short, fast legs—inside her head made her close it back. The End of Days was indeed upon them, if her bots agreed with that fool

Brian. Across the belt, Sophia raised her eyes, all mirth gone from her gaze.

"That's *Captain* Heathen to you, *doctor*. And yes, we know we might all die."

Penelope sat up. That was new. Her sister usually sided with Dr. Asshole. She'd never contested his assignment there despite his lackluster credentials—he had none of the survival skills required for life out there. But the decision had been made back on Earth from someone way higher on the food chain than any of them. And now she'd just spat out Brian's title as if it were manure. Standing ovation from Penelope's nanobots. *Shut up and go away*, she wanted to scream, but bit her tongue. If she slammed her head against the wall to make them go away, would she scare the other two people in the room?

Sophia turned to Penelope, her eyes warmer, and flipped open the cover of her tablet. "So, Private Secondborn. How much should I put you in for?" Her gaze scanned a list. "The odds are good for a repeat of the Europa incident, nerve gas, and some flesh-eating virus. There are also other entries like 'zombies from outer space', but that's pathetic even for trolls."

Penelope looked away. The deep-seated warmth of their once-affectionate monikers of Captain Firstborn and Private Secondborn had waned in the last few years. She didn't even recall when one of them had last used them. Funny how Sophia would revert to their old ways now that... Penelope stifled a sigh. Meanwhile, the rest of humanity, safe in their homes, comfortable in the practical immortality of the Panacea code, had fun placing bets on how and when the poor slobs on the Mars station would die.

"What's the point? It's not as if I'll get to spend any earnings. I still have eight months on my sentence, assuming we survive this."

"No, but I can set up a future purchase for you. Something nice to wait for you when you get home?"

Penelope's heart clenched. *Home.* She'd never see home again. When the Panacea code was released as freeware, and effectively resulted in the collapse of the health industry, Dr. Edhi and her team of coders and analysts had become cyber-terrorists to those who pulled the strings. In theory everyone wanted a life unburdened by disease; except for those who profited from it. Her former comrades had gone into hiding, occasionally updating the code from the darkest corners of the Dark Web, while she'd been snitched on and sentenced to three years of "community service" on Mars. The maximum sentence for a non-violent crime, and registered in the cyber-terrorist data-base for life. No respectable employer would hire her after that.

If they died here, would they know of her passing? And what would they hear? That she died poking an alien artifact? She blinked the rising moisture away—mostly frustration, really. A crew of nanobots with mops rushed behind her eyelids. *Get lost, imps.* She squeezed her eyes. Her hallucinations grew more ridiculous by the minute. She shouldn't be surprised, really. All that experimenting with mind-altering substances in her early twenties had returned to bite her forty-something ass...well, brain.

"Fine, put me down for a brain-eating virus." It had already started, hadn't it? If the mopping nanobots were any indication, her brain was turning slowly but steadily to mush. "In two weeks. Twenty creds." Fourteen days: that's how long it had taken the europavirus to kill off one fifth of Earth's population twenty years ago. But that was before even the first generation nanobots, and certainly before the Panacea code. Before their updated—and in Penelope's case, whimsical and opinionated—nanobots eradicated most diseases. But did Earth Central stop drilling where they shouldn't? As, in the Europa frozen wastelands? *Did they?*

"Twenty, done, two-weeks, done, brain-eating bug, done." Sophia raised her eyes to Penelope, her cheek twitching a little. "I'll record a message for Mama and Baba later on. We're ordered to maintain radio silence now, but...just in case. Would you..." She looked away. "Would you stop by to do it together?"

Penelope lowered her face so her sister wouldn't see her frown. She'd done her best to act civil in the close proximity of her Judas sister. Sophia was in charge of this tin can of a station, and she had to somehow make things tolerable for everyone out here. But now Firstborn wanted to play family again?

It wasn't their parents' fault, though. They might get to lose both their children in the next few weeks. So she gulped down all the bitter words that crowded at the tip of her tongue and managed, "Sure." A deep breath, and she added, "Why the radio silence? It's not as if we're going to post snapshots of the damned thing on social media. We're on quarantine, and Earth Central monitors all our communications anyway."

Sophia shrugged, avoiding eye-contact. "They want the channels open to monitor our vitals and update the code, if the need arises."

A lone nanobot tiptoeing on Penelope's optical nerve stuck its tongue out. Penelope just gawked. Her own sister, lying to her face. As if Penelope wasn't one of the analysts of the team that had created the original code. No team that Earth Central assembled could be up to such a task. Good thing she'd opened a back channel to reach Dr. Edhi, once she'd been told of the cube; her old mentor might be in her nineties now, the rerouted signal might have to cross the entire solar system and bounce off two dozen satellites before it reached Earth, but it gave her some solace that she wasn't alone in this.

"You're both idiots," Brian grunted. "Yes, mess with the code again. Ruin more lives. Be like that meddling Iraqi woman, who wouldn't listen to her betters five years ago. Why can't you get into your thick heads that we shouldn't be trying to get that thing open? Why can't you rocks-for-brains do the smart thing, for once?" He chewed on his nails, as if the biting and spitting could muffle his mumbling about having stupid women do a man's job.

Sophia glared. The entirety of Penelope's nanobots booed. Of course they did. That idiot had just cussed their mother.

Ye gods, no. Not "Your Mama" jabs inside my skull. I'd rather bang my head against that hellish cube and be done with it.

"Doctor. Septic tank duty. Now." Penelope had never seen Sophia so pale-faced, so thin-lipped, so Fury-eyed.

Apparently, neither had Brian, who scurried away mumbling more bigoted nonsense under his breath. It still made no sense to Penelope that Sophia had accepted this assignment. Off-world COs had the right to veto any potential member to avoid disruptive behavior in limited spaces such as space stations. And Brian was the very embodiment of disruption, the gift that kept on giving with his snide remarks to everyone he thought beneath him. Namely, everyone else.

Poor, poor Brian—*not*. Rich white middle-aged doctor, whose world of entitlement had turned upside down when the code became freeware and his trade as a neurologist became obsolete. He kept lamenting his past life where every man wanted to be him, and every woman wanted to fuck him. Apparently he still had some contacts in high places, people who owed him, otherwise he wouldn't have landed even this one job, working with plebes and worse—convicts like Penelope.

"Hey. Poppi? I think we've poked the thing enough."

Sophia's steady hand cupped Penelope's. Only then did she realize that she'd been poking the box repeatedly for the last five minutes or so, as impulsively as Brian had bitten his nails. Her face burned as she curled her index finger back into the fist it belonged. Beside her, Sophia sucked in a deep breath. Deep lines wrinkled her forehead, twin lines as deep and as prominent as the lines of office on her collar.

"Let's seal this area now, and let the scanners examine the cube from hell. You know, as we were supposed to have done half an hour ago when the quarantine protocol confined us." Before Penelope could poke it one last time, Sophia's firm grip on her arm guided Penelope out of the cargo screening area and into the corridor. "Come on, girl. Let's get to the mess hall. I hear the Russians who got stuck here with us have vodka."

The moment Penelope's mind processed the prospect of

alcohol, a group of nanobots formed a picket line, hefting banners with stop-signs on bottles around her cerebellum.

"Earth Central can shove their regs while we wait. Back in the old days, daily rations of vodka in all the Russian Federation outposts were standard procedure," said Sophia with a chuckle. "Or so I've heard."

Another picket line appeared in Penelope's head, this one holding signs in favor of booze. In a split second, the two groups started to slap each other silly with their signs.

Stop it! Penelope's headache waxed with every nanobot screech. *Stop it!* She squeezed her eyes shut, she rubbed her temples, but nothing cleared her head. She shrugged. "Just tired."

Sophia managed a strained grin. "Aren't we all? Let's see if the vodka rumors are true, then, and give the computers back home some screwed-up readings to decipher."

Penelope stopped in her tracks. *Oh crap.* That detail of the quarantine protocol had failed to register in her mind. Earth Central would be monitoring every fart, every burp, every trickle of pee to detect anything out of the ordinary. If the accumulated data suggested a new outbreak like that of the europavirus, they'd blast the station to hell and call it an accident, so to not endanger their precious immortality. It had happened before—Dr. Edhi had showed her the evidence, when she'd signed her up. And what if they could somehow detect her hallucinations? Penelope's stomach made a dive for her feet, while terror constricted her chest, each breath a painstaking chore. *Have I killed us all?* And a crew of nanobots in outdated nurses' uniforms slid through her veins towards her heart carrying tiny pumps and miniature stethoscopes.

Go away. It's all your fault. Penelope's head snapped up to meet Sophia's concerned gaze. *Good heavens, I didn't say that aloud?*

"Something *is* wrong." Not a question.

Penelope's mouth twisted. "You know what's wrong. You ratted me out." She raised her hand, to stop any objections her sister dared to raise. "Okay. Fine. Let's not get into another round of that again. I'll just go wash up a little and pop down an aspirin or something. Then I'll meet you at the mess hall." A lie. But was it an adequate lie?

A moment of silence, then a nod. "Fine. But hurry. This tin can was built for a skeleton crew, and its air filters can handle only so much farting from all of us stuck here in the quarantine zone." She laughed at her own joke. Captain Firstborn always resorted to toilet humor when frustrated or embarrassed, and only she found those jokes funny. "I wonder if anyone has put in 'methane poisoning' in the pool? If not, I think I should enter it..." Sophia's nervous chuckles trailed off as she made her way towards the mess hall. Penelope sucked in a deep breath. A lone nanobot lay belly up in her head, still laughing at the captain's fart jokes.

"Classy, aren't we?" Penelope mumbled, and the nanobot dove into her bloodstream with a hurt expression on its metallic face. Her shoulders slumped. If anything, her hallucinations were original. No demons with pitchforks, no bugs crawling up the walls, no creepy twin girls staring at her from the end of the corridors, no hatch doors letting in rivers of blood. She'd barely finished her thought, when a tiny pitchfork emerged from between the folds of her brain.

"Don't even try."

Thank the gods of all the stars, her trolling nanobots scurried back into hiding. Penelope made her way back to the screening area. It should be deserted by now, and she needed a quiet place to collect her thoughts before vodka killed half her brain cells. Perhaps shoot another message to Dr. Edhi, to see if she registered any anomalies from her readings.

If Earth Central hadn't detected her nanobots' malfunction, or whatever those hallucinations came from, they'd find out soon. There would be changes in her brain waves, adrenaline levels, something to clue them in that she was losing it. Not an issue if they were dying anyway, but what if they didn't? If that damned box proved to be some alien ashtray or something equally harmless, she could easily end up a lab rat in some unmarked scientific facility that studied anomalies like her. Worse yet, they might consider it a sign of infection and incinerate them all. She had her issues with her sister, but she didn't want her to die. Mama and Baba would be crushed, especially Baba who'd never been given nanobots to begin with. The loss could kill him.

Like a kick in the gut, that thought made her double up, engulfed by sudden heartburn. *Focus*, she ordered herself, and a crew of nanobots, now dressed up as firemen carrying hoses and extinguishers, rushed to her aid. Good God, it actually helped. What if they weren't just hallucinations?

Insanity starts with denial, she reminded herself as she neared the hatch door...that loomed open. What the fuck? She had locked it. She knew she had. She wasn't that far gone. Yet. She tiptoed closer and dared a peek inside. What the hell was Brian doing there?

He sat huddled by the magnetic material conveyor, an arm's length away from the sample scanner console. The communications panel at the wall had been ripped open, leaving cables exposed. Had he tried to bypass the radio silence protocol? He'd done some rewiring, judging by the abundance of duct tape. Now Brian clutched the cube on his chest, rocking his body back and forth in a slow, steady rhythm. Drool clung from the left corner of his mouth down to his chest as he muttered, his eyes wild and unfocused.

"It's fine now...it's done. Finally. As it should be. I'll get my just dues. At last."

Holy shit, what had happened to him? Brian, despite his flaws, had lots of skills, but hacking wasn't one of them. Who had showed him how to do this? Instead of offering their opinions, her usually meddling nanobots scurried away through her bloodstream. They amassed in deep caves hidden in the canyons of her brain, burrowed in the shafts and tunnels of her liver, squeezed through the pores of her bones. Their stampede generated pulses of burning pain in the center of her eyeballs. Panicked nanobots *and* deranged Brian? She couldn't handle both. What the hell had happened here? Who had hacked into their system?

The cube? No, it had never been a cube, but a container. A box, and Brian had spilled its contents. Its *denizens*.

Sudden pain made her knees wobble and her hand sought support against the wall. The pricks of countless needles set her skull alight as a crew of babbling, wild-eyed nanobots rushed in with pliers and duct tape and screwdrivers. They stomped on each other, with cursing chirps and frequent tongue-sticking, but they adjusted her eye and auditory nerves to this new reality.

Her hallucinations escaped the confines of her brain. A swarm of dark critters, too similar to big fat roaches for comfort—too alike to her own nanobots. These evil twins, of sorts, carried hammers, battering rams and set up miniature catapults. If Penelope's skin wasn't crawling with intertwined terror and disgust, she might think this amusing. But not today. Not like this, with Brian clearly insane across the room, not at the presence of that box from Europa's icy hell. What emerged next from the box crushed all possibilities that she might one day laugh at all this.

Another kind of monster crawled out: long, light-hungry ribbons as if made of liquid darkness. They reached out, caressed the wiring of the communication box, entangling within the red and green and blue cables, murmuring softly. Other entities followed, amber blobs of amorphous flesh, bubbling and reaching out with clumsy pseudopods, exploring their surroundings. Then their forms boiled and took oddly familiar forms: chimeras, hydras, birds with steels talons and deadly beaks, harpies and monstrous hybrids, half-children, half-serpents lashing their forked tongues at her.

Penelope slumped down on the floor. They were all going to be devoured by the monsters from her childhood mythology books. Had anyone added that to the betting pool? Did she have time to go add it now? Half her brain wanted to slap her silly and banish such absurd thoughts. The other half wanted to sit and watch what else would come out. Inside her head, her bots had hidden. All but one. This lone critter jumped up and down on her cortex, pointing and chirping in a frenzy. In one heartbeat it did its frantic dance, in the next it fell down with an ice pack on its head and a long-outdated mercury thermometer in its mouth.

"Oh, shut up. Leave me alone. We're dead anyway." Persistent little rascal. It kept doing that, pointing at the slew of its evil brethren amassing at the communication panel. Penelope sat up, struggling to focus. What was it trying to tell her? Listening to her hallucinations couldn't amount to anything good. But what did she have to lose?

Her home. Her future. Mama and Baba. Even Sophia. Another—deeper, duller—kind of ache purged the fog from her brain with a moment of painful clarity. The bot showed her sickness. Disease? Were those critters some alien viruses? But that was not news. They'd feared this scenario from the moment the First Contact alarm rang in the station, when that damned thing had been loaded on the conveyor belt. Her nanobot kept jumping up and down, each jump generating waves of static in her ears.

"What? What? I don't know! I don't understand!" The bot stopped its jumps, and pulled a minuscule tablet from its ass and pointed at the swarm of dark critters assaulting the communications panel, then back at the tablet. Back and forth. Back and forth.

Siege. And the enemy came with viruses of the malware kind. Was the box some sort of digital booby trap left behind by a long-extinct alien race? Once those roach-bots breached their firewalls and their safety protocols, once they found a backdoor into their communication grid, what then?

Crap. The nanobot network. The lone bot inside her head cheered, set off a couple of fireworks that added a nice edge of nausea to Penelope's headache, and hid back into the folds of her brain. This was not a random incident.

After the Panacea code, humans with nanobots were interlinked with a global network to receive updates and fixes to new threats of the organic kind, and radio silence and quarantine protocols didn't shut them out from that network. It lingered somewhere between the regular and the Dark Web, separate from both, and had firewalls upon firewalls to keep the code safe from idiots who thought they could hack into it. And the idiots had tried. Oh, how much they'd tried to bring disease back to humankind. But whatever this box was, it wasn't made by idiots. Or humans.

She had to stop this. Before they breached the firewalls. Before they reached Earth.

Penelope gritted her teeth and crawled to the gutted communications panel. She tried to pull away the dark ribbons, slap away the roach-bots, but grasped nothing. *You dumbass! There are no monsters here, at least none you can stomp on the floor. Those are pieces of code your short-wired brain translates as monsters. Get a grip!* She kept stomping on those quivering blobs, just in case. She had to do something. Trying to flatten them was something.

A cackle behind her, the malevolent laughter of all the cartoon villains of her childhood. She glanced over her shoulder. A black and spiky sponge-like creature had emerged from the cube in Brian's palms and had crawled on top of his head. It cackled, and countless serpentine heads sprang from its body, each glaring at her. A hydra? *Cut one head, and two grow in its place.* With a low hiss, it tugged on the ribbons, leaped into the wiring and vanished inside the network with a slurping sound.

"No!"

She lunged after it. The crash against the floor pushed the air out of her lungs. *Stupid, stupid woman!* Of course she wouldn't catch anything—not with her bare hands. No evil creature had crawled out of the box or leaped into the wires, only malware code that now wormed its way to Earth, to every human near a wireless connection. The horde of roach-bots cheered. The firewalls had fallen. She had to alert Earth. She had to—

A tug on her leg. They were coming for her. She squeezed her eyes shut. *No. I won't look. I don't want to look.* At the third tug, she gulped down the taste of bile and forced her eyes open.

One of the blobs had grown a head and thin limbs; no legs—only four long arms with delicate little fingers that now tugged at her pants. No eyes, no ears on a flat head with matted hair and a lip-less hole for a mouth that whispered uncomfortable truths. On the second tag, it shifted to a different form: a hunchbacked hag, her limbs gnarled, her snarl toothless. Her left hand grew long, delicate fingers to measure the thread of Penelope's life. In her right, her hand morphed to scissors of bone to cut its length.

You would never stop the Harbinger, you fool. There's nothing you can do now, just sit there, the worthless hide that you are. Now just sit there and mope while I count your deeds and number your days.

Fresh out of its digital womb, it crawled to nest in the curve of Penelope's curled-up body. She'd battled its kind before; pre-code doctors labeled such critters Depression and Neurosis and a shitload of long, fancy titles. What would they call it now, in this new form with the same ancient voice?

She kicked it off. Nothing. Of course nothing. It wasn't really there. And she'd only fail again. She always failed. The critter said so, over and over again, in soft little sighs. She'd failed Dr. Edhi; she had been caught. She'd failed her parents; she had given them her stigma to live with. She'd failed even this lousy job; she had let the enemy through. She'd failed humanity; the Panacea code would soon be useless. Big Pharma had won.

The thought choked her and her lone bot rushed in with tissues and a mop, chirping softly. The entity crawling closer to her chest snarled at it. The bot screeched, tossed away the mop and hid again.

Around her, the other blobs changed to slimy, ugly creatures too. One curled around Brian's body. An octopus-like creature, with long tentacles curling around his neck and head, and at the tip of each tentacle a mouth with luscious lips, whispering sweet little lies to the drooling idiot. *Good boy,* it told him, *doing as you were told. Good boy, doing your masters' bidding.* He could be great again, treating all the miserable fools who'd line up for days, weeks, months to beg him and pay him and blow him.

Others, over there, siblings: baby Scylla and baby Charybdis, engaged in a mock—or not—fight. Another one, a tiny minotaur huddled in a corner whining about the world being mean, and that chubby little cherub had two faces on its head, one sobbing and one giggling, and that other one, with no limbs and lidless eyes on a serpentine body, Echidna's hatchling, coiled and uncoiled its length.

Many more squirmed and wiggled around her, awaiting for their turn to squeeze through the communication channels and enter the nanobot network bearing their deadly gifts. Too late now. Too late for everything. She leaned back and rested her head against the cold hard surface. Perhaps she should open the cargo bay doors and just go for a stroll into the Martian wilderness. Or perhaps she should just lay here and wait, until the end came. There was nothing left she could do. No reason to fight any more. Just let go.

"No! My God, Poppi, what happened?" Sophia rushed to her side, dropped to her knees and hugged her. "What—"

It was nice there, in the warm embrace of a loved one— but she didn't really love her, did she? It was her fault she'd been caught. No, not just that. Worse.

"Leave me alone, traitor! *Ephialtes*! It's your fault the enemy got through! You're the reason that idiot Brian got here! Why? Why did you do that?" Penelope put all her remaining strength into her shoulders and pushed Sophia away…

…right into the arms of a new creature, freshly birthed from the box. Too thin, its limbs spidery, its eyes dark. It stretched upward, almost the height of a real person now, but too thin, with a mane of writhing snakes. Over garments of blood-red cloth, its eyes glowed as red—the eyes of a Fury. It held its right arm up, hefting a noose. Its left curled around Sophia's shoulders and pulled her closer, until its face nested at the crook of her neck and its lipless mouth breathed venom in her ears.

Sophia started sobbing. Penelope knew that creature that had latched onto her sister. She'd never set eyes on it—or anything like it—but she knew its name and the slow poison it released in the mind. Hadn't she tasted it, too, way too often?

Guilt.

Sophia sniffled and sobbed and forced words out of her trembling lips. "I'm sorry! I'm sorry! They promised... They promised the code for Baba, if..."

Penelope sat up, her mind struggling to focus. *What's the point*, a dark tendril whispered just behind her ear. The lone nanobot scurried close, parted jaws that would shame the biggest white shark, and bit right into it. The tendril whooshed away, and the nanobot bent over the nearest fold of her brain, retching. But the distraction helped her focus.

"What do you mean? What about Baba?" In the pre-code days, insurance companies refused nanobot treatment to patients with degenerative diseases, and their father had just been diagnosed with early-stages Alzheimer's. It was one of the main reasons she'd joined Dr. Edhi, so everyone would have a chance at immortality. But as far as Penelope knew, Baba had never been given a nanobot shot, the degeneration too advanced for even the updated versions.

Sophia wiped her nose with her sleeve. "They said their code could fix him, if I..." More sniffling. She shook her head. "It didn't. I gave you up, and now Baba is strong as an ox, with the mind of an infant. The doctors back home say he stands to live to be one-hundred-and-fifty, but...that's not life!" Sobs racked her chest, and she started pulling her hair. "I'm sorry! I'm sorry!"

Penelope banged the back of her head against the wall. So that's why. Baba was imprisoned in senile immortality, and Mama was chained at his side, her remaining years in servitude as his caretaker. And it was her fault. She'd taken on too powerful foes, and failed. She might as well go for the noose that abominable creature curled around her sister now dangled at her.

When her annoying little nanobot returned, she slapped her face to shoo it away. Everything was lost. Why wouldn't it go away? Unfettered, it screamed its nonsense inside her auditory nerve. "Go away," Penelope mumbled. "You're infected. We all are. Leave me alone."

No! Well. Others well! Hiding! Save. Must save!
"Hiding?"
Yes. There.
Penelope followed the nanobot's pointing finger—good grief, when did they grow fingers?—to a bright spot inside her brain. The hallucination grew more elaborate by the second. That spot turned to a silver screen playing her memories in a loop. Was her life passing before her eyes? Was she dying, at last? Because, right there, Sophia and her were building a castle on the sand, there Baba waved them off on their first day to school, there he watched her from afar being taken in cuffs to the Mars shuttle, and there, he read them tales from his favorite book of myths and legends.

Penelope sat up. The old tales. She squeezed her eyes shut. There was something important there, she could feel the memory slipping through her fingers. What was it?

That damned creature urged her to lay back down. What was the point? She'd fail again. But now, her stubborn eyes had spotted the alien box forgotten on the floor, a few feet away from Brian. And inside her head, bot after bot, her little rascals emerged from their hiding places and began shoveling coal to the slowed engine of her brain.

Think. Think about the box.

Not any box: a storage unit. *Think, woman. Think like the analyst you were, before all that.* What goes in a storage unit? What if…what if the race that had built it weren't the evil, Earth-invading monsters of human literature and film? What if they were actually *sensible* creatures? Hard to think so, with that creature curling its filthy body around hers, but didn't it make sense?

Sometimes a box was just a box. Where things are stored, for safekeeping.

Could this be a software unit, containing more than malware? An archive? If some long-gone alien race of sensible creatures had stored a shitload of viruses inside that thing, perhaps they'd stored the anti-virus software too. Problems and solutions.

Her nanobots cheered. Her brain bloomed with fireworks in all the colors of spring and filled her nostrils with the scent of Baba's aftershave.

Penelope gritted her teeth and crawled towards the box. With every breath, the roach-bots launched their offensive: her body weighed a ton and every motion released a torture of pins and needles and hot coals under her skin. Breath by breath, grunt by grunt, she made it there and grabbed the box with stiff fingers. Her fingertips traced the surface for a clue, her eyes now clouded by thick fog. There it was, a round indentation on its side, the one that looked too much like a button not to be a button, the one Brian had probably pressed once to release its horrors. The glittering markings formed entwined vines, or, rather, an ancient symbol: the caduceus--the double helix: a symbol of balance, wisdom and transformation. Whoever put that there, must have had the wits to not leave the contents unbalanced. At least, Penelope *hoped* as much.

For a split second, she thought she caught glimpse of fiery wings fluttering through the fog. One of her nanobots gave her a thumbs-up. A jolt of hesitation held her own thumb back.

If I release the fix, will you too vanish?

No answer from her nanobots. Was there a wave of tiny hands from the outer limits of her consciousness? If so, it too vanished in the advancing fog in her brain, and Penelope braced herself.

Burn, little cyberdemon spawn! And may your ashes drown in Lethe's waters!

Penelope raised her arm to bring it as close to the communications box as possible. She pressed the button, and uploaded Hope2.0 into the network.

The Fury of Mars

F. J. Doucet

*"And when I have withered you I will lead you off below, alive,
to pay the penalty for the matricide and its horror."*
— Aeschylus, *Eumenides*

The footage from tomorrow's first case, Your Ladyship."

The tightly-laced court aide waited for the nod to proceed, then loaded the footage. Judge Aguta Greywolf watched impassively, noting the impossibly slow progress of the one person craft wobbling across the screen. Intoxicated or elderly, she supposed. Most likely elderly, given the utmost care with which the ship ground to a hovering stop by the intersection.

"What am I seeing?"

"2221 Mitsubishi Wing X-10 piloted by one hundred and ten year old female. A tourist from Earth."

"Does she still have her license?"

"Probationary pending this year's eye exam. Restricted to her own nation on Earth."

Aguta grunted, discontented. With successful optic surgery rates, most eye tests came back positive into the hundred and twenties these days, but there were no guarantees. The old woman had arrogantly assumed her fitness to fly far from home.

"When did she arrive on Mars?"

"Her traveler's visa started on the Red Month and extends to the Green Month." The aide consulted her file. "Looks like she got here on Red 12."

About a month ago, then. "Has she been recorded driving the whole time?"

Another pause as the younger woman scanned her tablet. "Yes. Since day one."

"Fine. Continue footage."

The judge leaned into her black leather recliner, imported from Earth at an exorbitant cost. It was one of the few attractive objects in the bland Justice Ministry building, which had been designed for efficiency in a hostile environment, without any nod to beauty or luxury.

The video picked up from a three-dimensional intersection and showed the elderly pilot accelerating upwards perhaps two hundred meters before continuing horizontally. Though slow, there was still a certain assurance there, and the judge thought that the pilot had most likely been skilled in her younger years. She probably still considered herself capable.

A red Nissan Wing was cautiously easing into traffic approximately one hundred meters below the Mitsubishi. The accused started to drop into a lower lane and the other pilot slowed to give way. Both misjudged the distance, and the result resembled a disastrous underwater ballet. Despite exhaustive efforts from both Earther and Martian engineers, no one had yet managed to invent a total area artificial gravity system, and citizens still lived with the demanding effects of Mars' gravity, one-fourth that of Earth's. Under that influence, the impact of the old woman's craft crashing into the red Wing looked almost gentle, but as soon as the two crafts met, time sped up again. The Mitsubishi crushed the passenger side of the Nissan. The other pilot made some futile attempts to save his craft, then spun away from the camera.

"From the ground cameras." The aide loaded still footage onto the screen. The red Nissan Wing was a twisted, flaming mass on the ground. "The Nissan caught on fire, but the victim died on impact. Police took the other pilot into custody when she landed to examine the crash site."

That the old woman had landed and not fled the scene was something to take into consideration, and would perhaps merit some mercy, legally speaking. Aguta hardly thought it of much value. This clearly wasn't a murder, but could easily have been avoided if the older pilot hadn't been such a damned fool.

The judge opened the case file on her own screen. She considered herself a fair woman, and would go by the book. There might be some mitigating factors in the written report... Her scrolling hand contracted like a claw in front of the screen. The name of the accused fairly leaped out at her, its familiar long vowels heavy with meaning.

Isla Agnes Iversen. There she was. Citizen of Earth, of Danish and Scottish descent, born in Nuuk, Greenland, and current resident of Baffin Island, Nunavut, formerly a territory of Canada. Divorced. Mother of two.

Aguta's lips twisted. A glitch in the record. Neither child's name was recorded in the file, but this woman was mother of only one now. Isla Iversen's son had died more than sixty years ago, and Aguta could remember every detail of the day as if each had been etched in glass.

She opened the image file next to the name and stared at it for a long time. In Aguta's memory, Isla was beautifully dressed, curvy and vivacious, with a haughty, glorious voice and a laugh that could draw blood. When Aguta was a girl, there had been no one she had admired more than her mother. Her own name, though Inuit in origin, was inspired by her mother's Danish middle name of Agnes, yet the similarity had only come to remind them both of the vast gulf of personality between the charismatic mother and the sullen daughter. Aguta had wanted to *be* Isla; and, despite her own myriad successes, some part of her still refused to believe that she could ever live up to her mother's high-octane example.

"Wasn't this woman some kind of famous singer?" Aguta asked. She kept her tone neutral.

The aide stared at the photo. "Maybe? I'm not sure."

There almost couldn't be a better revenge than the expression of blank and uncaring incomprehension on the legal secretary's face, yet Aguta found herself persisting, digging for obscure cultural memory. "Yes—she sang techno opera. Had a string of big hits. I think she used a stage name. What was it again..."

"La Tisiphone!" the aide exclaimed. "I remember now. My nana really loved her. She had the one that went like daaa daaa laaa AAA." She did a fair impression of the famous old melody, but ended it with an unpleasant screech when she attempted to hit the high note.

"Yes, exactly," Aguta said dryly. *Tisiphone.* It meant "Avenger of murder" in ancient Greek, the name of one of the Furies. A myth that had caught her mother's fickle fancy, it now seemed almost a prophecy.

Aguta grimaced and waved at the aide. "Bring the accused for O-eight hundred hours tomorrow."

She sat back with a sigh when the door closed, relishing the renewed silence. The mugshot in her mother's case file hypnotized her. An intricate tracing of wrinkles covered Isla's skin, revealing a long, unspoken history of hard living. What had once been the seductive purse of perfect pink lips had sagged and paled. So too the huge, gorgeous grey eyes, now swallowed up by pouches of wrinkled fat.

Only Isla's long hair was still lush, but entirely white. There was no trace of that shocking, flaming red that her dark-haired daughter had once so desperately envied. The older woman's flawlessly trendy dress sense remained unchanged, but the stylish, tight white trousers and jacket hugged sagging bones and haphazard rolls of fat instead of sensuous curves. The resulting image was desperate and grotesque. If this hag had passed her on the street, Aguta would never have once suspected she was looking at her own mother, still forever glittering in the spotlight of memory.

Still, it behooved her not to involve herself in this case. The best course of action would be to alert her superiors that she had been given a conflict of interest in error, update her mother's file, and withdraw entirely. But there would be problems. The old woman would probably sit in a holding cell for another couple of weeks, physically uncomfortable and taking up precious resources, while the victim's family had already been waiting a week now for an available courtroom...

Another look at Isla's rotating 3D mug-shot decided the judge. She had no feeling about this pathetic creature and could sentence her just as impartially as any other man or woman on the bench. There was no need for delays.

The victim's family and the court officers were already seated when Aguta emerged from her chambers early the next morning. The bailiff cracked the hard floor with the sharp end of his ceremonial staff. "Judge Aguta Greywolf presiding. All rise."

The judge swept out slowly to mount her high seat. She knew how she looked, and pictured it in her mind as she glided forward. Tall, much taller than was usual for Inuit thanks to her mother's European blood and the effects of growing up in Mars' lower gravity. It was to the second that she owed the typically elongated, almost floppy appearance of her body and the hugely long head and jaw, which she knew were so unnerving to many Earthers. Aguta could recall a time in her girlhood when she too had been horrified by the changes Mars had wrought on her bones. She had appeared monstrous in her own view, inhuman and deformed, especially when she did not see the same kind of changes taking place in her father's adult body.

Yet in time she had grown reconciled to her new nature, and finally come to love the unassailable proof of belonging to this brutal planet. In her late middle age now, she considered the Martian form to possess the greater beauty, while Earthers appeared gnomish and rude. She enjoyed emphasizing the differences between them with her aesthetic choices. Her long, thick hair was still black, and she usually wore it coiled up on the top of her head in heavy, elaborate braids that enhanced the great skull and the exaggerated point of the classic Martian chin. Her formal judicial robes lent dignity to her late middle age, the black folds sweeping along in a queenly manner, billowing like smoke in the lower gravity and enhancing the alien allure of her spindly body. The effect was both compelling and conservative, appropriate, rather than the desperate air of a scantily-clad crone trying to hang on to her long-vanished youth and sex appeal.

This dignity had been her solemn father's gift to her. After the accident that had claimed his son's life, Grey Wolf had petitioned for custody of his daughter and been granted it. The courts had considered his famous wife too unstable, even if not technically responsible for the death of her only son. Embracing his new responsibilities as a single parent, Grey Wolf had uprooted himself from his beloved northlands and boarded a flight to the colony on Mars with his little daughter. He had worked hard to omit his ex-wife's famous name from their paperwork, paying bribes all around from their dwindling savings, and then paying even more to buy a place for Aguta in the very best girls' boarding school. Her father had encouraged her not to follow in the footsteps of either of her parents, but to pursue a stable profession outside of the arts. From the very beginning, Aguta had been drawn to the law and had pursued a successful career as a policewoman, before advancing age and decreasing athleticism had led her to switch tracks and enter law school.

Still the arts had been Grey Wolf's own unavoidable destiny, and his magnetic prints and tireless work ethic had attracted enough influential patronage that he had been able to wrangle Martian citizenship for himself and his child. Aguta's father never again went back to Nunavut, had seemed to want to put the past entirely behind him, but when he died at the age of ninety-eight his daughter had not been surprised that Grey Wolf's will had demanded his body be frozen and transported back to Baffin Island for burial.

Global warming had irrecoverably altered the Arctic landscape and brought millions rushing to take sanctuary from the rising oceans and killing heat waves further south. Grey Wolf had claimed not to care what had happened to Nunavut now that the vast empty spaces were being rapidly swallowed by towering cities, but Aguta did not believe that her father had ever really considered himself to be a true Martian, even after almost fifty years of living on the red planet. There were no wolves on Mars.

"Bring forth the accused," the judge commanded.

The electrified doors to the adjacent holding cell slid open, and two policemen accompanied the shuffling prisoner, followed by the court's doctor. Aguta fixed a stern expression on her face and took deep, quiet breaths through her nose to calm her racing heart. Would the old woman recognize her?

The mask of despair on the prisoner's face remained fixed, and Aguta felt a strange kind of bitter disappointment and relief. If the prisoner did suddenly recognize her daughter, she did not show it.

"Let the court be informed that I have reviewed the footage and determined that the accident that claimed the young life of Mr. Shinzo Manzoolas was avoidable and the result of reckless behavior on the part of the accused. Madam Iversen is therefore found guilty of manslaughter." Aguta was pleased with the droning, bureaucratic voice she heard emerging from her mouth. "Let the court further be informed that the accused did not flee the scene of the accident, but stopped to inform the authorities. The accused will also be questioned while wearing the Caput Veritatis to ascertain her motive and recollection of the events in question. All of these factors will be taken into account before sentencing is passed, should the victim's family decline to dismiss the charges."

Aguta looked over at the deceased's family. "If a parent, sibling or spouse is present here today, he or she may come forward to lead the questioning."

An angry-looking young woman descended from her box to stand beside the accused and the court doctor. The doctor determined that the Cap was functioning correctly by asking a series of standard test questions in front of the court. A rotating image of the accused's brain, projected in front of her, lit up as she answered the questions. The Caput Veritatis had evolved from early 21st century psychiatric research in dream control. The original purpose of the Cap had been to explore unconscious triggers in patients suffering from PTSD, but after researchers had observed that their invention could predict truth telling at a more than 90% rate of accuracy, they re-developed the project as a modern polygraph machine. The current iteration could map the complete neural network of any individual and very literally read a mind.

Aguta stared at the back of the court, trying not to hear the soft murmur of Isla's voice as it answered the test questions, but the melody of it assaulted her. She realized that she had not been entirely sure of this woman's identity until she heard the voice, clear and sweet as glass even at one hundred and ten years past birth. It was as if all the beauty that had fled from Isla's face had taken refuge in her throat.

"Functional, Your Ladyship."

"Very well. What is your relationship to the victim?" she asked the young woman.

"His wife, your Ladyship."

"You may proceed with the questioning."

This was all ceremonial. The girl would have been chosen hours ago and been given detailed instructions about her role. Aguta was not surprised when the wife showed no mercy, demanding a precise recounting of the events that had taken her husband's life. She asked the same questions repeatedly until the old woman started to shake with terror and confusion.

"Why did you do it? Why did you kill him?" the wife furiously demanded. Red faced, tears running down her cheeks, she was long past rationally recognizing that Isla had not actually intended to murder her husband. "Tell me!"

"I...don't know..." Isla sputtered. "I'm sorry." This last she whispered with wide eyes. Her obvious dental implants shone weirdly white and perfect under the harsh light of the court. Aguta stared at the back of the court to avoid looking at Isla's slack expression and squat body. Could this pathetic creature really be her passionate mother?

She only intervened when the wife started throwing foul curses. "Peace," Aguta said sternly. "Peace in the court or you will be dismissed. Return to your seat, madam." The young woman was escorted back to her seat, while Isla stood trembling like a threatened prey animal. "The victim's family may now choose to enforce the sentence determined by the court or to offer mercy to the accused. What decide you?"

A tall, middle aged man, perhaps in his early eighties, leaned forward into the microphone at the box. "We will enforce sentence, Your Ladyship."

"Noted. In light of the accused's conscientious decision to stop at the scene of the crime, it is the ruling of this court that the accused Isla Agnes Iversen be sentenced to only one sol of punitive illusion, to be carried out by the court medical authority. The length of the illusion is to be one half life sentence of 70 Martian years followed by permanent repatriation to Earth."

Hearing this, La Tisiphone held out her hands pleadingly and shuffled forward as if to walk to the judge's stand. The police restrained the elderly woman, firmly and not entirely gently.

"Sentence to be carried out immediately," Aguta added. This was unusual. Standard procedure was for the prisoner to be allowed a meal to fortify her body for the harrowing experience to come, but Aguta thought it prudent to skip this custom.

"Now? Don't I get an appeal?" The sad creature that had once been Aguta's mother looked around frantically, as if searching for a friend. *Earther,* Aguta thought scornfully. So many of them came to Mars ignorantly, without doing even the most basic research.

As she had expected, no one protested the irregularity. There was no room in the sealed, domed colonies of Mars for lengthy court trials or incarcerations. Even the simplest of buildings was erected at an exorbitant cost. In this way, Grey Wolf had reminded a young Aguta, Mars was very like the northlands on Earth had been in his youth. Resources were limited, life was harsh, and only the roughest of people could survive in either place. As in the once-frozen north, the barren wastelands of Mars attracted the desperate, the loners, the outcasts, all those people who wanted to leave memory behind them and say, when asked, *But that was another country.*

Such people were hard people, not the kind to waste money or time on extended incarcerations and appeals. The only concession to such gestures that the Martians made was in offering the families of the victims the opportunity to forgive the guilty and dismiss all charges if they so desired. But while most present day citizens had been born on the red planet, the hardness that had led their parents and grandparents to settle there had formed the bedrock of the Martian heart, and few were inclined to show that mercy. Most accepted and even encouraged the harshest possible sentences.

Still, compared to the physical tortures and mutilations experienced by the criminals of the past, modern punishments left no mark on the body. Criminals were now chastised through neurological illusions projected directly into the brain using the same technology that allowed the Caput Veritatis to function. The content was always different, and always the same: the most terrible moments of the offender's life played on repeat. And if the accused lacked memories terrible enough to fulfill the conditions of sentencing, the neuro-programmers could always come up with something creative.

To sentenced criminals the NPIs appeared to last for years, but in reality the illusions only played between one and three days before the guilty were either terminated—as in the case of capital crimes such as first degree murder and rape—or sent home to resume their lives, now hopefully terrified into being better citizens.

Sentenced to half a lifetime of nightmares, Isla Agnes Iversen was led out of the court by armed police. Just before she disappeared, she looked over her shoulder at her daughter, who sat so impassively on her high seat. And though she saw no mercy in the judge's long-jawed alien face, the old singer still opened her mouth on a plea. But when the melodic tongue flapped, it stayed as silent as an empty room.

Hours later, the judge sat in her chambers, listlessly examining file after file, unable to concentrate on any one thing for long. Every few minutes she asked her AI for the time. Each time she imagined what she would do the next day when the NPI was finished. Go to Isla directly in her holding cell and confront her? Or perhaps she might even claim to be low on staff and tell Isla that she was taking her to the docking bay herself. They would have privacy on the way for any number of conversations and outcomes. Aguta was considering just one of those myriad possibilities when she received a knock at the door of her office.

"Your Ladyship, your five o'clock is waiting," Aguta's aide informed her, poking her prim head into the judge's chambers.

Aguta stared intently at her own hands. They were folded neatly in front of her, still long and slim at eighty-six years, only lightly veined. Of course far longer than any Earther woman's hands, they sat like pale spiders on the polished, volcanic Martian desk.

"I am not feeling well," she said quietly. "Please inform the court officers that I cannot take the case now."

The aide blinked dumbly and opened her mouth twice before speaking. "But there's no one else to take the case..."

"Then it will have to wait, won't it?" She fixed the aide with a laser stare, and the officious woman backed down.

"Yes, I suppose it will, Your Ladyship."

As the door closed Aguta thought of how she had decided to accept her mother's case for fear of judicial delay.

But that was never the reason.

Aguta frowned. Strange how her own thoughts could sound like someone else's voice in her head. Disturbed, her hand reached to call the medical authorities before she consciously recognized the decision.

After two rings, someone answered and identified her from her authorization code. "How can we assist you, Your Ladyship?"

"How is the prisoner Isla Iversen's sentencing proceeding?"

A pause followed. "Ah, you were not informed, Your Ladyship?"

The judge tensed. "Informed of what?"

"The prisoner expired after the first ten years of her sentence. Emotional stress followed by cardiac arrest at 10:47 real Martian time." The breath drained from Aguta's throat, soft as a carbon cloud. "Your Ladyship? Your Ladyship?" Slowly, Aguta became aware of shouting from the speaker. "Your Ladyship, do you require assistance?" A murmured background conversation was barely audible. "*I'm going to send a paramedic.*"

"No!" she said sharply, then again more gently. "No. I'm well. No paramedic needed. I...broke a glass."

An absurd excuse, but the medic didn't pursue it. "The police have been informed, Your Ladyship. There will be a brief investigation, of course, but the guilty party was old, weak. I don't expect you'll see any trouble."

Aguta swallowed. "Yes, thank you." She hung up before the man responded. An investigation. It would take approximately five minutes before the police unearthed that she had sent Isla to her sentence without a meal or even a chance to rest. She knew from her own time in the force that the Martian police did not care much for Earthers, but they were also brutally efficient professionals. They would want to know why. They would start digging.

The sofa in Aguta's office looked suddenly very inviting, and she was tempted to lay down and let the whole wretched day simply go away. Yet the thought of waking up here, in the cold and silent night-time mausoleum of the court, with the proverbial axe hovering over her neck, was not appealing. Ultimately, she called for her Wing and set it to automatic pilot.

Aguta rode in the back seat, half-reclining, with a diaphanous black silk scarf from Earth folded double and draped over her face. The dome was climate-controlled, a clear necessity in the bitterly cold, inhospitable environment of the red planet, where even here at the equator it was never warmer than 20 degrees centigrade at summer's height, and usually considerably colder than zero. Even the amount of weak Martian light admitted was artificially adjusted over the course of the day. Inside the dome there was no need for sunglasses, or jackets, or any other weather-related paraphernalia. Still Aguta felt cold, and her eyes burned as if she had been cutting onions all day.

When she reached her complex, Aguta sent the Wing to park itself and headed straight for the condo, intending to sleep until the next day. Yet as she stepped out of the elevator onto the top floor, it was immediately evident that something was wrong. There was a strange smell in the air, like something had been burning, and dirty footprints disturbed the taupe hallway carpets. The prints were the color of rust, as if someone had been walking outside the dome and tracking in the ancient dust of the Martian wilderness.

Aguta stopped in front of her door. It was slightly but conspicuously cracked. Cautiously, the judge reached into a slit at the bottom of her right pocket to grasp the small pistol she kept strapped to her leg. In her position, she could not always expect a warm welcome.

The judge slipped inside, but was more disturbed than truly concerned. The sixth sense that she had cultivated during more than sixty years in law enforcement told her that the intruder was already gone. The red footsteps dried up just over the threshold, and the burning smell dissipated in the main lounge. It looked and smelled normal here, still the same familiar combination of mostly practical Martian furniture and luxurious decorative touches. She stopped in the middle of the room, looking around for clues, but there was nothing. Nor had anything changed in the rest of the house.

Aguta was so exhausted that her heart rate was barely elevated from the break-in. She decided to wait until morning before calling her security company.

Sleep was a black pit, utter and complete in its darkness, but not at all restful. The tiny, distant orb of the sun was just beginning to rise when Aguta struggled back to consciousness. Unsure of the exact time, she flipped open the heavy edge of her wine-colored curtain to stare sleepily at the typical Martian early morning sky, brightly flushed like a pink rose in full bloom.

Just as she dropped the curtain, plunging the room back into darkness, she heard the voices. They came from the hall outside of her bedroom, crafty whispers, planning and arguing in a register too high to track. Fury and terror electrified the judge, and she dropped down to the floor and under the boxy pre-fab bed, cursing herself for an old fool for not immediately reporting the break-in.

Quickly she freed her pistol from her pocket and fixed it at the door, planning to shoot at the intruders' legs. Yet the whispers continued for a long time before the door opened, and she was finally so tense that she started shooting before she saw anyone come inside. The gun made an awful crack and bang in her ears, and she flinched as she pulled on the trigger two more times before realizing that there was no one there.

Incredulous, she rolled out from under the bed and over to the door, peeking cautiously around the corner. The corridor was empty, and Aguta threw aside caution to run to the living room, which was also empty. When she tried the main door she found it locked from the inside. This time she made sure to check every closet and cranny of the house before calling her security company and demanding that they immediately attend her.

𝔸 ⸗ 𝕋 ℿ

The judge stood at the window watching the pale white sun hovering in a sky already losing its youthful roseate flush. She frowned while she waited, lifting one hand to her mouth as if to chew on a nail, only to immediately drop it again. She wondered if someone had reported the gunshots, or if she had been the only tenant awake so early.

It was only just past six am when the man from *AresTech* arrived. Though Aguta remained agitated, she still took the time to prepare a cup of tea for the technician while he checked the system and transferred a current copy of the security tapes to her personal interface.

"Has anyone seen these yet?" she asked.

"No, madam."

He hummed as he worked, and she realized with a kind of creeping horror that the song was one of her mother's hit singles.

"*Eumenides*," she whispered.

"Excuse me, madam?" the technician asked politely.

"Eumenides. It was the name of that song. It means "The Kindly Ones". A euphemism for The Furies, the Greek spirits of vengeance. The people were afraid to speak their names, lest they draw their attention."

"Like Voldemort," the man chuckled.

Imagine comparing chthonic myths from the dawn of civilization with 20th century pop fiction. Though of the two, most people were more likely to know the pop fiction saga with at least fifty different films based on it. "Yes, exactly like Voldemort," she agreed dryly. "How's that coming?" she added, nodding at the box in his hands.

"All done. Nothing seems to be tampered with. Let's look at your tapes."

Together with the technician, the judge watched herself leave for work, and then continued watching for the intruders. When they did not immediately see anything, Aguta told the man to fast-forward the tape. The footage sped by unnaturally for some time until the door opened.

"Finally—" she stopped mid-mutter, shocked the marrow to see herself enter the condo. "But that's not possible! I—try the rest of the apartment."

Patiently, the technician showed her the view from the start of the tape. Again there was nothing until she saw herself entering her own bedroom in the late afternoon. Sputtering with confusion, Aguta ordered the view switched to the hall outside of the bedroom, completely certain that she would at least see someone appearing to whisper and plot there, as she so clearly remembered.

Yet no one broke into the house in the night, and at five am by the time-stamp she heard gun-shots from behind the door of her bedroom, and then saw herself burst into the hallway. Frantic and disheveled, she appeared mad, aiming a pistol at shadows.

Though the security technician said nothing, Aguta could almost taste his thoughts, his amused pity. Her mouth drew into a tight line, and she walked away from the screen without a word.

In a bid to take her mind off of the entire disturbing experience, Aguta went into work just before seven in the morning. It was Sol 1, the start of the week and her regular day off. She had no scheduled cases, but thought that she might read ahead. But when she booted up her interface, the link to her mother's court medical file flashed onto the screen. The complete video of the interactive neuro-punitive illusion was attached. If she wished, she could watch it right up to the moment of Isla's death. Taking her state into consideration, she decided not to just yet.

"Download Monday's cases, and follow-ups from last week," she instructed her AI.

"There are no such files."

"Excuse me?"

"There are no such files." Suspecting a glitch in the audio system, she went in manually. All of her files were present.

"Computer interface, please recognize all currently displayed files."

"Yes, Your Ladyship. All files recognized."

"What was the problem before?"

"What problem, Your Ladyship?"

Aguta frowned. "You did not recognize these files."

"You are in error, Your Ladyship. I have always recognized these files."

There was no sense in arguing with software, no matter how intelligent. She would have the system inspected before her next paid work day.

"Loading file," the calm, soothing voice of the interface announced.

Aguta's face contracted with irritation. She must have a virus if the system was acting so erratically. "Identify file," she demanded.

The system did not respond verbally, but instead opened the file, and Aguta abruptly saw the world through the eyes of another. Harsh winds sang and whistled, obliterating the orderly confines of her office, and she saw the jagged cliffs, looming like the lip of the abyss over the Arctic Ocean on Earth. Two children played, a dark-haired boy chasing a plain and sullen Earther girl, not too close to the edge.

"Kids, lunch time!" That lovely voice was calling her to sit, drink sugared black tea and eat banaq, slightly sweet, fried bread lovingly packed for a spring picnic by her Inuit grandmother.

Aguta tried to move her hand or mouth, to close the file, but she was frozen in place.

The boy was laughing and the girl giggling, and Isla, unseen, laughed with them, putting one hand up to wave.

Aguta felt that she must be waving as well, and saw her own hand lifting in the periphery of her vision.

"Mama!" the little girl screamed. "Look at me, Mama!"

"Stop," the judge whispered with the greatest effort. "Stop file." It was loud enough for the sensitive interface to hear and obey, but the file continued playing.

Isla turned to arrange the food on the blanket, but looked back at the sound of loud bickering. Her children were fighting over a beautiful toy kite. The long red tails flapped in the wind and seemed to take on strange life, twisting in the radiant glare of the northern sun. They wrapped around the boy, tangling his slender body in their greedy lengths.

"It's mine!" the small girl shrieked before suddenly pushing her brother. Isla ran forward, hands already outstretched to catch her boy as his sister, in a fit of pique, sent him tumbling back in the open air.

How had they managed to come so close to the edge of the cliff? No matter. The boy fell, endlessly, and last of all went those awful, sanguine kite tails.

"Daniel!"

"Stop! Stop!" Aguta gasped, jerking furiously to the side. Unexpectedly, her body responded and the chair fell over from the force of her struggle. Stunned, she stared at the ceiling. A flicker in the room's lighting signaled that the file was not done, and the judge pulled herself up on her feet to firmly speak to the system. But when she looked at the screen it was blank.

"Computer, locate last played file in the interface."

"Yes, Your Ladyship. Loading."

To her dismay, the last file loaded was an academic research paper. A drop of sweat trickled down her forehead, landing in her eye, burning. What in hell was going on here? And how many times had the NPI forced her mother to watch Daniel die before Isla's heart simply couldn't take it anymore? Aguta wondered if she should have personally escorted her mother to her punishment. It would have been unusual, hardly procedure, but there were so many things that she had wanted to say, and many more things that she had wanted to hear.

"You killed him."

"What?" Aguta said, looking around the room for a speaker. That was not the voice of the interface.

"You killed him." The interface screen flickered and hummed, but the voice was organic, living, a woman's voice. "You killed Daniel."

"I didn't kill him," she retorted. "I was a child."

"Murderer!" the voice accused. "Child killer!"

"Child killer!" another woman's voice agreed.

"You killed him because you hated him," a third voice added.

"I didn't! I loved him."

"So you admit that you killed him," the first voice announced.

The last voice hissed. "Just like you killed your mother."

"No!" Aguta shouted. Her voice echoed on the ceiling.

"Your Ladyship?" the polite voice of her aide sounded from behind her closed office door. "Do you require assistance?"

The judge looked around frantically. She was crouched on the floor, rocking on her heels with her hands defensively held over her stomach. The screen had gone dark, but she thought she heard something still. Whispers, chattering like mad insects just after a huge, molten Earth sunset.

"No." She cleared her throat. "Yes, please call security. I think there might be an intruder here."

Court security came quickly to inspect her offices and all of the adjacent areas, but when they told her that they had found nothing, she felt only numb. A glimpse of her face in a polished window showed huge dark circles under too-large green eyes. She turned away from herself to carefully observe the armored men and women. Watching the police reminded Aguta of her own time in uniform, the brutal physical pleasures of pursuit and the immense gratification of capturing a resisting criminal. Some detective must be looking into Isla's case even now.

"It's only what you deserve," her aide told her.

Aguta looked around sharply. "Excuse me?"

"Would you like some tea, Your Ladyship?" The aide appeared no more than usually prim.

She quickly made a decision. "No, I think I'll take the day off after all. Upload the files for tomorrow before you leave." She didn't wait for the aide's response before briskly gathering her things.

"But what about the tape?" the security guard at the main entrance asked her solicitously.

Aguta stared at the armed woman. "The tape?"

"You need to delete the NPI from your system," the second guard on the other side of the door told her. "They'll

see that it was you who killed Daniel. And Isla took the blame
for it all these years..."

"Of course," the first guard added, "It's not the only copy."

Aguta ran down the fiberglass stairs. The low gravity
cushioned her bones and turned what might have been a
haphazard tumble on Earth into a series of long bounces
propelling her effortlessly to the rough ground. Landing far
below the level of the courts, she still heard the twin guards
laughing from above and behind her. They sounded inhuman,
like monstrous birds cawing guilt in her ear. Above the dome,
the normally butterscotch-colored sky of Mars at midday
showed streaks of red. The iron oxide in the air that gave the
Red Planet its name glared down at her like a furious eye from
a blood-soaked battlefield.

"Please," the judge whispered. It was an empty plea,
without direction, crafted from confusion. She had not the
slightest idea of what was happening, or what she could do
about it.

"Watch where you're going," another woman's voice
barked from behind her, and then a hard shoulder shoved her
to the ground.

𐎤 𐎟 𐎳 𐎲

*"It was an accident, Isla. She didn't mean it. She's just a child." Her
father pleaded with her mother, unseen.*

*"I know she's a child, Grey," the lovely, rich voice sobbed. "She's
still my daughter. But I can't even look at her. I can't bear it. You
weren't there. She killed our boy."*

*A long silence followed, and then— "You know I love you. If
you need me to, I'll take her away. But only until you feel better."*

Aguta woke with a gasp, sitting up in sweat-soaked sheets.
Her pulse was pounding so furiously that she feared she was
on the verge of a heart attack. Her breath sounded unnaturally
loud in the shadowed confines of her bedroom. The faintest
hint of light gleamed from behind the curtains, more gray
than rose. She peeked out the window and saw the frightful

movement of a dust storm hovering above the dome. There would be no ships leaving the planet today.

"Computer," she whispered.

"Yes, Your Ladyship?" The voice was soft, responding organically to her tone.

"Time."

"Five am, Ladyship. Sol 1," it added.

"Sol 1...but it was Sol 1 yesterday. It was my day off."

"No, Ladyship, you went to work."

"Yes, but on my day off."

"It is your day off today. Today is Sol 1."

"No," Aguta insisted. "I remember. I had the technician here to check the security system after the intruders and then I decided to go into work."

"There were no intruders. There was no technician."

"Sleep," the judge snapped at the system.

Yet had she dreamed it after all? No, the more reasonable explanation was that her computer systems were infected with a serious virus. Her home and work systems were largely separate, but she had synced her mail accounts and a few other things for quick data transfer. This was not precisely permitted, but all of her colleagues did it too. She would have to have someone in to look at the whole thing. Might a virus somehow have infected the security system additionally and caused her odd experience yesterday morning? It seemed unlikely, but what other explanation could there be?

Yet there were still the footprints, the smell of burning in the air. There must have been a real intruder after all, one who had broken in and then physically played with all of her systems. They could have redirected her security feed to a third party and might even now be watching her every move while attempting to confuse and terrorize her. If that were the case, they were succeeding. Her heart rate was still slightly high, though coming down under the persuasive force of reason. She would have her entire system inspected by an independent agency and checked for viruses and tampering. There was no need for panic.

By eight in the morning three computer engineers were investigating all three hardware sites, searching for back doors and foreign programming. Aguta gave the two professionals in her apartment tea and then withdrew to her kitchen to make dinners for her work week. She was wealthy enough these days not to constantly subsist on the usual Martian diet of reconstituted potato soup, multi-vitamins, and chalky calcium bars. At ten o'clock, she was just taking the first dish out of the oven when she heard a knock on the kitchen door.

"We've found something, Your Ladyship," said the jumpsuit-clad engineer.

"Tell me."

The younger woman led the judge out to the living room where half the guts of her system lay exposed on a tarp. She held up a beetle-shaped piece of carbon. "We've found one of these here and one in your office. The intruders were able to hijack your AI interface and alter the video feed of your security system. We've removed them from the hardware and are combing your software for viruses now."

Instead of terror and violation Aguta experienced a most profound sensation of relief. Though she had half convinced herself that some reasonable explanation to her troubles must exist, still there had been some niggling sense of doubt, of supernatural unease.

She smiled at the engineers. Both were women, as was the one in her office at work. That was slightly odd. Though women engineers were not precisely uncommon, most engineering fields remained dominated by men. But she felt more comfortable dealing with women anyway and wasn't about to complain.

"Thank you, Engineer Meghan," she said graciously, sneaking a tiny glance at the name sewn to the woman's jumpsuit. "I'm very grateful for your help."

Meghan smiled. "We're here to serve."

There was an odd echo in her voice as the other engineer said the same words at the same time. The judge turned to look at the tall, thin woman behind her. This one was much older, almost Aguta's own age. She glanced at the name-plate. "Thank you, Engineer Tiffany."

Tiffany smiled tightly. Her lips were a gray gash in the paper-thin skin of her long-jawed Martian face. "We are here to serve," she repeated gently.

By noon, all three engineers had put her work and home systems back together and left her with a warning not to connect them again. It was easy to break into synced systems, Meghan had warned her gravely.

The judge was soon yawning and tempted to lay down for a nap. She usually avoided sleeping in the afternoons, but then she did not normally rise quite so early. Surely a small nap wouldn't hurt much. Yet she found herself resisting the sloppiness of midday sleep, and sat on the sofa staring outside the window at the cold and flat Martian sky, still clouded by the persistent dust. She thought again about shuttles to Earth, but there was no sense alarming anyone on her mother's case by doing a search. There was still time to consider her options.

The storm on the outside darkened and quickened as she watched. As a young policewoman, Aguta had done training missions on the outside, tests of endurance and flexibility that easily could have killed her. She knew the landscape very well, had ridden as a conqueror over frosted banks and climbed the sides of forbidding mountains that dwarfed all the greatest ranges of Earth. But despite the training, no refugee from the law ever attempted to live out there. She would last only as long as her last gasp of tinned oxygen.

Aguta put the news on to distract herself, but the sleepiness persisted. With drooping eyelids, she watched the newscaster. Oddly, the woman looked like Tiffany, the engineer. Aguta was still watching the bony face when her eyes closed and her body slumped low on the sofa.

"*...the shocking story of a judge with a deadly secret and how she almost got away with murder—twice.*"

The voice from the screen roused her sometime later, but slowly, as if heard from underwater. Aguta shook her head and repeatedly blinked to clear the exhaustion from her brain. Except for the blue glare of the screen, the sitting room was utterly dark. Slowly, the judge sat up. Even in the static warmth she felt very cold, and sat briskly rubbing her arms with her hands crossed over her chest. Just how long had she slept, and why did she still feel so tired?

"Computer, time."

"2:45 am, Sol 3."

That was frankly impossible. There was no way that she had slept thirty-six hours, no matter how tired she was. The programming really needed urgent seeing to...except the engineers had already been here. Or the AI must have been wrong the first time, and yesterday had indeed been Sol 2. Except why had no one called her to work?

She looked back at the news. The anchor really looked so similar to the engineer. Hadn't she been watching the same woman before she fell asleep?

"*...the guilty...was convicted for the murders of her brother and mother....*"

She rubbed her arms again. What was that?

"Computer, play back the news broadcast."

"Yes, Aguta."

"Excuse me?" she asked sharply. Never before had the system referred to her by her name. It was not part of the programming. Unlike some people, Aguta had never given her AI interface a name or invited the software to make friends with her.

"Yes, Your Ladyship." It was too much to believe that she had imagined it, and she felt troubled. How many times had she had the system inspected now? What could possibly be wrong with it that it was still behaving so erratically?

"*A judge with a deadly secret,*" the broadly smiling woman on the screen told her with relish. "*She was sentenced to one thousand years of neuro-punitive imaging. And we all know that no one has survived more than six hundred, don't we?*" she asked casually. *"I mean, after that, it's just overkill."*

The judge swallowed against a suddenly intensely dry throat. "Computer, change channel."

"Changing channel." The screen flickered.

"You didn't think you could get away that easily, did you?" It was the third engineer, the one who had inspected her work system. Her name was thickly embroidered on her jumpsuit. *Alice.*

"Change channel." The screen flickered again, and the engineer Meghan appeared, licking her lush, pink lips.

"We know how to claim our rights."

Aguta shook her head and considered leaving the sofa, but found herself strangely bound to it. "Change channel."

Tiffany smiled at her from the newscaster's seat. "There will be no protesting your innocence. We will not be robbed. Slayer of brother, slayer of mother. Murderer of blood kin."

The channel changed again, though Aguta said nothing. This time, all three women stood together. Each was a slightly different height and weight, but all of them were green eyed and staring. Their tongues flickered out in unison to lick their mouths, and Aguta noted that all three had unusually long teeth.

"Look," the women whispered in unison, in chorus. "Look upon your deeds."

Together they reached down, under the visible half of the screen. Impossible, but Aguta knew what was coming, what must come, and tried with all of her will to escape. She could not even close her eyes. Even screaming was beyond her power.

The three women on the screen were growing taller now, and slowly a pattern of scales appeared on their visible skin, multiplying, thickening, and darkening—now red, now the sickly brown of old blood. Great, webbed wings sprouted from behind their shoulders, unfolding to fill the screen from corner to corner. Like lizards, their tongues flickered together, tasting the air, and all three she-demons were grinning when they lifted their unseen burden to the front of the screen.

It was Daniel, of course. How light-limbed and lovely he was, face slack but almost smiling with the cherubic mask of young boyhood. Yet his flesh was unnaturally still, slightly blue in color, frozen as if he had been left out in the long night of the desert on Mars—or dropped in a sea of ice on Earth.

"You will give us our due," Meghan said slowly.

Not Meghan at all, Aguta knew now. There were names for these creatures, names older than cities and civilizations. *Meghera*, the jealous. *Tisiphone*, the avenger. *Alecto*, the angry one. These were the Furies who hunted the murderers of blood kin and drove them mad. Once the ancient ones caught the scent, there was nowhere the guilty could escape to. Even those most distant, barren corners of the world, where only the mad and the desperate go, would be no refuge.

Like the past, the Furies would always find you.

"Yes," Tisiphone repeated. "You will give us our due."

Alecto's mouth stretched impossibly wide. "And we will give you yours."

Oh, no, no. They could not be planning to do as she feared. *No.*

But they were planning it, and they did. All three opened monstrously broad jaws and leaned over the defenseless little body of lost Daniel. Only when the Furies had started their awful feast did they finally permit Aguta to scream.

The eating went on for a very long time.

𐎛 𐎟 𐎗 𐎁

"You know she almost got away with it," the technician said over his potato soup.

"Who, the judge?" the court doctor asked.

"Mm." He swallowed. "Did away with the brother when she was just a kid. Then after the mother kicked it in the NPI, she took sick. Feverish and raving. Ended up in hospital for a week. So the mother's case file had to be re-opened by her stand-in to add the death notes. So anyway, get this." The tech waved his spoon through the air with relish. "The stand-in decides to be a lookey-loo and watches the NPI tape. Figures the whole thing out and alerts the cops. They gather all the evidence they need while she's still out of it, and when her ladyship wakes up in hospital she's handcuffed to the bed. They processed her within hours."

"Remarkable," the doctor murmured. She sipped her tea. "And the open monitor?"

"Oh, that. Yeah. The sentencing judge ruled that we need to watch the entire simulation unfold in case there's anyone else she might have bumped off. Anyway, it's a death sentence so there's no point respecting her privacy."

"I suppose not. What's this mythology stuff in the NPI?"

"Her mother was some kind of famous singer on Earth, back in the day, and she took a stage name from this old story about demons that haunt people who kill their families. I couldn't resist programming it in. I mean, it was like being handed justice on a *platter*." He laughed and drummed the plastic rim of his bowl for emphasis. "I don't normally get so creative, but the ideas just keep coming out of thin air. Really gruesome stuff. Maybe she'll kick the bucket in record time and stop taking up resources."

The doctor shrugged, already losing interest. She looked at her watch. "Break's almost up. I'll head back now."

"Yeah. Catch you in couple of minutes. I'm just going to fill my tea again."

The tech drained his cup and strolled over to the machine for a refill, chuckling softly to himself. The cafeteria was almost empty and quickly emptying even further. The area by the tea and coffee machine was unoccupied, and the tech stopped chuckling in reluctant respect of the almost echoing silence. He filled his cup with a frown, noting the unusually slow trickle of brown liquid emerging from the spout. By the time it reached the rim of the mug, he was sure that he was the only one left in the room.

"Damn thing," he muttered.

"Excuse me," a woman's voice said politely from behind him. "I'm here to fix the machine."

The tech jumped precipitously. "I didn't even hear you coming!"

The woman smiled. "You must have been dreaming." She reached over with a long-nailed hand and offered it to shake. "Hello. My name is Meghan."

Out of Tauris

Alexander Jablokov

Iphigenia saw him coming. He was just a wavering shape far off across the plain, and she might have imagined seeing the bundle he carried. She knew it had to be there, for there was only one reason a man came to Vravron.

He would have started while the stars were still in the sky to get all the way across Attica before Mt. Hymettos turned purple. He was a busy man, after all, with a farm in the countryside or a shop in Athens, a dead wife and, perhaps, a living child still unweaned. But he knew what had to be done, and had set about doing it at the first opportunity. If he owned a donkey, it couldn't be spared from its tasks. He walked slowly and steadily, a man who knew that heroism was not the way real work got done.

She left the girls at their games in the high-walled courtyard, and went out of the gate toward him. They met just at the ancient fig tree that marked the corner of the temple grounds. She led him to the spring and filled a wooden cup with water for him. He drank it too fast and shuddered at the cold. They sat together then, in the shade of the tree, and he set the bundle of cloth down.

"What was her name?" she said.

For a moment he was unwilling to say it. And this was perhaps the last time he would ever say it. "Leucothea, daughter of Dymos, of Keramikos."

"Ah!" Sometimes there was still some surprise left, after all these years. "We had her here, eleven years ago. I remember her. The fastest of her year. Leucothea won all the races, and we had some fast girls that year. She was not as good a dancer as she was a runner, but decently graceful."

He was flabbergasted. "Leucothea...ran?"

She knew what he was remembering. A woman who shuffled down the street with her basket, black-cloaked and veiled. A woman who slid silently up the stairs to the women's quarters when the work of the day was over, while he and his friends drank and sang to dry their sweat. A woman who, heavy with child in her last days, needed to stop and lean against a tree or a wall to catch a breath, on her way back from market or field.

She smiled. "A girl that age is so light her feet barely touch the ground. You've never known a woman who was not burdened by something."

He scowled at that, and looked away, lest he offend against the goddess Artemis, in the person of her priestess. Out in his world a woman's smile always meant secret knowledge, and thus public trouble. She didn't smile again, keeping her secrets to herself.

Girls came to the Temple of Artemis at Vravron from all over Hellas, the year before they were old enough to be wed. Here they lived together, played, sang, and ran, ran like a Scythian horse across an endless steppe. They fell down laughing, unable to stay on their feet. They were solemn at the ceremonies of the goddess, peering into the darkness of the temple to catch a glimpse of the twisted statue of Artemis that Iphigenia had brought with her when she first came here. They pretended to be other people, or animals. Bears, mostly. They pretended to be bears, and roared and hugged each other.

Then, wet with each other's tears, they went back out into the world to meet their fates as women.

She herself had been young when she came, not the bundle of sticks bound with tattered parchment that she was now, with all of those other women who had been forced to serve the goddess amid the rocks above the Black Sea. Together, they had brought Artemis Tauropolos through the narrow passages of Bosporus, the Propontis, the Hellespont, past crashing rocks and sullen pirates, out into the warm Aegean, all the way here, to Hellas itself, and dedicated her temple here, at the spot where the spring poured into the sea.

"And the child?" she said.

"The girl died as well, and is buried with her mother."

"Surrender what you have brought."

At that last moment, she could tell, he was reluctant to give them up, though he had probably cursed their weight as the rough road had climbed the shoulder of Hymettos on the way from Athens to Vravron, and he had met the heat of the rising sun. Then he picked up the bundle and handed it to her. She pulled it apart. The clothing had been packed while still soaked with sweat, blood, and amniotic fluid, and the stiff layers parted only reluctantly. It included a beautiful patterned peplos, sewn up the right side in the Attic fashion. The fibulas that had held the shoulders together had already been removed, and were probably even now being used to hold together someone else's garment. There was also a himation, a cloak old and worn, no doubt something of long comfort to the women of family, passed down from one to the other, providing a luck that had always worked before.

No amphora could pour out wine indefinitely. The lees finally came.

She put her face in the clothing and breathed in. The smell of pain and panic was still in the fabric. The goddess would accept it, hold it in her bloody hands, let it expire.

"Come with me," she said.

Men were unused to being told what to do by a woman, and usually bridled. Here they were grateful for it. She led him to the temple, and into the vast room where the clothing brought as offerings to the goddess was stored, the garments of women who had died in childbirth. Outside, the shriek of girls at play came over the walls.

He sucked a breath at the vast mounds of cloth, the simple shifts torn by fingernails in an extremity of pain, the richly embroidered himatia in dark red purple, the sandal straps bearing deep teeth marks, all brought here by men and left behind. He put his own dead wife's clothing down amid the rest.

Over the last few mornings, she had awakened in great pain. The activities of each day had made it recede. Now it returned still more fiercely, and she finally recognized it. She had felt this pain of the goddess as she had lifted her statue in the temple, the last day she was among the Taurians; when she left, and led the women away.

So it was without much surprise that she watched herself fumble among the old leather sacks piled on a shelf, as mesmerized as any sacrificial victim, to find what she had used so often at the Temple of Artemis Tauropolos, above the malignant waters of the Black Sea, and remember who she had once been.

He turned, to find the old lady standing before him with a long, narrow sword in her hand.

"You are Iphigenia," he said. "Daughter of Agamemnon, sister of Orestes, priestess of Artemis Tauropolos, and now priestess at Vravron. We give you sacrifice. We honor you."

She smiled. She retained a surprising number of teeth, and so still enjoyed smiling. "I have been Iphigenia for a very long time. You may be the last man I will welcome here with the clothes of a woman who died in childbirth, so I am Iphigenia for the last few moments left me. I will tell you how Artemis came to Vravron, and when I am finished, you can tell me if you still wish to give me sacrifice."

The vast school of silvery bonito slid past the shore. They circled the Black Sea once a year and always passed the same place on the same day of the year. They filled the water out to the horizon, their splash when they came to the surface a slower sound than expected, as if the water had grown as thick as honey. They could supposedly lift incautious ships up out of the water on their myriads of backs, the fishermen too frightened by their intended prey to dare drop nets.

She could no longer remember how many times that swirling silver in the dark water had passed since she had been brought to this place.

The long staircase down ended here, on a beach of round stones scattered with driftwood, dead fish, and the occasional piece of boat. She did not interest herself in what washed up, even should that oar there have come from the *Argo*, in which Jason and his men had long ago traversed this sea to Colchis, to rob the people there of their gold and princess and then return to Hellas through endless and fraught seas. Even the smallest town on the Black Sea had an oar from the *Argo* hidden away somewhere: the ship must have been as leggy as a millipede.

She knew the women thought she came here to remember home, as they constantly did. But she had no memory of any home at all. She clambered down here because the base of the cliff was the one place she couldn't see the temple on its promontory. All that was visible from this spot was the tuft of grass at the cliff's edge, the spot where the sea of grass that stretched from the mouth of the Ister in the west all the way past the Tanais in the east pushed its way south through the mountains of the Taurians, only to meet its match in the sea. Here she could stand, feel the clammy wind brush indifferently past her, and for a moment feel that nothing was required of her.

A sail rose at the horizon. It had the rakish cheer of a Hellenic ship, creeping into this sea as if they could not be seen, anxious to explore, raid, and abscond with the wealth of the Taurians, their gold, their wood, and their horses. She watched it as it slowly made its way around to the east, their most common angle of approach, seeking to conceal themselves in the wilds there. They could surely see the dark stone of the temple to the north, but paid it no mind.

The women would once again look up from their work, and despite their many disappointments, despite the fact that the Hellenes themselves had sold them up here, despite themselves, would feel hope.

It was her job to make sure that their hope remained forever unsatisfied.

The moment of peace had passed. There would be more work, and there was still last week's Hellene to be taken care of. She took a deep breath and started back up the stairs.

"Are you married?" she asked him.

"Not...yet."

The prisoner had been captured almost immediately. Several of his comrades had been killed, the rest had rowed away without ever coming ashore, leaving him alone to satisfy the goddess.

"Who?"

"My niece. But not...yet."

"Problems?"

He shrugged. "Drought. Disease. And disputes. Property."

He was not in his first youth, and his hair was thinning. He had a nervous, worn look. Marrying a niece would keep existing land in the family. But simply not losing wasn't enough, the reason he had gone out on an expedition to the Black Sea rather than just getting back behind his plow.

"You haven't farmed your whole life. Did you see it? Did you go back to see Troy on your way to the Hellespont?"

She could hear his breath in the silent temple. The space, with its ranks of black columns, was both vast and crowded, the stone beams invisible in the darkness overhead. Despite the fact that he was alone with one small woman, unfettered and unguarded, he did not make a move on her. None of them ever did. They sensed the cult statue of the goddess in its secret chamber in the temple's heart, on its three sets of steps. It was not necessary to force them to do anything. They could be guided by a gentle touch.

"The weather was fair for the passage through to the Black Sea," he said. "No reason to stop in there, though I have heard that some tribes from the interior have come and settled there."

Even the victors dreaded the spot. Only those with no memory of Troy would ever live among the blackened ruins.

"Your niece. Your wife to be. A pretty, useful girl?"

"I don't...yes. Of course. Well taught, and a good hand with a weaving."

"What do you remember that is important about your life?"

What she wanted wasn't the war so much, though she would listen to stories of single combat, climbing siege ladders, and burning farmsteads if that was what still occupied his mind. But she was more interested in the stories that could not be told, but sometimes stuck to the underside of other tales. The men who had gone off to the war may have been killed or maimed by it, but they had been able to *see* it. What she wanted were the experiences of others, those for whom the war had been a collapse of wet earth, a rotting of roofbeams, or a creeping plague that killed the sheep, a blind destruction without a sensible origin. A decade of war had torn human connections all around the inland seas, leaving behind it landless and fatherless men, women who had to sell themselves to eat, and children for whom tugging Hector's battered corpse about the walls, in the form of a dead dog, was just how they started their games.

"I remember Achilles crying," he said.

"Of course." She knew the stories. "Over the death of his friend Patroclus."

He shook his head vehemently. "Much earlier. At the beginning. Before the beginning. At Aulis."

"What caused the hero's grief?"

"He had been used by the King, by Agamemnon. To lure a girl to our camp, supposedly to marry her. To marry the great Achilles! Odysseus, who could persuade anyone of anything, had played that trick on both him and the girl, and so had twice as much fun as anyone else. So she and her mother came to Aulis, only to discover that Achilles knew nothing about it. It was Agamemnon who required her presence."

"You were there?"

"We were all there. All the warriors of Hellas, the entire fleet gathered together, trapped by a contrary wind, because Agamemnon had offended the goddess Artemis." He paused, as if realizing for the first time that he too had now offended Artemis. A bond between him and his dead King, then. "The goddess required a sacrifice before she would relent. The girl was that sacrifice."

"And Achilles wept because he was the cause."

"He wept because he could do nothing. The army demanded the sacrifice. She even pulled off the beautiful wedding garments her mother had dressed her in, so that she stood before us in pure nakedness, like a goddess herself. No one took pity on her. She was forced onto the altar, and the goddess received what she required."

His eyes focused on the past, the altar high above the army of the Argives, the unforgiving sun in the sky, the hills of Euboea across the strait, the black-hulled ships becalmed in their harbor. As he talked, she removed her own clothes, her deer-hide trousers and linen chiton with its many folds, and now stood before him naked herself.

He came to the present in shock. "You—"

The sword she held was as thin as a needle, made of rare hard iron. If she was not careful how she used it, it could hit bone and bend.

She was always careful how she used it. He died quickly, like a man finally realizing something that should have been obvious. His niece would marry some other uncle, and the property would endure.

In the inner chamber, the statue of the goddess received some blood in a bowl, as she had once received Iphigenia's. No army sailed off to sack Troy this time, but each sacrifice helped keep the eternally angry and disappointed goddess from destroying them all.

By the time she was done with the goddess, the women had come out: Kleio, the big Thessalian, as sturdy as the horses they raised there, and Ione, the sly dark Cretan, with the air of secrets kept from the crude northern Hellenes who had conquered her people. They brought hot water, sponges, and oil.

They sluiced the hot water over her as she stood, arms upraised like a small child. The blood had grown sticky while she mollified the goddess, and it took a while for the water on the floor to run clear. The steam brought the pink out into her skin. They dried her, then oiled her. No one spoke, and no one mentioned the unfinished tattoos on her back that no one believed were birthmarks, but the two women maneuvered neatly around each other, making sure her hair was clean, that nothing was left in any crevice of her skin. She found herself relaxing, for, despite herself, each man's death rubbed its way through that mysteriously inked skin, leaving a painful sore.

They did this with work-hardened hands that had been deliberately and slowly softened beforehand, calluses pumiced down, and thick oil worked into the skin, even though the man that had just died might easily have been one of their kinsmen, for each of these women had come from Hellas as well, sold to the Taurians by improvident owners.

Kyra had been taken while harvesting reeds along the shores of Corfu, Actë at her weaving when pirates stormed ashore at Lindos, Iphimedeia tending wounded men when her small city beneath Mt. Ossa fell to besieging troops from a more prosperous town in the Vale of Tempe. Theano had been nursing her child in the sun near Abdera when men hired by a neighbor had seized and sold her to settle a debt.

And then, when their new masters ran short, had a bad harvest, or found themselves otherwise unable to maintain the household they had acquired, each of them had been sold up into the land of the Taurians. The Taurians did not set forth on the sea, they did not storm fortresses, they did not sweat in the sun, staring at the hind end of an ox, digging furrows in the hope that wheat would grow again. They just went down to the mouth of the Bosporus once a year, not quite daring to leave their own sea, and the Hellenes came to them and exchanged women for the gold, iron, lumber, and horses that the Taurians had in abundance.

She had listened to each woman's stories, beginning to end, with their full burden of neighbors and relatives, squabbles and love affairs, soil rich and poor, favorite sandals and disliked slopes back up to the house from the stream, where the water jug always threatened to slip from wet fingers and cause disaster. She had lived all those lives, spoken all those dialects, lain with all those men, and disciplined all those children, so that she felt almost like one of them.

Every one of them believed, somehow, that, despite her rank and role, this high priestess must have grown up in her town, or just the next one on the other side of the ridge, or somewhere near that farm worked by her uncle. She knew, as well as they did, where there was a hollow in the base of an ancient olive tree where you could wrap a cloak around yourself and safely rest, under which steep bank the best swimming was, and at which hidden spot on the path the women could gather and exchange gossip without being seen.

"Will you take us with you when you go?" Kleio asked. She was younger, barely a child when taken, and after a year of crying, seemed to have settled down. But perhaps not.

"We are here, with the goddess," she said.

"The statue may not always be here."

"Stop it." Ione had a clever flick of her fingers that really hurt.

"Ow!" Kleio rubbed her waist. "It's true. The Hellenes are after more than gold...."

"'The Hellenes'. You be careful. Don't forget who you are."

This time Kleio dodged. "You aren't even quite Hellene, Ione. But just you be careful. We'll leave you behind when we go. You'll have to service all these men on your own. Are you up to it?"

"Ah, you are a fool." But once the thought was presented, it could not be ignored. "What Olympian would order someone to come for Artemis Tauropolos?"

"The real question is, what hero would they send? Do they have any left down there that are not dead like Achilles, lost like Odysseus, or unwilling to ever leave home again, like Menelaus?"

She let the names wash over her. The women still talked of heroes. Heroes did not come to the land of the Taurians. Only slave traders and thieves.

A voice called from outside. She turned her head. "What is it?"

"I have something to tell you."

"Is it that herdsman?" Ione was contemptuous. "He is insolent. He talks like a Scythian, the way a horse shits, not caring where it lands."

"And what would you know about that?" Kleio said. "Besides, I think he's funny. He doesn't like the Taurians any better than we do, and sometimes he has news from the seas or the steppes. He is free, and that lets him talk freely."

"Free talk causes trouble."

"Neither of us ever talked, Ione. Did that save us from trouble?"

Now that she was dry, they dressed her, pulling on the peplos, the himation over it, and giving her a hood she could choose to throw over her head if she needed the extra authority.

She didn't need the extra authority. Not with the herdsman.

"We've captured a couple for you," the herdsman said. "For Artemis."

The day was ending outside, and the heavy clouds were tinged with gold. "Why not leave that kind of thing to the Taurians? What business is it of yours?"

He squatted down with a grunt. Age had done little to reduce his warrior-like size, or his flexibility, and she chose to regard his refusal to loom over her as a courtesy. But he had clearly been growing tired of late, and could not stay long on his feet.

"Usually, no business at all," he said. "We leave them be."

"That angers the Taurians, you know, that you are so lax about intruders."

"Then let them come down and talk it over with us."

"Don't be too clever," she said. "They will instead take their anger and need out on the women."

"The one area where they give up on their indolence."

"The worst is that they will then expect sympathy in return." She wasn't sure why she was instead trying to elicit sympathy from *him*. He had an odd affection for her, but that did not extend to anyone else up here at the temple, not even the poor women brought to serve here. Ione was right to dislike him.

"This time the intrusion was impossible to overlook," he said. "Two Hellenes, clearly warriors from their arms and clothes, hid in the cave above where the purple fishers toss their used shells. We were bringing our cattle down to the ocean—"

"Do cattle really drink salt water?" She talked to this herdsman regularly, yet knew little about what his life was really like. Why did this suddenly feel like the time to learn about it?

He took the question seriously. "That would sicken them. No, we bathe them, wash the mud from their sides, take care of any injuries. And we bathe ourselves. And the children and dogs play. And that was the problem. These two had hidden to wait for nightfall, to do whatever it was they were here for. And the laughing children, the lowing cattle, the barking dogs woke them up. The shorter of them ran out screaming and waving his sword and tried to assault us. His taller friend came out and tried to restrain him. When he failed, he had to join the shorter one in attacking us, because supporting a famous prince in his madness is, after all, more important than preserving the lives of innocent women and children. We ran away, but they chased us. We had to take care of them."

This finally made her laugh. He was such a braggart. "Are you saying that you and your fellow herdsmen defeated two armed Hellene warriors?"

He shrugged, refusing to be insulted. "Some of us have more of a history with such things than you know. But they knew nothing of the land on which they fought, or of the slings we always carry to protect our herds and bring down small game. From a distance, we smacked them with stones, which drove them into a frenzy, and they ran around until they were tired. Then a couple of us came close. They gave chase and fell into a ravine hidden from their sight by shrubs and vines. When they tried to climb out we dropped rocks on them until they quieted down, then hobbled and tied them. The short one is clearly of royal blood; the taller also a prince, but still filling the role of helper and nursemaid."

"Royal blood? How do you know that?"

"Kings incognito still expect deference, and show a peculiar rage when they do not get it. I will say, he was tutored well in rhetoric at his court. At least I managed to learn a few new phrases to spice up my Hellenic."

The herdsman certainly knew more languages than a man who spent his days slapping the flanks of cows should. She had certainly seen him in a mood of easy familiarity talking with Scythians in troops, both men and women, in caftans, trousers, and pointed caps. The Taurians hated the Scythians, and hid behind their walls when the horse archers came through the mountain passes from the steppe to the north, which may have been why he denied any knowledge of Scythian, Cimmerian, or Sarmatian: "Why would I need to know any of those tongues? Cows barely talk at all."

So, in addition to everything else, she had to remain conscious of his tendency to lie. "So that's what you know?" she said. "A royal personage and a princely servant?"

"That's just the start. We also know who they are and why they are here. They are Orestes of Argos, and his cousin Pylades, of Crisa, beneath Parnassus. Apollo has assigned them to come and steal the statue of the goddess, reflection and image of his sister Artemis, and bring her back to Athens."

"How can you possibly know this?" she almost shrieked. "Did you bear him up on your shoulder to watch his older sister Iphigenia sacrificed so that the fleet could leave for Troy? Did you hold his mother Clytemnestra down when Orestes killed her? Did you turn Erinys and pursue him through the woods and fields to make sure he felt his guilt for what he had done?"

"I am much too old for Fury duty." The herdsman was sour. "As for the rest, Orestes was forced to suffer his tragedies and commit his outrages without any help from me. I do see that you have kept yourself informed of goings on in the Hellenic world. They do like to talk, and I suppose just dispatching efficiently can get old."

"If they talk so much, did they tell you this all themselves?"

He shrugged. He had many such gestures, all with the same import: *I am a useless block of wood, a mere blot on an otherwise pleasing landscape, it is useless to get me to think or to explain anything coherently.*

Now she had offended him, this old man who was the closest thing to a friend that she had in these parts, someone who seemed to bear an odd knowledge of her, but never admitted to knowing anything. His muteness surpassed eloquence. "Oh, please. Think of these poor women. With this new sacrifice, they will be on duty again, for these Taurians are religious, and always observe the rituals."

He finally allowed himself some sympathy. "You are too good for this work, priestess. As are your poor friends."

"And you are too smart for yours."

"Keeping cattle alive and happy is harder than it looks. After the life I have lived, I am glad of some work that spurs reflection."

"So who put the word abroad about these two?"

"Do you think they sailed up here alone on a roof beam? They have a ship, a nice wide one, well-pitched and fully crewed. There are only a few places to pull up further on that coast, and we know them all. We found them all resting in the shade of some big oaks, a spot we enjoy too. Such are always willing to talk in return for a jug of milk or a piece of cheese, though, really, they will mostly talk for the listening. And we certainly listen, for the world's news reaches here only rarely."

The true stories were not told by the poets and chieftains in the great room after the fine roasted lamb had been eaten but by their grooms and slaves in the kitchen and out in the yard, as tougher cuts stewed in the pot. The greatest of heroes can find that even the best armor fails to adequately cover their backsides.

"Bring them in," she said. "And you can go."

He waited a moment. Just as she was about to order him more harshly, he said, "Listen to their story, and they will listen to yours. If you can find a way to turn those two stories into the same story, you should do it, never mind the parts that don't quite fit. Things are changing, both in the steppes, and among the Hellenes beyond the Hellespont. This will no longer be a place for you. If you are gone before I come here again, I thank you for your kindness."

"I haven't been kind."

"Well, then. For your honesty."

The stocky short one wore a cap that perched on top of his round head, the lean tall one a tunic that barely reached his hips. If they hoped to delude her as to who was Orestes, prince of Argos, and who Pylades, the loyal friend, this was not an impressive start. But longtime friends are often unaware that everyone but them is in on the joke.

"Are you now near what you came here for?" she said.

"You mean death?" Pylades was a bit impudent, as suited a prince's friend. Such men knew it was the only way even an approximation of truth could ever be told. "You know better than I if that is to be found here."

"Why travel across the opaque waters of our sea to seek death?" she said. "From what I understand of Hellenes' domestic life, it lies as near to hand as the linen."

Orestes sucked in an enraged breath, and even the calm Pylades looked offended. After all, these men sought to be tragic heroes, doing the bidding of the gods, and could not concern themselves with how the laundry got folded.

For a moment she felt an almost intolerable weariness at dealing with anyone who saw the gods as anything other than biting flies that had somehow grown vast beyond comprehension.

Usually she just let this kind of man go ahead and herself became what they thought they had been told to seek. Then, when the moment came, she poked their hearts out with a stick.

But she had learned to listen to the herdsman, who knew how to trim a painful hoof. These two, grim and dutiful though they were, really did seem to have a solution for her.

"We had a visitor recently," she said. "He crossed the sea in the black ships to serve his king at Troy."

"Do you remember his name?" Pylades was clearly one of those belated men who thought they would never fight in a war as great as that of Troy, and so collected the names, acts, and deaths of the men of their fathers' generation in preference to their own.

"We do not ask names," she said. "The goddess does not care about them. Any more than I have asked yours." Perhaps they had worked on plausible names to give. If so, she wasn't about to give them the satisfaction of using them. "He talked to me of Aulis," she continued. "Of the sacrifice. Have you heard of what happened there?" The two men exchanged a glance. But she knew that Orestes could no more resist telling the story than he could escape the consequences of it.

"Odysseus came to Argos," Orestes said. "He told the King's family that Iphigenia, the oldest daughter, was to marry the great hero Achilles. At Aulis, in Boeotia, on the Euripus strait. He flirted with Clytemnestra, wife of Agamemnon and the girl's mother, and still more with her little brother, who was delighted and charmed by the great, clever hero, who entertained him all the way on the journey from Argos to Aulis. They beautified the girl in the early morning before the final journey down into Aulis, put flowers in her hair, and a patterned peplos of finest cotton."

Even if she hadn't already known who he was, she might have guessed the identity of that little boy, bewitched by Odysseus, as so many had been, most of them to their sorrow. A man loved by storytellers, if by no one else.

"But when mother, daughter, and brother got to the place, it was a dense, desperate camp, stinking of shit and unwashed men. And then, like that, Odysseus was gone, and was never seen again. The ships rotted at anchor. And the wind blew and blew against them, chopping the water, because Agamemnon had offended Artemis by killing a deer in her sacred grove and boasting of his skill afterward, the power of his great bow, and the fact that no prey, once chosen, could ever escape him."

"I don't think anyone ever agreed on what had angered the goddess," Pylades said. "Everyone just knew that she was angry. The gods always gave their fierce attention to Agamemnon, but it was the attention of a gambler to a spinning die, utterly important until the instant it lands, then just a bone cube with dots on it."

"Achilles had known nothing of this false marriage, but he raged and wept in vain. Achilles's own men, the Myrmidons, closest companions of his fights, threatened to stone him to death if he did anything to stop the sacrifice. The entire army, desperate to try the walls of Troy, were as one in this."

"So Achilles, who feared no enemy, feared the disapproval of his companions," she said.

"Of course...." Orestes stared at her in wonder. "That look...the line between the eyebrows...she would have that look, my sister, when wondering why something everyone said was good was not. It never had any anger in it, only... wonder. Iphigenia felt that wonder that day. It was the last expression I ever saw on her face."

"Did they grab her then, screaming, and shove her down onto the altar?"

"No!" Orestes was shocked. "There was always honor, even in this. In the end she agreed. She saw the necessity of it. She walked quietly to her death, doing what was needful. The entire army was silent in awe and gratitude."

She sucked air in through her nostrils, slowly. It wouldn't do to just kill them now. "A good priestess knows how to gentle the sacrifice, to make all seem necessary, so there is never a question that anything could ever be different. After she had taken her wedding clothes off, in one last, vain attempt at arousing pity, she lay down there and exposed her soft throat to the knife."

"Yes! You were there?"

"I can see it now as if it is before me. Her blood poured down over the altar, the wind changed, and the waters were clear for Troy. Within the hour, the harbor was empty, the camp abandoned, with only a mother and the corpse of her daughter to show that anything at all had happened there."

"But she did not die! There was no corpse. At the last moment, the goddess took pity on her."

"Artemis?" She served Artemis here in her Tauric temple, and could not imagine a goddess with less pity.

"Yes! As smoke obscured the sacrifice, the girl on the altar was replaced by a slaughtered doe, its wide eyes already blank, blood flowing down its flank."

"And Iphigenia? What happened to her?"

"No one saw. The smoke blew in our faces, and when the air was clear again, there was nothing but the deer. Everyone was scrambling for the ships, shouting, raising sail, no one saw, no one paid attention."

"And what happened to those men, the ones who got their wish, and got to war?" she said. "What of Agamemnon?"

"My father came home to my mother, Clytemnestra, who had taken over rule of Argos in his absence, and she killed him when he returned."

Unable to resist, Orestes had worked his way into his own story, though not enough to acknowledge Clytemnestra's own, separate rights to Argos. Perhaps only daughters learned that particular detail. So she finished that story for him: "After long travels, as Agamemnon stepped across his own threshold and threw off his traveling cloak, he died on the floor of that beautiful front hall, with its mosaic of the Nereids riding dolphins through the sea. And what of the great Odysseus, who so misled poor Iphigenia, and was so slippery?"

"He wanders the seas, blown here and there by contending gods."

"A good fate for him. May he continue to provide stories and never come to rest. And does Clytemnestra now rule Argos in peace?"

"No!" Orestes wailed. "She is dead. Killed by her own son, who is now pursued endlessly by Furies and his own self, never to rest."

Pylades, who had surely heard that particular story too often, was suddenly more interested in hers. "How did you come to this place, priestess?"

She laughed at that. "No man in your position has ever asked me about *my* history. Most are only interested in themselves."

"We are definitely interested in ourselves," Pylades said. "As well as in our duty to the gods. But the question has pertinence. Even I only saw that mosaic floor once, when I entered that palace the day of Clytemnestra's death. Agamemnon's blood still reddened the Nereids' sea."

"I come from somewhere other than here, but I don't remember where. As far as I know, I have always been raised by the women here. All I have is wind whipping past, and the endless churning of the face of the earth. A harsh sun. Hard hands. And then here."

"You came straight from Aulis," Orestes said.

"And who are you to say that?"

"I am Orestes!"

She was careful to give him no satisfaction of recognition, even feigned recognition. "You are Orestes? And who has sent you here, to the temple of Artemis Tauropolos, to steal the dread statue of the goddess?"

She realized she was starting to tell stories herself, or at least, speak in the language of stories, which is sometimes the only way to recognize what is a story, and what isn't.

"You know this?" For the first time in his role as the hero's bluff and humorous companion, Pylades looked afraid.

"The gods do not act in secret," she said. "Even if they have no understanding of why they act."

"Apollo has sent me," Orestes said. "Us. It is part of my cleansing from the death of my mother. Our mother, Iphigenia."

She suspected the gods had long ago cleansed Orestes. The stain was now his own, and they no longer concerned themselves with it. So this was part of some larger plan, a plan into which Orestes happened to fit, as he fit into hers. "Artemis is Apollo's sister. But there are many temples and shrines to her in Hellas. What need to come here, to the torn edge of the Black Sea, for this tortured, sky-fallen statue?"

"The gods of the outer lands are being hunted down," Pylades said. "One by one. And brought home to Hellas from each mountain cave, each thick-leaved grove, each spring, and every windswept shore. There was a time when the gods were just powerful children, who embarrassed us even as they tormented us and forced us to do their bidding. But within living memory, as they have incorporated those other gods into their own essence, they have grown too complex for us to understand. I have to say, they are beginning to seem almost… divine."

"Iphigenia." Orestes took her hand. "I can show you who you are. I can persuade you."

Perhaps he had spoken with that same gentle voice to his mother Clytemnestra, as she gazed out through the half-open door, wondering at the grown man in the courtyard who so reminded her of the small boy she had once delighted in making laugh, as behind her lover, the new King of Argos, Aegisthus, asked irritably who it could possibly be at this hour….

"You made a weaving," he said. "From the history of the family. The making of it caused much trouble, not least with our mother. The center of the weaving was a golden ram, an object of contention between our ancestors. I used to come into your room to look at it. It gleamed so bright, even in the dimness of a girl's room."

"The gold thread was the problem," she said. "For the fleece. Even though the family was royal, that was still an extravagance. Certainly for a girl child, even the eldest. But eventually Clytemnestra gave in, and the weaving was made the way it should be."

"So you do remember!"

She didn't. It was just a reasonable conclusion. She knew how these things worked. As she knew how this had to work. Even a girl of the steppe, though she was a potential warrior of horse and bow, knew the power of gold thread amid the other colors of a weaving.

"You are to be sacrificed tomorrow." Despite herself, she took a wicked delight in how their faces fell. She did not let them suffer long. "But I will come to your cell tonight, and free you. There is always a celebration before a sacrifice, twice so for two. All will be asleep by the lowest point of night, and we can take the statue with us and leave. But you have to agree to one thing...."

They discussed the details, like old friends and conspirators, until the shadows grew, and the two men were taken away to await tomorrow's fate.

All was now quiet and dark. Depending on which way the wind puffed, she could smell the dry herbs of the steppe to the north, or the brine of the sea to the south. Bats squeaked and tumbled somewhere in the darkness above her. A fox barked in the hills. The horizon was silvered with approaching moonrise.

Her feet knew the path, with all of its bumps and twists, over roots and rocks, through spots that filled with water when it rained, past dangling branches that scraped across the skin. All was darkness, but some parts of it were darker than others, with the temple darkest of all, gathering all the force of night into a thick knot. From there came a kind of malign silence, one that dared her to speak. There the statue of the goddess waited for her.

She turned aside. Men to be sacrificed were held in caves just below the temple mount, carved a bit larger over the years, and stopped with metal grates. She rolled the rock off the grate's foot, swung it open, and slipped into the cell. Orestes sat on the floor, staring out at what he could see of the stars, while Pylades, hunched uncomfortably against the low ceiling, stood over him.

She had long thought about leaving. But she had not known where to go...or who she would arrive as when she got there. And, despite herself, despite the loathing, terror, and pain it brought her, she had not wanted to leave the tortured statue of Artemis Tauropolos. It had fallen from the sky many years ago, and a temple had built around it. But what of her? Had she too fallen from the sky? She could not remember, and no one could, or would say.

Now these two young men, one the killer of his own mother, the other who strove to give that particular crime some kind of deeper meaning, had arrived with a solution. Iphigenia had served the goddess in Aulis, and she now served the goddess in the form in which she had fallen to earth in the land of the Taurians, and she would continue to serve the goddess, somehow, in Hellas. She would be Iphigenia. She *was* Iphigenia. These two interlopers had provided the simple solution to what had seemed an impossible problem.

"The stairs lead to the ocean, at the cliff base," she said. "Your ship can come up there, and be loaded. I will get the statue. And I will get all of the unransomed women, and they will come with me. They will not return to their homes, they will belong to no man. They will join me at wherever the goddess chooses in Hellas."

This was a difficult thing for them to grant. They would leave with only what they came for, the statue of the goddess.

Anything more would be too much weight, and nothing a god had demanded, or needed. Still, she sensed their impatience, their sullen reluctance. Even when doing a god's bidding, a man was a man. She would always have to remember that.

"Go, Pylades, go to the ship and tell them to push off from shore." Suddenly, Orestes was all royal command. "My sister will take the statue, and I will stand ready to defend her."

Pylades, eager and ready, ran off. The moon had risen, and, resting on its couch of glowing clouds, provided just enough light. She and Orestes climbed the hill to the temple.

There had been noise up here before. Laughter, cries, song, the clink of clay vessels, and, once at least, male voices raised in anger, fighting because what they already had no longer satisfied them.

Now it was silent and dark. She slipped off her sandals and entered the space without a sound. Orestes stood guard outside.

She had watched the women, sometimes, preparing, fixing each other's cosmetics, trading scarves and jewelry, reassuring a sobbing younger woman, who still perhaps treasured a memory of her native village and a day when all she had to deal with was an ordained husband not to her taste. At last, aromatic, colorful, supporting each other even when that was not needed, they climbed the steps of the temple to do their duty, and she would sit alone, without even a lamp, awaiting the moment that the sea again became distinct from the sky, the two blues separated themselves, and the women emerged into the sunlight to dry their tears in the cool morning breeze.

Bodies, clothed and naked, lay sleeping on the pillows and cushions were scattered on the stone floor. The flames in the braziers had died down to coals, but enough light came from a few hanging oil lamps for her to pick her way between them. She could see the wine-stained hairy bellies of the men, like half-inflated sheep's bladders. Their snores creaked like ships' hawsers. Happy and satisfied, faces smeared with food, penises with the already drying fluids of women, they did not move as she stepped over them. The air stank of sex and cooling lamb fat.

The women's eyes glittered in the darkness. They watched her and said nothing.

Someone grabbed her. She froze. It was the rough hand of a man, beringed fingers closing completely around her ankle. He pulled himself forward, raised himself on an elbow...then released her and lay back in a new position, satisfied with his accomplishment.

She stepped up into the chamber that held the statue.

It had fallen from the sky, and been instantly recognized for what it was. But sometimes she could not imagine why. It was barely a human shape, twisted and burned, of a kind of fiber that seemed neither plant nor rock. Dirt still clung to it, though whether that was from where it had landed, or from where it had come from, she had never known. Without hesitating, though she had never done this before, she reached out and picked it up.

It hissed and spat like green wood being thrown into a fire. She felt a prickle, then a deep shocking pain as it wrapped itself around her. She sucked in a breath, but did not cry out. She waited for the feeling to fade. It didn't. In a sense, it would never leave her. She knew that without understanding how.

She turned. A figure loomed out of the darkness. She smelled blood. With the pain of the goddess searing through her, she could only stand still and wait.

It was the herdsman. Hanging in his arms was the bloody corpse of a roe deer. A doe, no bigger than one of those curs the herdsmen used to protect their villages. The black, lolling tongue seemed much too large to have ever fit into its mouth.

"None of us killed it," he said. "Some distant bowshot of a galloping hunter of the steppe. Not deep enough to kill immediately, so it ran a long way before lying down to die at the sea, just as the sun set. If the gods ever send us signs, this is one." She just breathed and watched as he carried the deer up and laid it exactly where the statue of the goddess had been.

"Who am I to you?" she said.

"Your mother, Otrere, conceived you the night she killed her first enemy. Your father, a great warrior himself, died not too long after. She became our chief, and we followed her. A drought struck the steppe, our animals starved, the rivers turned to rivulets amid cracked earth. The goddess lacked a priestess, and promised rain in return for one who satisfied her. Otrere, wise and without pity, gave up her own daughter to serve the bow-wielding goddess at the sea. I was given the task to take you here, and to ensure your safety."

She looked at the dead deer and, for a moment, saw that poor, powerless girl at Aulis, her limbs dangling over the altar on which she had been stretched, the priest's bronze knife held over the smooth skin of her chest, her ribs disappearing and then reappearing one final time as she pulled in her breath.

Then it was just a dead deer, a sacrifice the goddess could accept, because the world was changing, and the gods knew they had to change with it. As Pylades said, the gods were becoming divine.

"You stayed," she said.

"I grew to like the sea, and the women of the sea. Even as you took your place as the priestess, and my protection no longer seemed necessary, I remained. And now Otrere herself is dead, your sisters and brothers dispersed to the winds. Other tribes ride the grasses, the world is changed, and this place is for me to deal with... Go with your torturing goddess and your tormented Hellenes. Leave the Taurians to us."

He had to know that, like flies, Hellenes would be back. They never left for long, for they tired of their homes as soon as they returned to them. But they wouldn't favor this rocky place, she thought. They preferred spots they could pull their ships up on shore, where the inland inhabitants could come out and trade, and where there was wealth to be looted. This dark spot amid the cliffs would not entice them. The herdsman and his people could attack the Taurians, take their place, and, perhaps, deal with the Hellenes as equals, until they inevitably became Hellenes themselves.

She left the herdsman, head bent over the dead deer as if it was really her lying there, and went down the steps.

She retraced her path between the sleeping figures, only

shifting to evade the man who had grabbed her. As she passed, each of the women stood, corrected her hair, smoothed her clothing, and picked up the small bag of possessions she had smuggled into the temple, to follow after her.

Orestes was startled by the bleak, screaming statue of the goddess, she could see that. He glanced over the women, but, of no use to him, in his eyes they might as well have been a herd of mountain sheep, huddled together in the fold, none to be distinguished from another.

"The ship must have cast off by this time," he said. "I have been listening for it, but the wind blows too strong." Indeed, the wind had risen. She could hear its whistle, and the distant crash of the waves.

They all followed Orestes down the long stairs to the ocean, and Iphigenia came last.

Now, decades later, she stood at Vravron with a grieving man and a sword that she had kept nearby, though its use was forbidden by this new Artemis, with her clean Hellenic temple and her running, laughing girls, who liked pretending to be bears.

"No one remembers who I might have been," she said.

"But you are Iphigenia," he said.

"Certainly, I have been so for longer than I have been anyone else."

He had seen his dead wife's stained cloak join the vast piles of fabric in the temple. His job was done here, and he saw no reason why he had to be sacrificed to some old sense of the sacred.

"You never told anyone otherwise." Then the young man thought he saw the point of the story. "But even if you aren't, it doesn't matter. It is as if Iphigenia did not die there at all, above the narrow waters of the strait at Aulis, as if she really had been whisked off to the land of the Taurians and replaced by a slaughtered deer, just as the tender poets said. As if it all had been completely true. For Orestes did come to the

Temple of Artemis Tauropolos, he and Pylades did rescue the priestess there, and they did return to Hellas with the sky-fallen statue of the goddess. Artemis did make her new place here at the spring of Vravron. Iphigenia lives yet."

She was ancient, her limbs creaking like a willow tree in a gale. He was young and had walked the sweaty distance from Athens here, needing only to be refreshed by the spring to reflush with life. He could roll a rock from his field and chase down a desperate escaped ewe. Still, when she moved, it was as if he was bound and laid down on the altar, able only to roll his eyes.

The point of the sword, narrow and sharp, rested on his chest, just below his nipple. He barely breathed, lest he push himself up onto it. The statue of the goddess still stood in a hidden spot, balked of blood in the new dispensation, subsisting on symbols and tears. Perhaps a hot gush of arterial blood would be a welcome reminder of old times.

"An innocent young girl was lied to and killed," the priestess said. "This was done to her to balance accounts with a vengeful goddess and let a heroic king lead his invading army to crush an offending city across the sea. All this was done to her, and she was forced to pretend, in the face of the men and for all time, that it was, in the end, her *own* desire, the final culmination of her duty. Everyone needed to know that she wanted to do it. This has always been the greatest torture men inflict on women, to take away choice and then make them pretend that the choice was always theirs. And then someone drove a sword right into her soft skin, like...this."

But she did not do it. Instead, she released him and he stepped away from her.

"So don't say that Iphigenia did not die." She was weak. The sword fell to the floor, and she slowly sat back against the wall. "She, the daughter and first-born of Agamemnon and Clytemnestra, that cursed king and queen, has been choking and gasping in Hades all the years since that fleet left for Troy. Very soon, perhaps even today, I will arrive there too, so that I can finally lie down next to her and hold her hand."

Little Bird

Kelly Jennings

I was born in the year 1531 P.D., a child of Walker House in Kadir-Walker-Jeon Combine on the planet Hayek, the third system out from Earth and the oldest House among all the Combines.

Kidege is my milk name. My register name is Walin278, but no one uses register names for the hatched. Depending on the run there might be four or eight or sixteen to any given name—in my case, eight. Milk names are given in nursery. Nana Oki gave me mine, because she said when it was feeding time, there I would be, mouth wide like a little bird. That's what Kidege means, Little Bird.

Since I was small, my path kept veering from the other Walin278s. This has to do with how I broke my leg, and with Melia Walker Hayek. She was third in line to inherit the Primary Board Seat of Walker House, and exactly my age. We were born ten minutes apart, I in the House Clinic and she in Combine Surgery.

Walin278s are gymnasts—we win for Walker House at all the Games. I was in training when I broke my leg, learning a new routine off the overheads. I missed the bar on my return, and then missed the net as well. Properly, I should have tucked and rolled as I fell, but I thought I could catch the net. I landed badly, and the break—a transverse fracture of my right femur—was very serious indeed. Nana Oki came running down to the Clinic as they carried me in. I wasn't in pain, since they'd done a block first thing, and I wasn't worried. It's true none of the other Walins had ever broken a bone, except when Fern broke her nose that time. But from animates I knew that broken bones were easily mended.

"Oh, Deggy," Nana Oki said. She tried to hug me without moving me on the cot. I hadn't seen her in months—she stopped being our nana when we moved out of the nursery, but she always visited at New Year. She petted my hair, which of course was kept short then. "Oh, my little bird."

"It doesn't hurt," I said. She tried to smile, but her eyes winced crooked. "It's only a broken bone," I added uncertainly. Nana kept petting me and sending panicked glances at the medics, standing talking by the doctor-machine which had my tests on it. I felt a sting of uneasiness.

The clinic door opened again, and Dr. Walker Jeon came in. I knew Dr. Walker Jeon—everyone did. She was the current Primary Seat holder. Also, she often came to our training sessions, to talk to us about proper meals, and hard work, and honor. I respected her, but she was no novelty. That day, I only paid mind to Amelia Walker Hayek, walking beside her.

Melia even then was not pretty, being stocky and round-faced, though she had clear brown skin and wonderfully silky black hair. But there was an intensity to her eyes, and something about the way she held her mouth, even then, that made everyone watch, as if at any moment she might say something you would want to hear. Also, she always knew what she wanted. There is power in that.

Her mother headed for the medics. Melia came to me. "You're hurt."

"I missed the bar," I explained. "I know what I did wrong, but the medics say I might not be able to compete again for a long time. The damage might be too serious."

Nana was still holding my hand, and I felt her grip tighten. I gave her a curious look. Melia did too. Then she looked toward her mother, who was speaking with the medics. Her mouth folded hard, and she marched over to them. I couldn't hear what anyone was saying—some sort of sound baffle was between us and them—but I could see when Melia started arguing. And I could see her mother try to make her be quiet. Good luck with that. No one ever stopped Melia from doing anything she wanted to do.

"What's going on?" I asked Nana, who murmured soothingly. One of the medics saw us watching, and came over to give me a patch. This put me to sleep, even though I struggled against it. And when I woke up, I was in Melia's suite, in a little room right off her bedroom, meant just for me. I had three medics to take care of me, as well as a maid I shared with Melia. We were going to be best friends, Melia told me.

And this turned out to be true. We shared everything— meals, tutors, clothing, secrets. We went to parties together. We slept with our heads on the same pillow. When her family took their yearly vacations at Waikato or Gagarin, I went with them. Since Melia might well one day hold the Primary Board Seat, she had to spend more time studying than most Walker House children, and I studied with her. Together, we learned economics, diplomacy, and history, as well the primary languages both of KWJ Combine (Classic and Public French) and of Walker House (Korean and Malay).

But Melia's true love was art. She spent as much time as she could creating animates. Thought I had no hand at drawing, I helped with the detail work—coloring and borders and lining. We both spent hours watching our favorite animates. Also, I was able to help her with gymnastics, which she chose for her daily exercise. I would never be Walin278 good, but I was good enough to coach Melia. Though I started out as her bonded worker, by the time we took her Preliminaries, we were as close as any sisters—closer than Melia was to her own sisters, I knew.

This was only natural. Melia's older sisters, Kaia and Tully, were engineered twins, a common tactic in Combine Houses. Once a genetically desirable blastocyst has been created, a parent—especially one high in the line of inheritance—often has the blastocyst split before implantation. This creates an heir and a spare without any additional trouble—and even for Combines, genetic editing of the germline is tricky, not to mention expensive, mainly due to bribes: editing of the germline is technically prohibited in Republic space.

Melia and her sisters did not live together. When they were in residence, Kaia and Tully lived on the top floor of Walker House, in the same suite as Dr. Walker Jeon. Melia and I lived across the park on the nineteenth floor of the annex. Often Kaia and Tully's instructors took them off for months at a time, to Earth or Acre or some other planet for tutorials. So mostly we only saw them at parties or other rare occasions. Melia said this was also common. You didn't keep all your heirs in one basket, she said. But I always thought, privately, that Dr. Walker Jeon did not value Melia sufficiently.

Not that Kaia and Tully weren't friendly. When we did meet, at parties or Board evaluations, they were always pleasant. Unlike Melia, they were tall and spare, their dark eyes perfectly shaped, their fingers long and graceful. But they were not Melia. They lacked her fierceness, the way that nothing stopped her. Dr. Walker Jeon never seemed to notice this.

When Melia was nineteen, Walker House started negotiations for an alliance, sealed by a marriage between Melia and Tiru Kadir Walker. I traveled with her to Kadir House, on Varma. Varma is technically a Core planet, but it is far from out from Earth, six jumps, one of them a double. We traveled for almost eleven weeks.

When we reached Kadir-1, the primary station at Varma, Kadir House sent an attaché to greet us. They also had a shuttle waiting. We were in Kadir House in time for supper, installed in a suite that seemed to have been designed for Melia and her delegation. Everything was just as it should have been.

The merger was a good one, Tiru being heir presumptive to the Primary seat of Kadir House. We met her the morning after we arrived, at an informal tea. She was tall and slender as a crane, with long dark hair which she wore braided with ribbons and rich dark rubies, gleaming like drops of blood.

Her eyes were a startling clear blue—I knew, from my studies with Melia, that this meant she had inherited one of the genetic defects that had spread through the Combines, ocular albinism. There were several such defects that had become common to the Combines over the past 1500 years. The Combines blamed it on the effects of pollution and radiation from the Devastation, but Melia told me really it was caused by their strict endogamy resulting from their zeal to maintain genetic purity. "Genetic purity," Melia scoffed. "Inbreeding, more like."

The Combines practiced genetic sorting now—checking blastocysts before implantation to weed out embryos that carried one of the known genetic problems. But this caused their gene pool to grow ever more limited, so that lately they had only been weeding out the most egregious defects, and mending the others, after birth, with genetic engineering on the somatic level. With Tiru, they had probably selected for female zygotes, and left it at that—women inherited the defect, but it didn't usually cause them harm. Her children would have to be females, though, or genetically mended post-birth.

The marriage gift she had brought to Melia was a gold ring inset with a ruby very like those gleaming in Tiru's hair. Melia's gift to her was a shiftable drone. These were new that year—a shiny toy put out by Walker House R&D. Made in the shape of a kestrel, the drone could fly almost anywhere. When it encountered an obstacle, such a building or a river, it shifted to the shape of a caterpillar or trout and continued its investigations. Everywhere it went, it captured image, sound, scent, and samples of soil or other substances from the world around it. "A spy mecha," Tiru said, watching the bird buzz about the sunroom where we were meeting.

Melia made her eyes wide. "I never considered that use. It's designed for gathering scientific data. This one is a prototype, clearly. Those meant for exploring settlement planets will be less decorative."

I watched from under my lashes. By that time, I'd lived

and slept beside Melia for nearly fifteen years. I had learned as well as she had to let your opposition underestimate you. But as a child of the Combines, Tiru had surely been taught the same lessons.

Tiru smiled as if Melia were the sweetest violet ever. Then she took her hand and slid on the ring. "It is set to adapt to your finger. You will tell me if it seems too tight."

That evening, in our rooms, Melia gave the ring to Njema, head of her Security, who took it away for a bit. When she brought it back her long mouth was tucked down at one corner. "Chipped?" Melia asked.

"Oh, yes. We shorted it out. Could have happened while you were washing your hands."

"Ha." Melia put the ring back on. "I'll find occasion to lose it, nonetheless."

This, you understand, was the Combines. If the two Houses *hadn't* been trying to spy on one another, it would be remarkable. A little healthy intra-House espionage was just a hearty immune system doing its job. So the negotiations proceeded, and so the alliance was made. As part of the agreement, Melia took residence at Kadir House. Three days after the wedding, everyone from her delegation except her Security crew returned to Walker House.

I stayed as well. Melia insisted. I'd half expected either Tiru or Dr. Walker Jeon to protest. I had no real function in Melia's household, after all. But no one on either side of the table raised the slightest objection. At the time, I was too relieved to wonder.

The trouble began slowly, and almost at once. At first the incidents were the sort we could not be sure about. By "we" I mean Njema and I, not Melia and I. This was the main point that made me uneasy. After the delegation left, Tiru took Melia to her quarters to live. She replaced Melia's servants and Security with her own. "But only when I'm in her quarters," Melia said, when Njema objected. "You know that's reasonable. You're bonded to Walker House. Anything you learn, Walker House will know."

"This was not part of the accord," Njema insisted. "You were to maintain your own household, and your household was to maintain its own authority."

"I am perfectly safe," Melia said. "Kadir House has excellent security."

Which was not at all the point, and also not something Melia—our Melia—would say. I tried to speak with her, the few times we were alone, until she told me to stop. "I have always given you liberty," is what she actually said, "and now I see I have gone too far. You will cease to question me in this fashion."

Melia never talked like this. Melia *would never* talk like this, not to anyone, and clearly not to me. I went to Njema about it. She thanked me for the information. I knew enough about Security officers by then to know that Njema was on the edge of red alert herself. So I returned to my quarters very troubled.

That night we were all taken into custody. 'Protective custody,' according to Kadir House Security. "Protection against what?" Njema demanded, as their Security hauled her away from us. I was locked in what I hesitate to call a cell. The bed was luxurious; the terrace door opened out onto a lovely garden, though with high walls and a glass roof; the galley was fully stocked. There was even a tablet with games and animates. No access, though, not even to the House bank. And the door would not open to me.

I do not know how long I was held here—eleven days, if the light and dark of the light in the garden could be trusted. But I do not know if that light was real or virtual. On the afternoon of the eleventh day, Tiru entered, along with two of her Security Officers. I had been in the garden, where I often was, watching the little spotted beetles fly from flower to flower. I came inside to greet her. "Is your family well?" I asked, lowering my head.

"My wife enjoys her usual health," Tiru said, answering the question I meant rather than the one I asked. "She worries about you."

I looked at Tiru warily. "And I about her."

Those odd crystalline eyes stared at me, unblinking. "My wife asks a favor from me, and I can refuse her nothing. She wants you at her side." Tiru must have seen eagerness light my face. Her sharp smile tightened. "But you understand. I cannot allow the seditious talk that landed us in this situation." She gestured at the cell around us.

"With respect," I said, lowering my head further, "I mean no sedition. My concern is only for Melia."

"Quarrelsome and petulant. I cannot allow such a divisive tongue in our household. Fisal."

I looked up, since this last word was spoken as a command; but not swiftly enough. The two Security converged on me, one seizing my arms and the other, Fisal, getting a grip on my hair. He yanked my head down and held me while Tiru came near. I didn't struggle. Of course I didn't. Her long fingers moving deliberately, Tiru slid open my blouse, brushed me between my shoulder blades with something cold, and put a surgical gun against the spot. A hard thunk, a sharp mean pain. I cried out: the last sound I ever made.

Melia's suite—like my cell—was beautiful. A beautiful cage. It had its own garden; a sunroom; a sauna; everything anyone might want, except access of any sort. No ports in the study and no access available on any of the tablets. Nor was she allowed to leave the suite except under escort by Tiru's Security.

When Tiru first brought me to Melia, she was in the atelier, working at an easel much better than that she had used in Walker House. The animate she was at work on was new to me—filled with flowers, and bright colors, and featuring, as I would soon learn, a sweet young girl in the first year of her marriage to a powerful king, whom she adored. It was tagged as historical fiction, set on Earth before the Devastation.

"Kidege," she said, and rose to embrace me. She always called me Deggy, and we *never* hugged. "Thank you," she said to Tiru. "I can hardly think without her beside me."

"Anything to clear your thoughts," Tiru said. Melia kept hold of my hand. I could see, from the side of my eye, how carefully Tiru watched her, those ice-clear eyes unblinking.

After Tiru left us alone (well, alone but for the feeds in every room, sending a constant stream of data to Tiru's security), Melia pulled me close again. "I've missed you."

I opened my mouth, and no sound emerged. This was the first I knew what Tiru had done. Even then I didn't fully understand. I knew she had stopped my speech, but I didn't know how. Melia stared at me, dismayed; but she said nothing. With the spies and feeds around her, she had to guard what she said. It took me time to understand this, I am ashamed to admit. At first, I was puzzled by her changed behavior. Why did she not ask about Njema? Why did she not demand that Tiru explain what she had done to me? Why was she acting so sweet and sunny, like the stupid character in that stupid animate she was wasting her time drawing?

The next morning when a second easel arrived, Melia put me to work on the animate. I did what I usually did— coloring in flat background colors, like broad swaths of lawns or flowers, as well as the fussy intricate repetitive work: decorative borders on buildings or clothing or gutters—the spaces around frames in an animate. Such decorative work needs to be exactly duplicated from frame to frame, or they flicker and distract the audience. Often these are left blank for just that reason, but it's a point of pride among true artists to create intricate designs in these spaces.

The gutter frame I was reproducing for this episode was not the usual geometric shapes. Instead, it was random letters in Hangul—the Korean script. Ever since we were eight or nine, Melia and I used Hangul to write messages to one another, partly in Classic French, and partly in Korean, all mixed with Walker House dialect and joke-words known only to the two of us.

In this gutter design, the Hangul letters were very stylized, and no matter how I read them they did not spell out anything. Shooting a glance at Melia from the side of my eye, I continued reproducing the border, and meanwhile examined the rest of the frame. Now that I was looking for them, I saw Hangul letters everywhere: around the rims of urns beside doorways, on the hems of children's tunics, in the leaf-shadows thrown by the great tree leaning over the garden wall. Like those in the pattern around the gutter, none of these made words; but when I passed my draft to Melia for approval, I added the Hangul letters for K and S in one corner of the picture. This was how Melia and I wrote the Classic French word *casser*. In Walker House, casser meant something so good it would break your heart in half. Hangul didn't have a letter for the hard C sound, so we had to use K. When Melia passed the draft back to my easel, she had erased the letters. I glanced up, and found her smiling at me, a faint sly smile of approval.

Over the next several days, while we worked at the animate, Melia and I told one another our stories. As you know—or perhaps you don't, if you've never seen artists work—creating a animate sequence just a few moments long requires lengthy prep work in the form of thumbnail sketches, character sketches, background, layouts, costume design, and many other details, all of which come together in the final product, the animate uploaded to the nexus for viewing. (This last was an obstacle, since we had no network access.)

So Melia and I had plenty of chances, while making and refining sketches, to communicate via Hangul in borders and gutters and a hundred other places. She would pass a sketch to my easel, and I would pass mine to hers, always erasing the layer that had our scribbled bit of communication on it before we did. In this way she learned what had been done to me—as much as I knew of it—and I learned that she knew what Tiru had done to me.

It was a genetically engineered somatic rebuild, loaded

onto a virus. That was what Tiru had injected me with, the virus loaded with targeted genetic edits. One edit paralyzed the nerves controlling my vocal cords; another destroyed a specific area of my brain, the one responsible for generating speech. Kadir House had designed these edits. They were used to create—as Kadir House put it—trustworthy bond servants. No speech, no spies, Kadir House said.

<Did they not think I could read and write?> I demanded, scandalized.

<I doubt they considered it,> Melia wrote back. <Most bonded labor can't.>

Which was true—in those days, bonded workers meant to serve as tutors or physicians were taught to read and write Public French, and perhaps another specific classical language related to their field, such as English for historians. But for someone such as I—a cull, a gymnastics scrub—there was no reason Tiru would think I had been taught to read, much less write. She knew only what Melia's mother had told her about Melia, and as I've noted, Dr. Walker Jeon spent almost no time with her least-loved child.

We also spent time discussing what Tiru was doing—what she wanted from Melia. Tiru was the heir to the Primary Seat of the Kadir House Board. That seat was currently held by Daiki Kadir Walker, Tiru's aunt.

Melia was third in line to the Walker House Primary Seat. Their marriage, this alliance between Walker House and Kadir House through the two of them, had been aimed at consolidating power in later generations. Any children Melia and Tiru had would be high in the line to inherit the Primary Seat in both Houses, allowing both Kadir and Walker House to gain more leverage in controlling all of Kadir-Walker-Jeon Combine. And if the alliance continued, with the children of Melia and Tiru marrying the children of Melia's sisters and Tiru's younger cousins, this consolidation would strengthen further.

But Tiru had no interest in maneuvering for power for her descendants. She wanted power now, for herself. Specifically, she wanted to disinherit Melia's sisters. If Melia held the Primary Seat at Walker House, and Tiru the Primary Seat at Kadir House, Walker-Kadir House would control, by fiat, the entire KWJ Combine.

<But only once her aunt and your mother are gone,> I pointed out, my Hangul lettering faint patterns in the water of a brook in which our sunny heroine was dabbing her fingers.

<Yes,> Melia replied, *<we would have to disinherit them as well.>*

We wrote in the mix of languages we had used to speak to one another back in Walker House—bits of Korean, bits of our own catch-phrases, bits of Classical French. So when I read the plain Public term Melia had used, *disinherit*, I stared at it, wondering what I was meant to understand by that word. Erasing those letters, I finished the brook, and moved on to the border around the bench on which our sweet naïve heroine was sitting, having just been told by the local wise woman that she was pregnant, and dreaming of the beautiful child she would bear. In among the border pattern, I wrote *disinherit?*

I was worried that *disinherit* was yet another Combine way of saying *murder*. Like *cancel*, or *cull*—Combine citizens had countless words for killing. But as it turned out, Tiru actually meant disinherited. What information she had on her aunt I do not know; but for Dr. Walker Jeon and her two oldest children, there was the genetic engineering. True, editing the germline of their heirs was common for Combine parents; nevertheless, if evidence was brought forward which showed Melia's mother had engaged in such editing, and—worse yet—that her heirs were products of the process, the High Court might well be forced to disinherit all three of them. This would leave Melia holding the Primary Board Seat.

Tiru claimed she had the evidence. But she could not present it to the High Court—she had no standing. Melia or some other heir in line for the Primary Seat on the Walker House Board would have to do so. At first, Tiru had attempted to persuade Melia with her charm. When that failed, she turned to threats, aimed at me and her Security. Like us, Melia had been deprived of access from the beginning. Her mother would be alarmed at her silence eventually, she told me. However, considering what a valuable alliance this was, it might be months before Walker House raised questions about this silence. We were on our own.

As animate artists went, however, Melia was famous, and not only because of her place in the line to inherit at Walker House. Her viewers would be eagerly expecting her next release. Melia's plan was that we would embed a message in the frames—hide it in the layers. Since animate fans loved hunting for hidden bonuses, the odds were good someone would find the message. What about Tiru? Melia said Tiru didn't follow animates. Tiru thought they were something for children. The problem lay in uploading the episode once we had it finished. Without access, how to do that? I suggested wheedling Tiru into uploading it, but Melia thought, probably rightly, that this would arouse her suspicions.

No, she decided, we would construct a concise message. We would embed it in several places in the animate. We would finish the episode. And we would wait for our chance, which would surely come.

Well before the episode was done, however, Tiru sent her Security to escort Melia to the Kadir House clinic. Though I usually accompanied Melia to such examinations, Security barred me this time, taking her off alone. I could not cry out or protest, but I fought the one who held me, stamping my foot in panic. Melia looked back over her shoulder, her eyes wide and distant. I think she knew even then what Tiru had arranged.

Once she and her Security escort had vanished into the lift, the Security officer holding me let me go. I whirled to scowl at him, but his face was blank. When I turned back, there was Tiru, watching me steadily with her ghost's eyes.

I backed away, fighting to make my expression bland and helpless. Tiru made a small amused sound in her throat, and began to move around the suite, opening lockers, peering into the atelier, where our easels still glowed with the frames we had been working on. "Your presence here is a favor," Tiru said, "from me to my wife. You understand that, I assume?"

I said nothing – well, how could I? But I made no gesture either, just stared back at her.

"It is a favor I can rescind." Tiru turned to look at me, and I bit my lip, and lowered my head. "I expect you to encourage my wife toward loyalty. Toward wise choices. Two futures lie before us. Do you understand? In one, we are among the most powerful people in the Republic. We are safe in that power. Our children are safe. In the other, I die. Amelia dies. You die. Do you understand what I am saying to you?"

I lowered my head further. But I nodded. Tiru nodded back, and, her Security sweeping around her like a dark cloak, left the suite.

I was left alone. I went into the sunroom, my pulse thumping hard in my ears, and sank down on the bench by the north window. This sunroom overlooked the coast Kadir House had been built on. Though Varma had been settled more than nine hundred years before, Kadir House had done very little to rebuild it, relying on arkologies and domes to house their population, and using most of the planet as raw materials, mining minerals and agricultural chemicals through bots and drones. This coastal cliff and the wild sea below had not been rebuilt at all. Tumbled rocks, thick with black moss, covered the coastal land; the sea was a deep blood-red. The waves surged up huge and ragged, cresting against rocks that thrust up from the floor of the bay, their foam a carmine froth. I clenched my fists around the bench, thinking of the sunny fields around Walker House, the thick grass there, the shady pines, their sharp clean scent. A land I might never see again.

Melia was not returned until three days later, and when she was returned, she was groggy and confused. They had kept her sedated most of the time she was gone, she told me later.

We suspected at once what had been done to her. So when she began to sleep later and later, and to take long naps in the afternoons; when her back hurt too much for her to work at the easel; and when, after standing too quickly, she went grey with nausea, we knew why.

Of course her implant had been removed before we left Walker House, since one stipulation of the marriage was that she would produce the first heir. Tiru seemed content to allow Melia to host all their children, in fact, which had struck me as odd even during the preliminary negotiations. Usually when a marriage is between two women, one bears the heir, and the other the spare. This isn't done out of consideration for the other woman, as you would expect, but due to Combine beliefs about epigenetic influences. Combine Board members, especially, are fanatical about genetics, and the less they actually understand about how genes work, the more fanatical they are.

So we had expected Melia to bear children. But we did not expect those children to be implanted without her consent. Melia summoned her Security, and asked to be taken to see the physician. Once again, I was forced to stay behind. This time, she was gone only a few hours. When she returned, she was still pale, but her eyes were thoughtful, rather than shocked.

"Thank you, Tavi," Melia said to the Security officer. When he was gone, I mimed inquiry. She ignored me, walking away. Instead of going to the atelier as usual, she went out into the garden. Of course we had gardeners, but Melia often worked among them. Now she went to the kitchen garden, where the two under-gardeners were at work, mixing new compost in among the fallow patch they would plant soon. They stood straight as Melia approached and she waved them back to work, moving on to the end of the garden that was in full fruit. The smell of tomato plants lay rich in the air, melons and sage, basil, rosemary, lemongrass and thyme. Flowering plants grew among these: marigold, lavender, pansies, and yarrow. Melia ran her fingers over the golden yarrow, looked me directly in the eyes, and then bent to pluck a fat leaf from the sage plant. She sniffed it, and gave it to me to smell as well. "So lovely," she said blandly, and moved on to gather melons for our dinner.

From animates, I knew that certain herbs could be used to bring on a miscarriage. And I knew that yarrow was one of these. This had been a plot point in an historical animate we had watched as children. I was almost sure sage was another. I was worried, since after we had watched that animate, we had done research on the history of using herbs as abortifacients. I knew how dangerous such medicines were.

But as it developed, this was not her plan. In among her personal effects, Melia had a medkit—what Combine heir did not? The patches were all labeled benignly: immunoboosters; Dolorex for pain, Wasito for anxiety; Sominel to help with sleep. But hidden in among the others were six patches labeled as anti-inflammatories which were actually a mix meant to cause a chemical abortion. One of these was enough in the first ten weeks.

One morning well before dawn, Melia woke me from a troubled dream, filled with murder and death. Her sleep trousers were soaked with blood, and for a moment I thought I was still in the dream. "Get help," she said, her voice breaking. As I scrambled out of bed, she pressed something into my hand.

As I ran for the entrance to our cell, I hid it in the sleeve of my night dress without even looking. Later, during the fuss and clamor of the physician arriving and Tiru arriving and the outcry of servants and Security crowding about, I hid it more securely, up under my breast band, in a place only a very thorough search would discover.

"Kidege," Melia cried out, as the physician was arranging to have her transported to the Combine surgery. "Oh, Tiru, please! Kidege!"

I edged through the crowd and took her hand. Tiru, harried and—I will give her this—worried, made no objection this time. I rode with her up the lift to the clinic, and stayed with her, still holding her hand, all through the exam and the tests. When the physician said, very gently, that he was afraid this represented a miscarriage, Melia burst into tears. I tried to go to her, but Tiru moved in first, brushing her fingers over the tears on her face. "Now, now," she said. "Don't cry. It's all for the best, my love."

Tiru meant that genengineered embryos often fail because they have some flaw. This is not true, by the way—genengineered embryos are all screened before implantation. But as I said, the less Combine rulers knew, the more certain their beliefs.

Melia wailed louder, and I slipped out of the clinic door. My heart beat hard, and I was light-headed. Not until I was halfway along the corridor did I understand that I was angry, not afraid.

This was the primary clinic for Kadir House. A maze of corridors stretched around me, lined with rooms— examination rooms one way, patient rooms another, bays filled with medical equipment, techs buzzing everywhere. I walked like I knew where I was going until I found an empty room. It looked like a lounge for techs: sofas and a small galley with a sink piled with dirty crockery. The port in the corner was out of sight of door. I took out the data stick Melia had passed me, back in her suite.

ᚉ ᚎ ᚏ ᚐ

When I found my way back to Melia, she lay alone in the clinic bunk, tears running from her eyes. I knelt by the bed. Remembering Nana Oki, I petted her hair, wishing I could say soothing things. She cried harder, knotting her body into a circle. I climbed up into the bed and wrapped myself around her, hugging her tightly. "Oh, Deggy," she said. "My Deggy. What would I do without you?"

We still had no access, so we had no way to monitor what happened after I posted the animate. We did not know if readers had found our message, or what they did then. Later we would read the comment streams in which one reader discovered the message, and almost at the same time another reader did as well, and then hundreds of them were translating it and arguing about its meaning. We would see the moment someone suggested transmitting the message to Walker House. Arguing about that went on for some time, as you can imagine, most people not being eager to come to the attention of the Combines in any respect whatsoever, and clearly not when it was a case of two Combines in conflict.

But Melia's fans were both loyal and relentless. In the end, someone sent the message. The first we knew about any of this, however, was when Tiru stormed into our suite, a brace of Security at her heels. Tiru went straight for Melia; when I tried to move between them—honestly frightened at the fury in those ice-bright eyes—Fisal caught hold of me and wrapped me in his implacable grip.

Tiru shoved Melia into the wall. "What did you do? *What?*"

Melia widened her eyes. "Oh, has something happened, my love?" she asked, smug with triumph. Tiru stared at her, her muscles frozen. "Has someone arrived? Walker House Combat Security, perhaps?"

"They'll find nothing," Tiru said through her teeth. "They'll find your *bones.*"

Melia laughed, and Tiru began dragging her from the room, heading for the sunroom—I don't know what she thought to do. Break the glass? Die there in the poisonous air, the two of them together? Fling them both down to the rocks?

But even Tiru Kadir Walker could not have honestly thought she could slaughter a Walker House heir in full view of two Security Officers.

At the time, believe me, I was not so rational. Seeing Tiru yank my Melia from her feet, her face a rictus of fury, I struggled against Fisal's grip, my mouth open in a mute scream. "Stop," Fisal warned me, his voice louder than the hissing rush air which was the only sound I could make. "Stop it, now, or—"

Before he could finish his threats, though, the door crashed open behind us—literally crashed, banging into its recesses— and Security poured it, a flood of Security, only some of them wearing Kadir House colors. The rest, including the one who shoved her Lopaka Tac-20 in Fisal's face, wore Walker House's azure and yellow. Fisal dropped me so suddenly I fell to my knees. Scrambling up, I lunged toward Melia; but our Security had gotten there first. They had her safe, and Kadir House Security had seized hold of Tiru and were wrapping her wrists in restraints.

ᛘ ᚡ ᛯ ᛕ

The Walker House senior diplomat had traveled to Kadir House, along with three squads of Walker House Combat Security. Loret Crevier, the diplomat, had not seriously expected that they would need to mount an assault on Kadir House; or that three squads would be sufficient if they had. Her team had brought the Combat Security more as a gesture than anything—a gesture to show how seriously they were taking this.

As it developed, once Daiki Kadir Walker understood the purport of what Crevier had come to tell her, she was more than willing to arrest her niece. Not surprising, given that the most common way to vacate a Primary Seat on a Combine House Board was by assassination.

Daiki and Crevier ran the investigation together, though Daiki took the lead. The investigation took most of a month, and not just Melia and Tiru but all the servants in Tiru's household as well as her Security were interrogated, as was I. Tiru was present for my sessions, so I saw her surprise when she realized I was literate. Her own servants could not write or read, but they could gesture *yes* and *no*. This turned out to be sufficient.

The formal hearing took place in the Kadir Boardroom, and lasted less than an hour. Tiru was not allowed to speak. She sat slumped, those beautiful eyes dull. After her aunt pronounced the death sentence, Kadir Security pulled her to her feet. Melia stood in their way, her hollow gaze fixed on Tiru. "It's all for the best, my love," she said. "I would never bear a child with blood like yours."

At that, Tiru's expression, which had been beaten to dullness, sparked into bright anger. Before she could answer, though, Daiki snapped her fingers and Kadir Security took her away.

All this was long ago.

Melia has held the Primary Seat on the Walker House Board for almost thirty years now. This is a record. No one else, anywhere in the Combines, has held a Primary Seat longer. Her own mother, Dr. Walker Jeon, only lasted twenty years.

Her atelier sits unused—we have the top floor of Walker House now—and the last time I visited the room, dust lay thick on her easel. On the feeds, fans have long since stopped wondering if she will ever post another animate.

Dr. Walker Jeon and Melia's sisters all died in the same incident, an explosion and subsequent fire in their chalet on Gagarin. A local insurrectionist group was blamed, and six of their leaders executed. It was a weakness in Dr. Walker Jeon, the love for her two older daughters that kept them both with her. Melia always knew how to use a weakness.

I am Melia's own weakness, of course. But Melia has little to fear from me, a small, mute, powerless woman, my only network the servants of Walker House. I know she has considered this—whether to fear me. She looks for weakness and threats and advantages everywhere. That time in Kadir House changed her. She was always fierce. But she had also been kind, and quick to laugh, with a deep sense of justice. When we returned to Walker House, all this vanished. No laughter now, no softness at all. Sometimes when she fixed that intense gaze on me, I thought how her eyes had become like Tiru's, so clear and cold.

I know my sentiment is wrong-headed. Walker House needs a powerful Primary Seat holder; the Combine needs a leader who will do what must be done. Still, sometimes when we're alone in her quarters at night, I can't help a surge of sorrow for the child I knew. And this is the question that torments me—was this always what she would become? Was the Melia I knew as a child just the gawky, fluffy fledgling that would always become this fierce-eyed raptor? Or did another future lie before us once?

No idle questions: Melia has at last set about creating the children who will be her heirs—twins, as is the usual practice. To me, she has given the task of rearing them, in a nursery on a green jewel of an island far, far from Walker House. The children will be born soon; I have spent the last months hiring tutors and fitting out our island home with supplies. It is an immense task, and I am glad for the organizational skills Melia taught me.

But as you see, I will raise what may well be the next Primary Seat holder for Walker House. Since Melia took the seat, we are most powerful House in the most powerful Combine in the Republic. Her heirs will need to be strong to survive. I know this. Shall I raise them to be human as well?

A question that keeps me troubled, far into these silent nights, and one I will never, ever ask Melia.

Wings

Elana Gomel

She walked the empty streets of yet another town, walked slowly, because her glass shoes—the last, the very last pair, she hoped—were clouding with blood that seeped from her raw feet. At first, she thought it was early in the morning because there was no sun in the milky-white sky. But then she realized the transit had deposited her in a fifth-time zone. She spotted a small cafe and went in. A slovenly waitress, her coarse black hair falling in a solid mass onto her stooped shoulders, brought her a cup of spicy coffee and a stale puff-dough pastry.

Pounding music filled the cavernous room, coming from some clunky mechanical contraption she instantly despised. She was idly looking out the window, sipping her coffee (not bad, after all) when a group of laughing schoolgirls passed by. One of them looked back, her eyes the color of the sky over Thebes. Was it her daughter? She swallowed the familiar grief. No use wondering. Her daughter might pass her now and then in one of her myriad disguises: a laughing urchin, or a majestic swan; a swirl of fresh snow or a piano tune; a slim borzoi or a lady in a dress worth a kingdom's ransom. And she would never know, never recognize her own flesh and blood or be recognized by her.

She got up and went into the bathroom at the back of the café. Standing in front of the cracked mirror, she dragged a plastic comb through the tangle of her yellow curls. In proper sunlight they still shone like gold—the coin with which she had bought her immortality. Her beauty had not withered in her endless peregrinations but grown refined, her slender body pared down to the pure architecture of her bones. Her eyes were of an even purer blue than the eyes of the schoolgirl, but her skin had been burnished by the sun so that she looked almost like one of those barbarian slaves who used to serve in the Temple of her mother-in-law.

Never mind. When she found her husband, it would all be restored. Her love, her daughter, her complexion. Her world.

She washed her face, adjusted her tatty jeans and hoisting up her backpack, went out. In some fifth-time zones periods of light and darkness chased each other around like fighting cats but here the white dusk just went on and on.

She considered her options. The latest instructions, coming from her mother-in-law in a dream, as maddeningly vivid as it was obscure, seemed to suggest she had to cross a desert. Was it in this zone or the next one? Was it really a desert or some oblique symbol based on one of those childish word-games the immortals were so fond of? This was so much more difficult than the first time because there was no set task to fulfill, no definite obstacle to overcome, nothing except those horrible glass shoes, two pairs of which had already shattered on her travel-worn feet. There should be three pairs to wear out but what if the old horror, in a fit of senile pique, had decided to multiply the sacred number or had forgotten about it altogether? There was nobody to restrain her now, no higher authority to appeal to. The others were...she closed her eyes and saw heaps of jagged marble around a splintered banquet table, a perfectly formed stone hand poking out of the debris, the fingers clenched.

The street was deserted. She suspected that were she to go back to the cafe she would find it deserted as well. She plodded on.

The sullen quiet was broken by a flapping sound. Startled, she looked up. A flock of birds wheeled over her head, their plump bodies and pointed wings black against the colorless sky. Her heart gave a leap. Doves, her mother-in-law's flunkeys!

The doves alighted on the sidewalk in a perfect circle with her at the center. She was surrounded by pearly-gray bosoms and unblinking eyes the color of blood. Their cooing drummed in the dead air.

"What do you want?" She shouted, enraged. "Spying on me? Go tell your mistress I won't give up!"

No response but something did happen: a sudden shift like an intangible gust of wind. The doves stepped forward, hemming her in. No, they did not. The circle was shrinking because they were growing.

Was there no end to her mother-in-law's tricks? Wearily amused, she watched the doves balloon out. They became the size of chickens, eagles, ostriches. And still they kept on growing. Suddenly she was not amused any more. The acrid smell of bird shit clogged her nose. The doves loomed over her, their stubby beaks drooling. She drove her fist into the nearest bird-breast, but it drowned in the flea-infested down. The cooing rose to an unendurable pitch. She felt a sharp pain in her left shoulder and then a hot trickle down her back.

"You can't do this!" She yelled. "It's not part of the bargain!" But even as another peck penetrated her sleeve, she remembered that there had been no bargain.

She managed to push through what felt like a barricade of frowzy pillows and was running down the street when a thunderous whirring above made her realize the giant doves had taken to the air. Splats of guano fell around her like acid rain. She covered her head and angled toward the nearest house. But then the swirling of agitated air buffeted her, lifted her off her feet and slammed her against the hard pavement. From the corner of her eye she saw a larger shape swooping down among the cloud of panicky birds. And a dark curtain fell over her, cutting off the anemic light.

She came to lying on something warm and gritty. Sand. Sand and the sea; the deep aquamarine glow; the familiar tang of salt like a message from home. She sat up and saw an empty beach fringed by the dazzle of placid wavelets.

Turning around, she discovered a man meticulously going through the things in her backpack. She opened her mouth to protest when he looked up and shook the pack open. It had been reduced to a torn rag. The memory of the confrontation with the doves made her wince. So undignified!

"Are you OK?" the man asked.

She looked at him closely. Medium height; dressed in faded army fatigues. Black hair, dark eyes, eagle-face: all strong angles and hard restless lines. Some of them were age; older than he seemed at first glance.

"Have we transited?" she asked.

He shrugged. "If this is what you call it. We're in a different place."

"Different zone," she said. She looked around. The beach continued inland, dotted here and there with clumps of succulent plants and then rising into the folds of sand-dunes. The air was balmy and crystal clear.

"Are you hungry?" he asked.

She nodded. He spread a tablecloth on the sand and placed on it two apples, a flat loaf of white bread, a water-flask, and some stewed vegetables in a tin can. She would not eat apples because they were her mother-in-law's fruit. The tinned stuff was repulsive for a different reason, but she was ravenous.

She caught him staring at her and smiled inwardly. The magic was there; it was just the matter of using it properly. When the quest was over; when she sat on the golden throne and held the water-mirror; when the scattered pages of *Theogony* were put in the right order...everything would be as it should be. Again.

"What's your name?" she asked.

He shrugged again. "I don't know. Once I found myself in this...this," he made an expansive gesture, "I don't know who I am. Sometimes I suspect I must be dead or dreaming. It's not my world, that's for sure."

"It's nobody's world," she said.

"What do you mean?"

She brushed the crumbs off her shirt and stretched, aware that the movement set off the swell of her breasts.

"The gods have died. Most of them, anyway. When I was a child, I was taught the universe is a book written by the gods and each has a chapter to him- or herself. Well, the writers are dead, and the book has been torn apart. You have zones now, pages randomly glued together. And we are moved across them by chance or malice."

"Malice?"

"As I said, not all of them died. Too bad."

He looked sharply at her. *He really has interesting eyes*, she thought. *Bright and dark; dark and bright... Like morning and night mixed together.*

"So if the world is wrong, somebody must set it right."

"Yes," she said. "Somebody must set it right."

For the rest of the afternoon, they explored the beach. They climbed to the top of the dune and discovered a semi-desert scrubland. There was a tiny spring surrounded by low bushes with leathery leaves. They had fresh water, and the soldier's pack contained more tins. She made a face.

"It's very ingenious," he said in an aggrieved voice. "They keep forever."

"It's a barbarians' invention," she said. "They work in metal and smoke and create things that cough, and spatter, and stink. We make things of beauty."

They bathed in the sea. As she swam, she felt the gentle nudging of rainbow fish whose school followed her around. A dolphin came and smiled at her with his clownish mouth. And when she came out, water streaming down her perfect body like liquid draperies, she felt the warmth of the soldier's gaze on her skin.

He told her about his wanderings. Some zones he mentioned seemed familiar, but most were totally strange. A white city with straight boulevards shaded by broad-leafed trees—but the leaves bled, the sidewalks twitched, and the buildings were subdivided into tiny chambers like nautilus shells. A world of purple dusk populated by midgets with scarlet mouths and dead eyes. Dragons with blunt scaly faces, their heavy dewlaps sprinkled by fresh blood as they fought over the carcass of an emaciated woman.

"Chaos, who ruled the world before the gods, is rising again," she said.

It turned out he kept a diary. After some prodding, he took it out, a large notebook in a scuffed leather cover, and opened it with a bashfulness she found endearing. Uncomprehendingly, she looked at the twisted characters running across the page.

"I can't read this," she said.

"Aren't we speaking the same language?"

"Probably not."

"How come we understand each other?"

"Maybe it only seems to us we do. Or maybe with all the world-pages mixed together we all have the gift of tongues now. Anyway, what's that?"

"A poem," he said. "I found it in the ruins."

"What does it say?"

"The love that moves the sun and other stars."

"Yes!" she exclaimed. "Yes, this is exactly right!"

The sun was dropping toward the clear slash of the horizon separating the silver sea from the rose-tinted gentle sky. He put his hands on her shoulders, pulled her close and kissed her. She was gratified by this acknowledgment of her magic but that was enough for now, and with a tiny twitch of her finger she made him release her and shrink away. Seeing a mortified expression on his face—he, of course, felt that it was some failure of his manhood – she relented. "I'm a virgin," she said.

He blushed and stammered an apology. She laughed. "I have a husband and a daughter. But this is one of her cruel jokes. When you have Hymenaeus for brother-in-law, it does not take much to restore your maidenhead."

"Hymenaeus?"

"God of marriage, he calls himself. Prurient pasty-faced little sneak."

"And you are...?"

"I'm Psyche."

The sun hung just above the horizon, a soft orange ball amidst the glory of gold, velvety gray and royal blue.

"I've heard your story a long time ago."

"All the stories are mixed together now that *Theogony*, the Book of Gods, has been torn. Time is broken. Chronos' body has been dismembered; the pieces scattered."

"What I know...you were the beauty of the family and your father sold you..."

"I met her, that Beauty who married the Beast. She's not as pretty as she thinks. No, my father loved me and even my sisters... They envied me, true, but I don't think they ever really wanted to hurt me."

The smell of olive oil, and the blue shine of the cloudless sky, and her bare feet pattering on the marble, and her sister's scornful voice "You think you're so pretty!" and her own triumphant laughter. "I am!"

"Our family was rich, and our city was old and prosperous, and beginning to get paunchy round the middle. Like a middle-aged man, abandoning his wife and falling in love with a teenager. They looked for a new goddess and found me."

"They worshipped you?" He sounded scandalized by the idea and she thought: *he's a barbarian, after all.*

"Why not?"

"You are just a mortal." There was something in his voice that made her scan his face.

Could he be a godling, one of their scattered progeny? No! I would know. Too light, too dark. Too strange. Nobody like him among that degenerate crowd.

"It's not unusual. It wasn't the first time a girl was chosen to be crowned and anointed in the Temple. But nobody expected her wrath."

"Her?"

"The goddess of love. The ruler of nesting doves, spawning salmon, rutting deer and nursing babies. The Queen of the world. Aphrodite. My mother-in-law."

"Why does she hate you so much?"

"Because I'm more beautiful than she is."

He looked at her with those strange deep-seated eyes and she felt a shiver of disquiet run down her spine. What was it? She did not know; she was not good at categorizing ambiguous emotions because for so long she had lived within the simple clear-cut lines of love and hate.

"You are the most beautiful woman I have ever seen," he said quietly. She turned away, staring into the molten gold of the horizon. "I'm sorry," he said. "I shouldn't have... You are married."

"Marriage is a human thing. Gods don't care. Nature does not care. As long as babies keep coming...this is all that matters. Love keeps the world on track. 'The love that moves the sun and other stars'."

"It is not right," he said.

"Yes, it is. My brother-in-law Hymenaeus, he puts shackles on desire. My daughter sets it free."

"Your daughter?"

"Her name is Pleasure, Hedhoné. Born of the union of Eros and Psyche."

"I remember, as a child, going into the Temple, genuflecting before the pink-marble statue, of the goddess, touching her draperies, trying to sneak a peek into the water-mirror she held in her hand. The water that fertilizes the thirsty soil so that the crops may grow, and women conceive...it is under her command. Still."

They were lying on the blanket near the small fire that the soldier had built with pieces of driftwood. The indigo sky was sown with stars and the sea glowed with a faint greenish sheen.

"But when you saw her, was she like that? Like her Temple statue?"

"No, not at all. She was surrounded by stinking pigeons. She was stark naked, no draperies, and her body was running to fat. And her face was hungry – not the hunger of passion but of a perpetual petty dissatisfaction. She was getting old, like all of them, like all the gods, and she hated that. The gods have no memory; they are creatures of desire. But with their end approaching they suddenly desired the one thing that was denied them: the past."

The whispery silence was shattered by mighty splashes. Broken water cascaded off a giant body in a waterfall of stars. The beach was suddenly alive with thrashing orange tentacles, coiling and whipping through the air. The soldier jumped up, but Psyche stopped him.

"It is the Kraken," she said. "He no longer obeys her."

The soldier tried to push her behind his broad back, but Psyche stepped forward. A tentacle as thick as her waist wound itself around her. She patted the rough, pitted skin. The tentacle withdrew and the Kraken submerged again, leaving behind luminescent streaks of disturbed plankton.

"You see?" she said. "Her allies are abandoning her. She is old and spent. She can no longer make the ocean brim with fish and the air thrum with birds. She has lost her own desire and cannot kindle the desire that keeps the world alive. I can!"

The soldier stared at the sickle of the new moon that cradled the fiery ember of the evening star.

"Yes, they left me on the mountainside, tied to a post. It was after the drought, the fire, and the famine; after the oracle made it clear the goddess of love was outraged at the upstart girl taking her place and demanded a sacrifice."

"A human sacrifice?"

"It's done in Hellas."

He snorted disapprovingly. "Cattle," he said. "You were the gods' cattle."

"This is how it should be."

"No. There is another way. The way of fire and metal."

She frowned. "What do you mean?"

He shook his head in frustration. "I don't have the right words," he muttered. "I must have lost them somewhere… in another zone, as you call it. But I'll find them. The right words, the right story. My name."

They had slept briefly. Now there was a little graying in the east, and she could see his face better: a hard face, lines like scars, the face of a man on speaking terms with death. But now Death was dead as well, Hades slumped on his black throne.

"After the first hour of weeping and cursing I decided I was not going to let her see my tears anymore."

"To fight well you need to hate your enemy," he said.

"I was bored. Seems strange being bored while you're dying but so it was. I amused myself by watching the birds. Swallows, finches, robins. Only doves did not come. Well, they would have come later, together with vultures." The soldier nodded.

"I imagined myself growing wings and flying away. Then I must have fainted. But I saw the darkness in the sky, the winged shape coming toward me…" She fell silent. The sky blossomed in sullen reds and pearly pinks.

"Why did he lock you up with nobody for company?"

"It's not true!" Psyche cried. "He built a palace for me. It was floored with amber and walled with sardonyx; the pomegranates in the garden were filled with rubies; and the air was brighter than beaten gold. I had Smyrna figs to eat and Thessalian wines to drink! True, I had nobody to talk to because the slaves had their tongues cut out. But who needs talk when you have love?"

"You must have," the soldier said dryly, "because according to the tale I know, you asked him to bring your sisters over."

"I did not ask for them! He must have arranged their visit to please me."

"Didn't quite work out," the soldier pointed out.

"It was my fault! I should not have listened to them! A fool's words are poison."

"What did they say?"

"They wanted to know who I was married to."

"Rather natural, don't you think so?" Psyche turned away.

"Sorry," the soldier apologized. "My manners are not great, I know, but when you spend most of your time shivering or burning, you lose the knack of talking to ladies."

She went on with her tale, even though something in what he had said nagged at her. "They tried to convince me I was making love to a monster. I knew it was nonsense. The bedchamber was always pitch-dark, true, but I knew every inch of my lover's skin. I could have picked him out by touch in a crowd of thousands."

"It could have been an illusion," he said.

"Of course. But my pleasure was not an illusion, and neither was the baby in my womb."

"Then why...?"

"Because I wanted to *know*. Oh, he talked to me. He refused to give me his name or tell me who he was, but we talked. I did not have much to say then, a naive girl just out of my father's house with vague dreams and unfocused ambitions. But he told me wonderful tales: about speaking flowers and singing bees; about strange slimy creatures at the bottom of the sea that carry imperishable flame in their flesh; about birds crossing oceans to find a home that no longer exists; about lovers separated and reunited. He was sweet and wistful. He was not like *them*, the other gods; he was born in their twilight and inherited none of their swagger and brutality."

"So what did you do?"

"I hid an oil lamp in the bedchamber. And when he fell asleep, I lit it."

A feeble flame flaring in darkness and his face and body swimming up from the shadows. This redeemed it all: anger, frustration, fatigue, dingy inns, monsters and sunless days; they were all redeemed by that one moment of vision. If only she could make it the end of her story rather than the beginning…

"Did you scratch yourself on one of his arrows?"

"There are no arrows; it's a superstition. My husband does not spill blood. A touch of his wings is all it takes."

"Does he have wings? How could you possibly not know it while sleeping with him?"

"He was my first man," Psyche pouted, "how was I to know how it's supposed to be? But they were so lovely, his wings: huge, soft and rosy-white, spread on the bed like a pile of Persian silks. I wanted to stroke them, to find out how they moved, to feel the muscles that roped them to his body."

"But then…"

"But then a drop of oil fell upon his bare arm," said Psyche, getting up and staring into the sea that was growing dim as clouds veiled the sky. "You know the rest of the story. How he was burnt and had to fly away, under his mother's curse; how I followed him, swollen with my baby, to the abode of the immortals; how I faced my mother-in-law and forced her to set three tasks at the completion of which I would be reunited with my husband; how I fulfilled the tasks with the help of kind creatures, large and small—and trust me, it was not easy to haul the water of life in a bucket when my own water was about to break—and how the goddess had to wake her son from the enchanted sleep and allow him to embrace his wife; and how my divine daughter was born. I'm tired of talking. Do we have anything to eat?"

"So, what are you doing here?" the soldier asked.

Psyche did not answer, squinting into the pearly space where the cirrus-shrouded sky and the gray sea melted into each other. It was marred by circling dots.

"Doves!" she cried. "We have to move!"

The soldier shook his head. "These are gulls," he said.

"Still," she insisted, "we're going to transit soon. We'd better be prepared. I don't want to be stuck in a fifth-time zone again."

"What's that?"

"There are four times of day but there are zones in which a fifth is added. It is the worst: muddled and ambiguous, neither light nor darkness." The soldier started packing. She saw he was putting her spare clothing into his backpack. "Hey!" she protested.

"You did not answer my question," the soldier said. "In the tale I know you were reunited with Eros and accepted into the company of the immortals. The story was over. Finished. So how is that you're here and alone?"

Psyche bit her lips, tasting the ocean tang of blood. *What does it matter?* She told herself. *He might as well know the truth.* "It's the second time," she said.

"The second quest?"

"Yes. I told you, she hates me. And when the other gods died—the Sky-Father and his wife Hera—there was nobody to restrain her. She is the Queen now. You see the results."

"She did it again?"

"Yes. Took my daughter, separated me from my husband, and sent me on a new search for him."

The soldier hitched up his backpack. "So," he said, "you're tramping from zone to zone, attacked by monsters, fighting giant birds, wearing those horrible shoes—are they really glass? And all for this Eros, this boy wonder. And where is he? Hiding behind Mummy's skirts on Olympus?"

"Shut up!" Psyche flushed with anger. "You have no right to speak of him this way. What do you know? You're just a barbarian!"

"I may be," said the soldier levelly, "but I know what I see."

She turned her back on him. He came over and put his arms around her. Psyche buried her head in his shoulder, angry with herself for the tears that had always flown too freely, the heritage of the fierce temper tantrums of her childhood.

"Don't cry," the soldier whispered. "I love you."

Psyche started. "Don't say that!" she cried. "How long have you known me?"

"How long did it take you to fall in love with Eros? Do

you even remember his face?"

She disengaged herself. "We'd better go up the dunes," she said without looking at him. "Transits are easier when you are on a higher ground." They trudged up the slippery sand slope and Psyche tried to explain.

"Eros and Hymenaeus have no father. She needed no male because she was a force unto herself, equal sister to Sky-Father. But now she has become a malicious harridan, a petty mindless schemer. The world has fallen apart because the force that binds it is no more."

"'The love that moves the sun and other stars.' But Eros is Love. Where is he?"

Psyche grabbed his hand, pointing upwards. A jagged black line appeared in the sky. The line widened and the dune they stood on shuddered, sloughing rivulets of sand.

"Transit is coming!"

He hugged her hard, squeezing the breath out of her. "We'll go together!" he shouted.

And they did.

This was the desert.

They stood in the wilderness of red stone under the lowering sky of purple and orange. The terrain was folded and wrinkled like the skin of an old animal and colored in the shades of drying blood. There was no sun; the light was heavy as if ready at any moment to congeal into darkness. Twisted spires of rock thrust from piles of rubble.

Somehow, they had lost their clothes and all their belongings during the transit. They faced each other naked, a man and a woman. The syrupy light painted the soldier's chest hair black and tinged Psyche's body with rose. The glittering fragments of the glass shoes shone on the ground.

"My things!" she cried.

"You don't need them now," he said, "You're coming with me."

"I need to find my husband!"

"Your husband is dead."

"Yes," Psyche said. "He is dead because I killed him."

Scarlet drops of blood like scattered jewels on the rosy wings...
She turned away, staring into the furnace of the sky.

"He would not protect me. He would always take her side. He spent more time with her than he did with me and our daughter. I did not know you could kill a god. I wanted to teach him a lesson. But the gods were dying anyway..."

She felt the soldier's hand on her shoulder.

"I'll protect you," he said gently. "You see, it's all done now. Your quest is done. You are coming with me."

"You're not a god," she said.

"I will *make* myself a god. The last one, the new one. Look!"

He spread his arms wide and a glow of liquid silver flowed over his body from his toes up, subtly changing his proportions, streamlining him, smoothing out the bumps and valleys of old scars, melting his arms and solidifying them into the elegant scythe-shapes of narrow wings fringed with metallic feathers, and then flowing over his face like a veil and covering it with the shining bird-mask, its sharp alien features washed with blood as it reflected the red light. Dawn and dusk; beginning and ending; fire and ember.

"Lucifer!" she cried in recognition. "Lightbringer!"

He inclined his head—the liquid metal of his body as pliant as flesh. "This is my true name. But I am also known as Eosphoros and Hesperus."

"Morning star and evening star!"

"I will set this dull world on fire," he whispered, and his voice was like a clang of iron against iron; like a hiss of bellows in the forge; like the crackle of flame and the shriek of gale. "I'll make it new and wild. And you'll come with me, my love."

She stepped back. "No!" she said.

"But..."

"I am Psyche. The Book of Gods has been scattered but one story still endures: the tale of Soul's search for Love. As long as the story continues, there is hope. If I give up the sun will go out and the stars will fall from the sky. But if I find him, if I take his mother's place on the golden throne, the world may still be restored."

"He's dead!" Lucifer cried.

"When Death is dead, who is to keep him in the eternal darkness?"

"I can give you wings," he said. "My ambition will raise you higher than Olympus itself."

"I have wings of my own," she said. "Yours will burn but mine will endure because they are the wings of desire. And desire is immortal."

A distant rumble started in the hills, coming closer, gathering momentum, and the earth shook, as if the enormous animal on whose hide they perched were waking up. Shards of rock flew, the sky darkened.

Psyche opened up her arms and sprang into the air, borne on the iridescent butterfly wings that sprouted from her shoulders as frail as a soap bubble, shivering in the violent wind. But they bore her up as the terrain underneath convulsed and shattered, gaping fissures crisscrossing the hills, converging upon the silver figure that stood still, his face lifted up to her.

"How do you know I am not him?" he cried.

Startled, she tried to bank, to turn back. But the wind picked her up and hurled her into the star-studded void over the clashing pieces of the world; of light and dark; of seas, cities, and deserts; of birds and fish; and dying gods and spawning monsters. Caught in the maelstrom, Psyche flew on, tears drying on her face.

The Crack at the Border

Dimitra Nikolaidou

t's Good Thursday, and I have to help a dead man cross over. This is not what scares me. By now I have done it a few times already, enough to lose my fear of ghosts for good. No, what really scares me is that to reach this particular ghost I have to make my way through the yellow-lit, medieval streets of Nicosia's Old City. The Greek sector is safe, but if I take a wrong turn, I might accidentally cross the Green Line, the narrow no man's land separating us from the occupied Turkish part of the island. Best case I'll be detained, worst case I'll be shot. Of course, tonight I do want to cross over, but there is a special place to do so safely, and I can just make it out in the distance.

Hermes street. It used to be a bustling place before the Turkish invasion. Now it's cut in two by the bloody Green Line. In the Greek sector where I stand, pastel facades disguise the old warehouses behind them; two cherry trees bloom between marble benches, their petals unmoving in the night. The place would look like a theatre stage if not for the checkpoint at the end of the road, where the occupied part begins. No set designer could replicate the sense of abandonment beyond the rusted gate so perfectly, the weeds growing in the ruins, the gutted houses, the bullet holes in the derelict walls. Nor could they convey the threat emanating from the guardpost, dark under the red and white Turkish flags.

I hesitate. Beyond this ruined gate lies the reason I picked our abandoned family tradition and learned how to guide ghosts through; the one dead man whom I really long to liberate. And it's the week before Easter, so the walls are thin and porous and I know that I can make it, if only I find the courage to go through this cursed border.

The priest's mournful chant is soaking the stony alleys. It sounds different than any Easter chanting I am used to— and then I realize it is merging with the muezzin's call from beyond the border. I take this as a sign, and walk straight on.

I try not to stare, even as I walk straight towards the iron bars. I haven't been doing this kind of work long enough to be brave about it; my lips have almost crushed my unlit cigarette, my hands clutch at the offerings in my pocket. In my mind, the guard returns, sees me ready to trespass, reaches for his weapon. In my mind, I can hear shots. In my mind, my heart clenches and stops; blood wells up and soaks the black silk of my shirt. I gasp for breath and the cigarette drops from my lips. The pain spreads and the lights of Hermes street go out behind my back.

"That will be ten euros," the twin snakes say politely.

I gasp again, lift my hand to my breast. The silk is dry, my skin intact. My ears are still ringing from the shot, but nothing hurts. The snakes are still waiting, wrapped around a single column, the best-mannered Caduceus you will ever see.

Right. First I sigh, then the anger comes in waves. I pick a fresh cigarette from the hard white pack, and stick it between my lips with too much care. I tuck my long hair behind my ear; I straighten my tunic. Only then do I fish in my pockets for the entrance fee: a small tortoise shell, a miniature bottle of scotch snatched from a mini bar and a skeleton key. I drop them all in the silver plate glistening in front of the snake.

"Have a wonderful evening," the snakes offer. I turn around and walk into the darkness ahead of me.

Every single time; at some point I should stop falling for these tricks. For now, I try to forget the whole thing and go ahead. I pluck the cigarette off my lips, hold it between index and middle finger, extend my hands and separate the darkness like a curtain.

The bar I enter is half-lit and almost empty. There is a mirror on the wall, reflecting only the sleek wood-and-steel furniture, the single calla lilies on the glass tables, the amber-filled bottles on the industrial-themed shelves. What it does not reflect: me, the barwoman and the swarthy, bearded soldier having a drink of water at the bar. It is unsettling, but ghost borders are always like that.

I cross the room and sit at a table, the better to collect my thoughts before venturing on to the other side. An ashwood clock hangs on the wall, but it has four hands and none of them moves.

"So, someone did come."

I turn my face to the bar. The soldier's voice matches the depth of his black, slanted eyes. The uniform he wears looks new, his knee-high boots are as polished as the mirror behind us. They belong in a museum of course; no soldier has worn their likes since the fifties. He is not the man I am looking for, but he might know something about him.

"You were expecting me?" I ask.

"I expected someone from your family to show up, eventually."

They had other concerns, I want to tell him. There was the invasion, the war, the refugee camps. There were coups, marriages, divorces and life itself. But they made it out, and then they made me, and so here we are.

In the end, I keep my thoughts to myself. "I am here now," I say. "There is a man I need to help. A young soldier, around nineteen. Have you seen him, perhaps?"

"I have. He has been waiting for you."

I'm sorry, I want to say. But becoming a psychopomp is not something you learn through an app. Your family has to teach you, and mine had tasted enough death for a generation, and they had decided to leave the family traditions behind. So I had to teach myself, and that takes time.

Again, I say nothing. "Will you take me to him?"

"I will." Yet he keeps staring at me. "How is your grandmother?"

I look at him for a few seconds, confused. Then the story comes back to me, along with Grandma's soft, round face. *I used to dream of saints when I was young. Saint Mamas came to my sleep, once. He was dark, very dark and wore a soldier's uniform. He told me Come, come and let me show you my home. And I followed, to the next village, and he showed me where his house was.*

It would have been nothing but a strange dream. Only some years after, Grandma Anthe—now married with children—had gotten lost along in a nearby village where she had never been before. And what did she find there, but an old abandoned church dedicated to St Mamas, protector of the Akrites, Byzantium's border guards, and patron saint of the Madraites, who came to Cyprus from Anatolia and fought the Saracens off the land. All in all, a rather busy Saint.

She could have gotten in, answered the call then. But she had just lost her little brother to the English who were occupying the island back then, and her husband was out there, carrying messages for the resistance, and she didn't need any more ghosts in her life.

"She is fine. For a ninety year old woman. And she remembers you still."

He smiles without moving his lips. I cannot explain it—it is a borders thing. And he won't say anything else.

We step out the bar's back door together, into the misty borders of no man's land. The guards cannot see us here, between the worlds; we, however, can spy on their transparent silhouettes. The man on the Greek side is kissing a girl, who stands on tiptoe to reach his guardpost's window. The Turkish guard is looking at them across the Green Line, a sad smile on his face. Sounds cannot cross worlds though, so neither the priest's nor the muezzin's chant echo in the still air.

"Did you try to persuade her again?" I ask. It's neither here nor there but I might not have another chance to find out.

"I did. I burned a church for her."

Oh. I remember that story, too. She had dreamt of him again, knocking on her door. Telling her that she was asleep, while his house was burning. She got up and knew the old church would burn that night, that if she ran there she would save it, but in the room next door my father had just come back from the war, his leg full of bombshell fragments, and she could not leave him alone. Next morning, the little church had turned to ash. She mentions the story casually every time my father has to go to the hospital, so many decades after, to remove more fragments from his flesh.

"She had her reasons." I say. St Mamas does not comment further. Orthodox saints; let us just say that the icons do a very good work of recreating their gaze. "Is the man I'm looking for here?" I ask.

"He will be."

I wait; I kick a stone, but it does not move, my leg goes right through it. It used to spook me at first, the immateriality of the borders. Made me feel as if I was the dead one. Gives you perspective, when you get back home, but it does not last long. In the real world I have papers to grade and bills to pay, friends to meet and a partner to fight with. They weigh on me as if they matter.

"Was it you at Tylliria too?" I ask him. "Were you trying to recruit my father?"

"I did," St Mamas says. "Eosphoros was already there, so I asked him to deliver the message."

A few months before the invasion, dad was stationed at Tylliria. Sounds like something out of high fantasy but it was just a little village up the mountains. The army had rented the only empty house for them. And it was empty for a reason. A few years back, the doctor who had built it had gone insane and killed his family. The next family who moved in, the same thing happened to them. The house had stayed empty until the army moved the soldiers there.

I knew about Eosphoros too. Right across the cursed house, the soldiers soon learned, the village tailor was in the habit of summoning what he called Goetic demons for whomever brought him gifts. By day, the tailor sewed; by night, he cast his spells for the clients coming over all the way from Nicosia. Dad's commander got really involved with him, and they would summon Eosphoros at night together. The soldiers could hear them through the thin walls.

I can guess how St Mamas' invitation message went, too. One night father was at his guardpost, rifle in hand. He was not afraid of the Turks; them, he knew. They had never been friends, but they used to nod at each other in the streets, back when things were not that tense between the two communities. No, he was afraid of the things in the house, the things that made men kill their families in their beds. That is when he saw the shadow, cast from behind him. Tall, long, horned. He cocked his rifle, ready to die rather than go back and empty the weapon on those men he was supposed to guard.

But wait, he thought. *This is a shadow. And devils and ghosts cast no shadows. So, you cannot be a devil.* The shadow shortened and then it whimpered. He turned around and it was the commander's dog, now scurrying away.

I always wonder. He has chosen not to. He laughs, but he does not look at me when he tells the story.

"In hindsight," St Mamas says, "I should have chosen a better emissary."

I look at him and want to tell him that father would not have accepted anyway. His rifle had spewed too many bullets already, and he had his own ghosts to mourn.

𐤀 𐤉 𐤕 𐤌

"There he is," St Mamas says.

I freeze. Blood leaves my face. My family' stories dance in me, and I bargain with none other than myself.

You can do this. You can help. Both your parents would be glad to know, even if they chose to turn their eyes away in the end.

Go ahead.

The man—the boy—is crossing the Green Line a few meters ahead of us. His uniform is the National Guard uniform of the last thirty years. He is walking fast, an unlit cigarette in his mouth. He smiles.

He smiles because he will see his Turkish Cypriot friend, the man he is guarding us against, and exchange matches and magazines and a joke with him.

Idiot, I want to tell him. *Who told you this was a good idea? Didn't you know how this was going to end? Didn't your superiors scare you enough, didn't they hammer into you what this green line really means?*

I let go of my anger. I am not here to solve the world's problems. I am here for a single man, and between this and that I am nineteen years late as it is.

I approach, carefully, my own feet making no sound. His feet scrape flagstones riddled with mortar and bullets. He is in a rush. What was his name, again? I try to remember but I fail.

Nineteen years ago, I am at a jazz club, talking with a friend. Well, not any friend, but this is a story for another time. I am eighteen and he is one year older than me, and like any other Greek Cypriot he is serving at the National Guard before he can go off to the university. We have been at peace with the Turks for twenty-five years now and everything is going fine, even if our island is cut in two; our generation has only known the good times. I am a naive pampered first-year university student, and in my eyes he is mature and rugged. Sue me later if all this is too familiar. It does not matter, anyway. We are having a great time and we almost kiss but then he has to go back to the camp and we set up a date for the next night.

He never showed up, of course. I did go to his funeral a few days after. Even then, as I stood with the funeral flowers withering in my hands, I knew that for all the priest's chanting, part of him was still wandering the land. And I knew that I didn't have time to kiss him, but I could do this one thing for him, even if back then I didn't know how to do it.

It took years to find out what had happened, to find a witness. Apparently, while serving the boy I loved had made friends with a Turkish Cypriot guard across the no man's land. Every time the Turkish commander left the guardpost, his Turkish friend signaled him, and he crossed over; he brought his friend English magazines, and in return he got cigarettes, which were much cheaper on the Turkish side.

And on that night, the signal flashed, and the boy started crossing, only the Turkish commander had forgotten something and went back for it. And he saw this Greek Cypriot crossing the Green Line, and he picked his rifle, and he shot him in the gut.

He bled for hours, the witness told me, eyes red. *We could hear him across the Green Line. The UN soldiers tried to intervene, but the commander told them clearly that anyone trying to retrieve him would also get shot.*

And so they left him. Bleeding in the dark. Moaning for hours. Was he asking for his mother? Or am I only making that up now? Negotiations failed. The UN soldiers failed. I do not know what happened to the Turkish Cypriot guard, but our boy died out there, helpless, a few meters from his friends.

So here I am now, nineteen years after, an unlit cigarette in my mouth. I do not remember his name. I did not have the courage to pick up the phone and ask our common friends, bring the memory up again. Life, and marriages, and divorces, and everything in between. All we can do is save one person when we have to.

It will have to do.

I cross the few meters that divide us, and say "Hey." He turns. Thank my Grandmother's saints and everyone who can listen.

His face is youthful and flushed in all its deathly paleness, We would be roughly the same age now, but he is dead. He doesn't recognize me but he smiles. I remember that smile.

"Do you want a fire?" I ask, pointing at his unlit cigarette. He turns to look at his friend up the Turkish guardpost, but sees no-one there. Thankfully, he does not consider it long. Ghosts have their own line of thoughts and I got lucky.

He nods. I light my cigarette, inhale—I had to practice, since I do not really smoke—and I beckon him near me.

He presses his own cigarette on mine, and takes a drag through lungs long rotten. I nearly die there myself. But I made my choice when I started walking Nicosia's dark streets on a Good Thursday, so I manage not to faint.

He takes another drag. His cigarette is lit. "Thanks," he smiles. He turns to the enemy guardpost again, and just like that, he starts to fade. I linger. I smile to him as he smokes and lets the tobacco do its job and never questions what a woman is doing there, in the middle of no man's land, offering him her fire.

In the end, he is all gone. I turn to St Mamas and he turns back inside. I follow. My hands are trembling and I hold back tears and I want to call my mum and my dad and tell them that there are too many ghosts, too many unguarded borders, too many cracks in the world but tonight I came here and now there is one less. And as far as I know, this is all we can do, when we can do anything at all, and this is one more miracle than most people get in their lifetimes.

Unearthing Uncle Bud

Athena Andreadis

Based on an idea by Peter Cassidy

"Ooh, come take my hand,
We're riding out tonight to case the promised land…"
— Bruce Springsteen, Thunder Road

D anny Fenton raged down the street through drizzle stinking with scorched wood, grinding her teeth harder than usual. She had promised her mother, rest her soul, but this was it, the proverbial last straw. It was a mercy that Uncle Bud, her mom's kid brother, had not exercised his reproductive imperative. The Fentons were the quintessential walking wounded, a small army of troubled characters who routinely destroyed the lives of their spouses, spawned deranged progeny or failed to attract mates altogether. They were quiet alcoholics, matter-of-fact suicides, non-profit arsonists who torched McMansions that replaced community gardens, and blocked artists who expressed themselves as either cruiseship musicians or local graffiti legends.

All this said, there was no question that Uncle Bud (officially Benedict, trailed by a long string of saints' and heroes' names) was the worst of a very peculiar lot. When he was a kid, he insisted he had found a way to communicate with the woodchucks who were scarfing up his mother's sorry vegetable patch. In his teens, while his four male siblings were robbing liquor stores and getting laid in the back of cars, he was constantly being arrested for breaking into the nearby college observatory, using all the telescopes and leaving them out of focus. The irate Astronomy Department had to threaten the family with a lawsuit before he'd desist.

When Bud got drafted into the Air Force in World War II, his beleaguered mother prayed hard that he'd come back with a craft—if he came back. Initially it looked as though someone had been listening to her, because he became one of the few people who could both fly an airplane and repair it. But he was still a Fenton. First came his downing in North Africa, about which he kept stubbornly mum even to his commanding officers and the shrinks and chaplains they sicced on him. He got even stranger after being ordered to bomb a civil records depository in Vichy that the Germans and their French collaborators were using to track down undesirables. Bud got it into his head that there were still lots of records everywhere that could be used to track down unfortunate innocents and victims of circumstance.

This started a chain reaction. He began to fret about his birth certificate, his school transcripts, his Air Force files, his motor vehicle records. An episode during which he attempted to burn the archives on the base landed him an officer's disability pension. This allowed him to buy a small one-bedroom cedar-shingle cottage near the ocean in New London. To his neighbors' vocal disapproval, he painted it teal, the window shutters salmon-peach. Then he pretty much disappeared from everyone's radar—except for rare moments when he made an appearance at family functions.

Wakes he never missed. Rain or shine, he'd be there in his blue trench coat, a slight man with a dancer's taut body and oddly powerful hands that looked as if they could crush a stone. His narrow face had a becalmed, cloistered look, reinforced by the druidic long salt-and-pepper hair. His eyes, though, burned an almost phosphorescent green and had given sleepless nights to both his parents. One considered it the devil's color; the other wondered if his placid wife might possibly have wandered. When he was reliving missions over Europe and North Africa, he became articulate and animated. Otherwise he communicated mostly with frowns and monosyllables.

Danny was the only one of the younger generation who had actually listened to Uncle Bud's stories. Later, she'd played trumpet duets with him and learned the constellations and the names and stellar types of the major stars in both hemispheres. But when time came to enter the real world, Danny had no more time for Uncle Bud and cringed whenever college friends started discussing their families, expecting reciprocal revelations. She thought that by becoming a mortgage banker, she had entered a safe harbor. Home buyers were so distracted and scared that they were never curious about the inner lives of their bankers.

But there was the small matter of her promise to her mom. Danny's mother, neé Isabelle Fenton, had noticed her collecting straight As since first grade and listening raptly to her uncle, and cornered her when she became fifteen. "Take care of your uncle," she said. "You're the only one in the family with some sense." Shortly afterwards, she died in a freak accident on the boat that had acted as refuge for her and her beloved. He had accompanied her in the dark realms, just as he had abandoned the warm seas of Florida for the freezing ones of New England for her sake, becoming as adept at lobstering as he had been at sponge diving. A butane stove had been involved, and several relatives were still muttering darkly that this was a fitting punishment for a woman with a solid husband living in sin with a non-Catholic.

But not Uncle Bud: during Danny's dwindling visits, he spoke as if his sister were still alive, still leaving the porch light on to guide him home after his nocturnal forays to the observatory. And while Isabelle had been alive nobody had dared badmouth her in front of her kid brother. Not when her in-laws called her barren, not when she took up with the heretic with the funny name. So Danny could not abandon Uncle Bud now, no matter how much the exasperation.

The call had come from Connecticut Edison—and not from the usual office drone level, either. There had been constant blackouts in Uncle Bud's neighborhood. People couldn't use their A/C and hairdryer at the same time without overloading the circuits. Plus the power usage did not come remotely close to the numbers showing up on the meters. Finally they had sent teams up poles and down manholes to trace the leak.

And so Danny was raging down the street to confront her uncle, whipped on by the specter of respectability loss. She'd screeched to New London on two wheels all the way, for once oblivious to the risk of speeding tickets, and was now sprinting to the unassuming house, her mind's eye swarming with black helicopters and police in combat uniforms. She had left her car on the next street over. She could have parked smack in front of the house but didn't want her uncle's neighbors, already surly, to slash her tires—winter was coming and those radials had cost her close to a month's pay.

At her first knock on the door, it yawned open before her. Danny had so much momentum that she shot over the threshold and splatted on the floor. Muttering words that would scandalize her Boston Latin School teachers, she got back on her feet and stared around.

The room was uncluttered and scrupulously clean. Danny recognized the faux-mahogany curio shelves once crowding her grandma's tiny parlor, now bulging with books. She checked trouser knees for rips and palms for gashes (annoying, but nothing urgent), then glanced at the titles. The numerous spines bearing the name Antoine de Saint-Exupéry rang a loud bell. Uncle Bud had shoved *Wind, Sand and Stars* into her hands the moment she could parse words past *See Spot Run*. The bottom shelf looked to be entirely manuals and dictionaries but Danny was too jittery to check them closely.

The bathroom, kitchen and bedroom were just like the living room—spartan to the point of monasticism—but the duvet sported a large bulge. Stomach in her throat, Danny swept the duvet off to uncover an orthopedic pillow still retaining divots. At that point, her heart rate slowed down enough for her to register that both duvet and pillow were deepest indigo showered with stars. *Here's Orion…here's Lyra… but where's Benedict the windwalker?*

Danny checked the attic entrance—locked from the bottom, padlock undisturbed—then started inspecting the floors. In the back corner of the kitchen, behind the fridge, was an unusually large trapdoor. Metal, not the usual flimsy pine slats, nor aluminum either from the looks of it. She started yanking at its handle, fear overtaking annoyance. *Is he lying down there, dead a week or longer? But the Edison people told me the power drain's still going on—*

"Quit stompin' around up there, I'm tryin' to work!" You could take the man out of Boston, have him fly as far as the Maghrib, but you couldn't turf Boston out of the man. By now, Uncle Bud's legacy Elizabethan accent could only be heard in deepest, darkest Dorchester. Then the trapdoor opened slowly on silent hinges. It didn't improve Danny's mood to discern a network of red beams crisscrossing the dark square of the hole leading below.

"What's with the beams, Uncle Bud?"

"What do ya think, Einstein? Dontcha watch museum heist movies? Hold on a sec. Lasers off!" To Danny's resurging disquiet, the beams vanished at the voice command. Her uncle clambered out and carefully closed the trapdoor before turning to pin her with that otherworldly gaze of his. "What brings you to New London on a workday, Daya Meránthi Dieudonnée?"

Danny felt herself flush. After her mother's death, her uncle was the only one left who called her that. It was bad enough that Danny's mother had defiantly given her only child the Fenton surname, making it plain to the world and to the parish (the two being essentially co-extensive) that her legal husband had played no part whatsoever in Danny's making. But the first names were perpetual-motion humiliation engines. Danny had put as much effort into burying them as she had in erasing her townie accent.

"Got an urgent phone call from Conn Edison brass, know anything about that?" Danny checked out her uncle. He was wearing neat, faded work coveralls covered with a multicolored constellation of stains. From his breast pocket protruded a tiny turban made from the same indigo fabric as the duvet in the bedroom, sporting what looked like Ursa Major. Uncle Bud tracked Danny's gaze and dug into the pocket, producing a fist-sized stuffed polar bear upon whose ear the turban rested rakishly.

"Meet Titouan er Raisouli the Magnificent, my first mechanic!"

Humor him, maybe he'll take me downstairs so I can inspect the mess he's brewed. Good thing I wore my grotty old sneakers. "You guys putting together model airplanes?"

"Kinda," replied Uncle Bud, a smile lighting up the crags of his face.

"The Edison people traced a drain to this location that could power Manhattan. You must be building the mother of all model airplane fleets."

Uncle Bud looked at the jaunty little bear. "You think she can be trusted, Titouan?" He communed briefly with his first mechanic. "He likes you. Wanna see?" Danny nodded, marshaling her energy for dealing with whatever lay below.

There were more stairs to the bottom than she expected. A lot more. She smelled machine oil and kerosene underlined by a faint whiff of seawater. She also noticed that Uncle Bud turned the voice-activated lasers back on as soon as he closed the trapdoor. Then he hit a light switch. What came into view looked like a snugly constructed hangar containing...Danny blinked...*a flying fortress of some sort? Calm, calm, humor him a bit more so I can get him away from here before the authorities jump us. Gotta stop Edison from taking the house away as collateral for damages, why did I ever agree to be his proxy...*

"Great holo job—looks almost real!" Her uncle's smile grew wider and he motioned her to keep going. Danny put out her hand and pushed forward through the small drizzle of ceiling drips, expecting the illusion to eventually dissolve. But it didn't waver as she inched closer…and closer…and finally felt metal under her palm. "You built an entire airplane in a basement?" He nodded, suddenly looking as young as his WWII photos.

"B-17G, modified for a crew of one!"

"You hollowed out this cavern all by yourself?"

"Not as bad as it coulda been. Loose soil and lots of sinkholes this close to the water."

"But if it's mostly sand…" Danny looked up, adding the fear of a sudden avalanche to the long and still-lengthening worry list. The ceiling was covered with joined metal sheets. A series of articulated beams with gears along their length formed a corridor that flanked the plane and faded into the darkness ahead. "What are you planning to do, charge admission for make-believe flights?" She examined her uncle's creation more closely, her brain still not reconciled to what her eyes were telling her. Below the cockpit window, in ornate uncial script, she saw the words *Principessa Isabeau*. Once again, he had tracked her gaze.

"I kept the name. Worthy vessels, both. I always wanted to take her flying. You, too. Like your dad took the two of you sailing. To meet people who sing their stories."

"What people?" asked Danny, willing her voice not to crack from the weight of memories.

"I promised I'd go back. Gave my word. But I must bring a gift worthy enough, that's what guys are supposed to do. She's waited for me, I know it."

"Who, dammit!" He stroked her cheek with his fingertips, rough from tool use.

"Your namesake. Your mother chose Dieudonnée to spite all those assholes, Meránthi is your dad's mother, but Daya came from me. Both your parents asked me to be your godfather. Fine work I did of that, especially after…" He checked himself with an effort. "I'm sorry them names caused you so much grief, kid." He heaved a small sigh, as though he were awakening from a long sleep. "But you're on your way now, and I can be on mine."

"Can you talk sense? You—" Heavy banging on the trapdoor drowned out her words.

"Benedict Fenton? Police, open up!"

"Let's go sort this out, what do you say?" Danny put on her most coaxing voice. "I'm sure we'll get it worked out! Once they see what you managed to build…"

"Ya think?" She felt her throat close. No, she knew and so did he. A long stay in a locked ward was the likeliest outcome. *Tethered, his wings clipped for good—after I promised my mom…* "Here. I taught you the constellations with this." He handed her a dog-eared folded map held together with tape and staples.

"Mr. Fenton? Open up, sir, or we'll be forced to break down this door!"

"Go on, kid."

"Uncle Benedict—"

"Stay away from the house once you're above ground." *Is he planning a Viking funeral? Better than being buried alive, stuffed with thorazine and soaked in his own pee.*

"Take good care of your captain, Titouan!" She hugged her uncle hard, leaving one more stain on his coveralls, then started climbing the stairs under the deafening din of the blows against the trapdoor. The police yanked her up roughly. One of them prepared to jump into the opening but pulled away his hand with a howl as the top snapped shut, nearly obliterating his thumb. While the uniformed contingent continued its assault on the trapdoor, two plainclothes detectives took her to the parlor. The house was full of policemen and Edison workers milling around a figure familiar to Danny from her own job—a middle manager.

"Miss Fenton? We spoke this morning on the telephone."

"If you would only let me persuade my uncle—" she started when she felt vibrations through the soles of her feet.

"Is someone drilling through that trapdoor?" asked the suit.

"Negative, the drill team is on its way from New London station," replied one of the uniforms. The vibrations grew so strong that Danny felt her teeth rattle and she had to struggle to remain upright. Books fell out of the bookcase. The lighter furniture items started trundling across the floor, heading for the corner closest to the kitchen.

"What the fuck?" yelled the older of the two detectives. "Everybody out, now!"

Danny headed for the door as fast as everyone else. At least the rain had stopped—the sky was now awash with gauzy veils of cirrus. She ran to the front corner of her uncle's house lot, then turned around.

The entire lot, the street in front of it and the pebbly beach all the way up to the water's edge were steadily tilting up. The ground was shaking hard and a deep roar, rising in pitch, rose from the opening. The police and Edison men, now joined by neighbors, watched gaping as the B-17 emerged from the opening, skated briefly on the shallow water of the bay and took off at a steep angle. Danny took off her scarf, waved. *Fair winds, fair winds...* The airplane dipped its wings once, twice, then headed east.

Conn Edison took Benedict Fenton's house (still oceanfront property, no matter what the lot looked like after the B-17's takeoff) but Daya Meránthi Dieudonnée Fenton fought successfully to keep his books and the starry sky duvet. Inside one of the books, a Tamazight grammar full of margin notes, she found two faded sepia photos. In one, her uncle smiled in the company of half a dozen men who wore turbans and veils that covered their mouths. In the background, against scrub and dunes, was a small, battered propeller plane. In the other, he stood in front of a large decorated tent next to a formidably poised woman with bottomless eyes and high cheekbones who bore a king's ransom in gold coins on her chest.

The month following her uncle's burst out of his basement, Daya kept scanning the news for a story of a plane crash in the Atlantic. There was only a tiny item, buried deep in the back pages, about an alarm at an isolated Azores airstrip. Reportedly, the single airstrip attendant saw "a ghost plane" that appeared literally out of the blue. He said that its pilot raided the kerosene pumps and then took off as mysteriously as he had arrived. However, the local authorities suspected that the attendant had made up the story to cover selling the missing kerosene as farm tractor fuel on the side. The attendant indignantly brandished a blurry photo which everyone declared a clumsy doctoring.

Daya spent an evening in the library, trying to extrapolate the range of a B-17 that didn't carry the usual crew of ten or the full bomb load and checking distances on maps. Then she went over her bank statements, resigned from the bank and applied for a passport. She spent the next few months discovering that the heretic with the long, funny name who had contributed half her genes and half the kisses and laughter of her childhood had a large extended family, some in Tarpon Springs, some in Kálymnos—all adept seafarers, like him. The older Meránthi wept when she held her granddaughter in her arms, proof that not everything of her son's had perished in the fiery abyss that had consumed him and his beloved.

Daya was progressing past tourist phrases in her father's tongue when another article surfaced in the back pages of international news, about the Amazigh people acquiring their own independent air carrier (a fleet of one so far, said the report, but with plans to expand). Upon reading it, Daya hugged her grandma with a promise to return as often as she could and headed for Morocco. Asking right and left and showing photos and maps, one crisp dusk she found herself southeast of Ouarzazate, between an expanse of stony desert and the Atlas slopes, in front of a large decorated tent.

Gingerly, she scratched the front flap. She heard movement inside the tent and the flap lifted. The woman from the photo was older, her hips wider and her face weathered by wind and sun—but her eyes were still bottomless and she still carried a king's ransom in gold on her chest. She looked at Daya for a long moment, then smiled.

"My name, but his eyes," she said in English that carried the swells of her own tongue. "Good that you came. A man is alone without a motherclan, without sisters and sisters' children." She pointed towards a side plateau where several men were sitting cross-legged around a small fire under the shelter of the B-17, now showing signs of use. They all wore indigo turbans, the end of the cloth wrapped around the lower half of their faces. "Go make him glad, then come to eat and rest."

Daya walked towards the group. Closer up, she noticed that one of the headcloths was mirroring the stars that had started to glitter in the darkening sky. *Here's Orion...here's Lyra...* When he noticed her, he stood up and reached inside his breast pocket, withdrawing a small stuffed polar bear now as dust-streaked as the B-17—though its turban was still jauntily perched over one ear.

"You predicted she'd come. I knew I could trust your judgment, Titouan."

Notes

Titouan is the Occitan (Provençal) and Tamazight (Berber) version of Antoine (Anthony). Dieudonné(e) means Godgiven. Isabeau is a diminutive of Isabel/le. Maghrib is Arabic for west, a term for the part of Africa west of Egypt and north of the Sahara, but primarily for Morocco.

Mulai Ahmed er Raisouli (or Raisouni, 1871-1925) was a leader of the Jebala Amazigh, a combination of feudal baron and folk hero, reputedly the last of the Rif pirates. A heavily Hollywoodized version of his activities was shown in the film *The Wind and the Lion.*

Daya (or Dihya) Ult Yenfaq Tajrawt was a 7th century Amazigh military and religious leader who led her people against the Ummayad invasion of North Africa. She may have been of mixed Amazigh/Hellenic descent; her Arabic moniker was al-Kahina (Priestess/Seer). She was initially successful in repelling the Arab armies but after a series of tactical errors she died in battle. After that defeat, most Amazigh (originally polytheists, though some followed Orthodox Christianity, others Judaism) became Islamized and were major participants in the conquest of Spain. Several Amazigh groups (primarily the Tuareg, whose men don veils upon reaching adulthood) were traditionally matrilineal and the women owned all major property.

The Hellenic community in Tarpon Springs, Florida, comes almost exclusively from the Dodecanese islands of Kálymnos and Symi. Their traditional occupation was sponge diving. Their saga is movingly chronicled in *The Bellstone: The Greek Sponge Divers of the Aegean* by Michael Kalafatas.

The range of a traditional B-17 is 2,000 miles with full crew and bomb load. The distance between the Connecticut coast and the Azores is 2,500 miles.

The Transmutations and Their Originals

Into the Wine-Dark Sea   The Argonauts
Sirens   Atlantis
   (the Thera eruption and the fall of the Minoans)
Hide and Seek   Odyssey, Book 9 (the land of the Cyclopes)
The Sea of Stars   Odyssey, Book 11 (the descent to Hades)
Between the Rivers   Gilgamesh and Enkidu
Calando   Arion and the dolphins
One Box too Many   Pandora and Epimetheus
The Fury of Mars   Erinyes (Eumenides, Oresteia cycle)
Out of Tauris   Iphigenia Atreides (and the Scythian Amazons)
Little Bird   Philomela
Wings   Psyche
The Crack at the Border   Hermes Psychopomp
Unearthing Uncle Bud   Daedalus (and a very different Penelope)

About the Contributors

Athena Andreadis (editor)

Greek-born and -raised Athena Andreadis came to the US at age 18 to attend Harvard, then MIT. She spent much of her adult life doing basic research on human brain function at the molecular level. She's the author of *To Seek Out New Life: The Biology of Star Trek* and the engine behind the highly acclaimed SF anthologies *The Other Half of the Sky* and *To Shape the Dark*. Her poems, stories and essays have appeared in venues like *Harvard Review, Strange Horizons, Crossed Genres, Bull Spec, SF Signal, H+ Magazine, io9*, and her own site, Starship Reckless. She's the chief astrogator of swashbuckling small press Candlemark & Gleam.

JAMES L. CAMBIAS

James L. Cambias is a science fiction writer and game designer. Originally from New Orleans, he was educated at the University of Chicago and lives in western Massachusetts. His first novel, *A Darkling Sea*, was published by Tor Books in 2014, followed by *Corsair* in 2015. *Arkad's World*, his most recent novel, was published by Baen Books in 2019. His short stories have appeared in *The Magazine of Fantasy & Science Fiction, Shimmer, Nature*, and several original anthologies—including the collection *Hieroglyph* (eds. Kathryn Cramer and Ed Finn). Most recently, his story "Treatment Option" was featured on the XPrize foundation's "Seat 14C" Web site. He has written for Steve Jackson Games, Hero Games, and other roleplaying publishers, and is a partner in Zygote Games, a small company specializing in science and nature-based games. His most recent game title is *Weird War I,* from Pinnacle Entertainment Group. His blog is at www.jamescambias.com.

F. J. DOUCET

F. J. Doucet was born and grew up in the shadow of Niagara Falls, and though she has since lived in the cultivated cities of both Europe and Asia, fierce natural forces and landscapes continue to greatly influence her writing. "The Fury of Mars" was inspired not only by the chthonic Greek myths, but by a year and a half spent living and working among the Inuit people in the Canadian arctic. Her poetry has previously been published in print and online sources, including *Ascent Aspirations* publications, *Hamilton Arts and Letters, The Saving Banister, Red Bird* chapbooks, and *The Lyric* and *Grey Borders* magazines, with work forthcoming in *Daddy: A Cultural Anthology* by Grey Borders Books. This is her first printed short story.

ELANA GOMEL

Elana Gomel is the author of five non-fiction books published by Routledge, Macmillan and others, and of numerous articles on subjects ranging from science fiction and fantasy to posthumanism and Victorian literature. She has published more than 30 fantasy and science fiction stories, in such magazines as *New Horizons, Bewildering Stories, Timeless Tales, The Singularity, New Realm, Mythic,* and *The Fantasist;* and in anthologies *The Apex Book of World SF, People of the Book, Twelve Days of Christmas,* among others. Her speculative novels *A Tale of Three Cities* and *The Hungry Ones* were published in 2013 and 2019, respectively. She can be found at https://www.citiesoflightanddarkness.com/.

ALEXANDER JABLOKOV

Alexander Jablokov is the author of six novels, with *Brain Thief* the most recent, and a number of short stories. His story "Bad Day on Boscobel" appeared in *The Other Half of the Sky* and was reprinted in *Year's Best Science Fiction 31* (ed. Gardner Dozois). His day job is writing technical marketing content, which often informs his science fiction—but please do not tell his clients. He is fascinated by history and by the stories people tell to make sense of it.

KELLY JENNINGS

Raised in New Orleans, Kelly Jennings is a member and co-founder of the Boston Mountain Writers Group. Her short fiction has appeared in many venues, including *The Magazine of Fantasy & Science Fiction*, and the anthology *The Other Half of The Sky*. Her story in that anthology, "Velocity's Ghost," received an honorable mention in *Year's Best Science Fiction 31* (ed. Gardner Dozois). She co-edited the anthology *Menial: Skilled Labor in SF* (Crossed Genres, 2012). Her first novel, *Broken Slate*, was published by Crossed Genres (2011) followed by *Fault Line*s, based on "Velocity's Ghost", from Candlemark & Gleam (2018). Visit her at http://delagar.blogspot.com/.

SHARIANN LEWITT

Author of 17 novels under five different names, Shariann Lewitt (aka S.N. Lewitt, Nina Harper, Rick North and Gordon Kendall) has written literary hard science fiction, high fantasy, young adult, military science fiction and urban fantasy. She has published 40 short stories in anthologies including *Decopunk* (eds. Tom Easton and Judith Dial), *Gifts of Darkover* (ed. Deborah Ross), *Otherwhere* (eds. Keith DeCandido and

Laura Anne Gilman), *The Confidential Casebook of Sherlock Holmes* (ed. Marvin Kaye), and *Bending the Landscape vol. 2, Science Fiction* (eds. Stephen Pagel and Nicole Griffiths). Lewitt has formal background in Population Genetics and Group Theory, and learned that fieldwork was just a bit too applied (also too dirty!) for her as an undergrad. She currently teaches at MIT.

CHRISTINE LUCAS

Christine Lucas lives in Greece with her husband and a horde of spoiled animals. A retired Air Force officer and mostly self-taught in English, she has had her work appear in many SF/F magazines, including *Daily Science Fiction, Pseudopod*, and *Nature: Futures*. Her stories appear in highly-claimed anthologies; among them *Tails of Wonder and Imagination* ("Dominion", Night Shade 2010, ed. Ellen Datlow), and *The Other Half of the Sky* ("Ouroboros", Candlemark & Gleam 2013, ed. Athena Andreadis). She was a finalist for the 2017 WSFA award; her story "Χίλια Μύρια Κύματα" ("A Thousand Waves from Home") won the 2017 Φανταστιcon Award; her story collection *Fates and Furies* came out in 2019 from the Candlemark & Gleam Reckless imprint; and she's working on her first novel. Visit her at http://werecat99.wordpress.com/.

DIMITRA NIKOLAIDOU

Dimitra Nikolaidou is a Greek Cypriot, born and living in Greece. She is the head editor at Archetypo Publications, teaches creative writing focused on speculative fiction at Tales of the Wyrd, and works on her PhD researching role-playing games and the literature of the fantastic. Her short stories "Any Old Disease", "Blindness", "Horns of Gold and Hands of Silver", "Heart of Vesta" and "Blue Wedding" have been published in *Metaphorosis, See the Elephant, Gallery of Curiosities, Starship Sofa*, and in the *After the Happily Ever After* anthology respectively. She has published non-fiction at Cracked.com and Atlas Obscura, as well as in many Greek books and periodicals. She is always planning a holiday somewhere in Europe.

MELISSA SCOTT

Melissa Scott was born and raised in Little Rock, Arkansas, studied history at Harvard College, and earned her PhD from Brandeis University. She has published more than 30 original novels and several short stories, most with queer themes and characters, as well as authorized tie-in novels for *Star Trek: DS9, Star Trek: Voyager, Stargate SG-1, Stargate Atlantis*, and *Star Wars Rebels*. She won the John W. Campbell Award for Best New Writer in 1986; Lambda Literary Awards for *Trouble and Her Friends, Shadow Man, Point of Dreams* (with long-time partner and collaborator, the late Lisa A. Barnett), and *Death By Silver* (with Amy Griswold); and Spectrum Awards for *Death By Silver, Fairs' Point, Shadow Man* and the short story "The Rocky Side of the Sky". She has also been shortlisted for the Tiptree Award. Her short stories "Finders" (*The Other Half of the Sky*, Candlemark & Gleam 2013, ed. Athena Andreadis) and "Firstborn, Lastborn" (*To Shape the Dark*, Candlemark & Gleam 2016, ed. Athena Andreadis) were both selected for Gardner Dozois's *Years Best SF* anthologies. Her novel *Finders*, based on the eponymous short story and first in a projected tetralogy, appeared in December 2018. Visit her at http://melissa-scott.com.

JUDITH TARR

Judith Tarr is the author of over forty novels of fantasy, science fiction, and historical fiction. She holds an MA in Classics from Cambridge and a PhD in Medieval Studies from Yale. Her novels have won the Crawford Award and been nominated for the Locus Award and the World Fantasy Award. She lives in Arizona, USA, with a herd of Lipizzan horses, a clowder of cats, and a blue-eyed dog.

A.M. TUOMALA

A.M. Tuomala lives in western New York, somewhere between Niagara Gorge and the Eternal Flame. In addition to hiking those sublime landscapes, Tuomala enjoys researching Gothic fiction, collecting rocks, and building new worlds. Tuomala's debut novel *Erekos* (Candlemark & Gleam, 2010) was named among the best SF/fantasy novels of the year by *Publishers Weekly* and won the Benjamin Franklin Silver Medal from the Independent Book Publishers of America. Tuomala's most recent novel, the historical high fantasy *Drakon* (Candlemark & Gleam 2016), was a top-Ten SF/F selection of Booklist in 2017. Visit the author at http:// amtuomala.com/.

GENEVIEVE WILLIAMS

Genevieve Williams's short fiction has appeared in *Asimov's, Strange Horizons, See the Elephant, Analog*, and other publications. She has an MFA in Popular Fiction from the Stonecoast program at the University of Southern Maine. She lives in Seattle.

ELENI TSAMI (COVER ARTIST)

Eleni Tsami studied linguistics at the University of Athens and art at AKTO. She started painting in the early 2000s with a love for fantasy and science fiction. Her work has been featured in many book covers (Night Shade Books,

Hieroglyphic Press, Candlemark & Gleam), Digital Artist magazine, and various online galleries. Her Candlemark covers include the highly acclaimed SF anthologies *The Other Half of the Sky* (2013) and *To Shape the Dark* (2016), as well as Melissa Scott's SF novel *Finders* (2018). When she's not working or plugged into the internet, she likes to read, play games, and hike. She lives in Athens, Greece. Visit her at http://www.planewalk.net/.